Knit in Comfort

Also by Isabel Sharpe

As Good As It Got
Women on the Edge of a Nervous Breakthrough

Knit
in
Comfort

ISABEL SHARPE

AVON

An Imprint of HarperCollins*Publishers*

KNIT IN COMFORT. Copyright © 2010 by Muna Shehadi Sill. All rights reserved. Printed in the United States of America. No part of this book may be used or reproduced in any manner whatsoever without written permission except in the case of brief quotations embodied in critical articles and reviews. For information address HarperCollins Publishers, 10 East 53rd Street, New York, NY 10022.

HarperCollins books may be purchased for educational, business, or sales promotional use. For information please write: Special Markets Department, HarperCollins Publishers, 10 East 53rd Street, New York, NY 10022.

FIRST AVON PAPERBACK EDITION PUBLISHED 2010.

Designed by Diahann Sturge

Library of Congress Cataloging-in-Publication Data
  Sharpe, Isabel.
    Knit in comfort : a novel / by Isabel Sharpe.
      p. cm.
    ISBN 978-0-06-176549-0 (pbk.)
    1. North Carolina—Fiction. 2. Knitting—North Carolina—Fiction.
    3. Lace and lace making—North Carolina—Fiction. 4. Women—North
    Carolina—Fiction. I. Title.
  PS3619.H356645K59 2010
  813'.6—dc22   2009052869

10 11 12 13 14 OV/RRD 10 9 8 7 6 5 4 3 2 1

*Heartfelt thanks so Lucia Macro and
the wonderful women of the Whine and Dine breakfast group
for their unending cheerleading and support.*

Chapter One

Fiona Tulloch lives with her family on the far western coast of Shetland Island, two hundred miles northeast of Scotland and the same southeast of Norway, in a community of crofters who rent land for crops and grazing from the local laird. Their house is a typical two-room low stone building with a turf and thatch roof, flagstone floors and walls coated with plaster stained with smoke from peat fires burned for warmth, cooking and for drying meat and fish.

In 1925 Fiona is sixteen, a blue-eyed beauty with blond curls and smooth cheeks pink from sea winds, strong and hardworking like all Shetland women. She has a way with Shetland horses—"ponies" to non-islanders—and the small, hardy Shetland sheep, and can coax grain, potatoes and vegetables out of the island's poor soil.

Fiona spins exceptionally fine wool, six thousand yards from a single ounce, for the delicate lace shawls she, her mum, Granny Nessa and Aunt Charlotte knit. From thicker wool are made stockings, caps, mitts and sweaters for the family and for sale to supplement the family income. With sheaths attached to their belts holding one needle steady, they can knit with one hand, even walking and doing chores.

While women care for house, animals, children and crops, most Shetland men, including Fiona's father, fish to sell and feed the family. Anchored in the warm Gulf Stream, the islands don't suffer from extremes in temperature, but winds blow fiercely across their treeless surface, and storms are strong and unpredictable.

Most of the week men are at sea in their small, colorful double-prowed sailboats. When they return from a trip, wives, daughters and sisters sigh with relief and put a hot dinner of fish, potatoes and oats on the table. But there are days some women linger alone on the shore, still scanning the sea for boats that never appear, for husbands, brothers or sons who never come home.

If she can steal an hour, Fiona walks along Eshaness's cliffs covered with summer wildflowers—bird's-foot trefoil, buttercup, daisy and squill—gazing out at the Atlantic, bright blue, turquoise or cobalt, depending on its mood, smelling the salt and peat and heathery freshness on the clothes-catching wind, watching white spray foam and crash against the black rock far below, and hundreds of birds wheeling, diving, leaving and returning to their cliffside nests. Sometimes she talks to her older brother *whose body is still somewhere under the waves. Sometimes she sings for the birds and the seals and the sheep and horses around her or simply for herself.*

Fiona and her family are poor, the storms fierce, the clouds many, but the air and water are clean, the fish plentiful, the crops thriving and Fiona is in love. Calum Jamieson is a fisherman five years older. She's loved him since she was a curious eight-year-old watching men readying their boats to put to sea from the sloping southern shore of the town. He'd tweaked her curls, told her she had the bluest eyes he'd ever seen, and Fiona had fallen right there. Someday soon she'll marry him, it's understood, though they haven't yet spoken of it. Already he is changing, from treating her like a little sister to recognizing her as the nearly grown woman she is.

"I'm just about done! One more to go!" Sally held up her ten-by-ten-inch square of multicolored green which she'd chosen to knit in a simple pattern of stockinette stitch with occasional purl-row stripes. "Dorene, how much more do y'all have?"

Dorene frowned at her violet square decorated with wobbly vertical cables. "I should be done this one in a few days."

Megan bent over her blue square, shading navy toward teal in a modified Acre lace pattern. Seven colors of the rainbow: red, green, blue and violet being knit here tonight; orange and yellow already finished last week in a crazed hurry, before Jocelyn and Cara's trip to Vegas; and back home, Megan's mother-in-law, Vera, worked on indigo. Five squares assigned to each knitter in her chosen color, any design she wanted. Eventually the squares would be assembled into same-shaded rows, then the rows joined into a rainbow blanket, the Purls Before Wine knitting group's entry into the annual Comfort Craft Fair contest.

They wouldn't win. Everyone knew that as long as Roy Aldernack was judging, the contestant who slept with him or at least flirted the most outrageously would prevail. But the Purls Before Wine knitters entered every year anyway, then sold the craft at the banquet silent auction and donated the proceeds to a homeless shelter in Asheville.

"I still can't believe Cara and Jocelyn went to Vegas in July." Ella shook back her dark chin-length bob, fingers flying over her red square shot with silver thread. "They're going to cook in that heat."

"Jocelyn said they get the best deals in the summer." Dorene yanked up another length of violet yarn, needles moving painstakingly slowly. "And Cara was crowing about getting away so poor Frank finds out what being a mom is like when the kids aren't in school."

"Cara told me they're crashing two conventions while they're there." Sally giggled, shoving back a curling blond strand from her forehead. "Ready for this? Plastic surgeons and bodybuilders!"

Ella lifted a perfectly shaped eyebrow. "Big bucks and big biceps?"

"One to wed, one to bed." Dorene burst into laughter, always louder than anyone else's, especially at her own jokes.

Megan took a sip of her passion-fruit iced tea. Cara had married Dorene's brother right out of high school, otherwise Megan was pretty sure the others wouldn't have included Dorene in their group. Megan wouldn't be in either if Sally hadn't invited her, an invitation Megan still wasn't sure the other members were too happy about. An invitation she still wasn't sure she should have accepted, except that Sally was so sweet and Megan loved to knit.

"Hey, Sally." Dorene put down her blanket square and grabbed her wineglass, giggling already over whatever she was about to say. "Did you use your shower present from Cara yet?"

"Oh." Sally looked up from her green and blushed. "No, not yet. Maybe after the wedding . . ."

"His and hers lingerie! Tab A! Slot B!" Dorene thumped her flat chest and guffawed, showing a half inch of gum above her teeth. "And the husband-training kit from Jocelyn! I thought I was going to pee myself laughing. Those were the best presents."

"And the worst?" Ella worked her red wool which matched her nail polish nearly perfectly, part of her effortless chic—nothing dared clash with her. "Your pin-on buttons, Dorene. 'Groom,' 'mother-of-the-bride,' 'grandfather-of-the-groom'? Where in God's name did you find those?"

"Hey, now, I thought those were cute." Dorene lifted her large chin defiantly. "They're so everyone knows who everyone is."

"Sweet Jesus, Dorene, this is Comfort. Everyone knows who everyone is already." Ella stretched her mile-long legs halfway across Sally's worn brown carpet. "And who'd want to pin a red-striped button on a summer wedding dress anyway? Totally ruins the look."

Megan kept her fingers working, her face peaceful. Sometimes she despaired at the level of conversation at Purls meetings, though it was far better without Jocelyn and Cara. Megan had once suggested a combined knitting and book group, so they'd have something interesting to talk about while they worked, but that idea had been met with all the enthusiasm of women facing pelvic exams. "Speaking of dresses, when will you get yours, Sally?"

"Mm, the end of this or early next week, I think." Sally put her wineglass down, blue eyes sparkling wide. This would be her second marriage, but her first church wedding; she eloped after high school and was widowed by the Iraq war a decade later. Rough years until she and Foster, her Comfort High sweetheart, rediscovered each other after his divorce. "It's off-white with a full skirt, lots of pearl and lace trim. It's so beautiful. I'll feel like Princess Diana."

"But you practically had to throw a fit before Foster's mama would get the dress you wanted," Dorene said.

"What did she want you to buy?" Megan asked.

"A plain strapless silk sheath—without even a veil. I know she has incredible taste, and I'm sure the dress was gorgeous, but I can't wear strapless for one thing, because of my scars, and I really wanted the whole frou-frou Cinderella getup, puffy sleeves and train and the whole works."

"She shouldn't be dictating what you wear to your own wedding," Ella said.

"She's paying for the dress . . ."

"So?" Ella exchanged her knitting for her wine. "Stand up for what you want. I should lend you my copy of *When Women Rule.*"

Everyone laughed, uncomfortably, because they all knew David, and what his wife's book did to their marriage.

Megan turned her square to start her next row. "I'm glad you got the dress you wanted, Sally. It's sweet of Foster's mom to buy it for you."

"I think she's just horrified at the idea of the dress I could afford. In front of all her Asheville country-club friends." Sally shuddered comically. "Bet you could feed a family with teenage boys for a year on what this dress costs. It doesn't seem right."

Ella shrugged. "It's her money to waste."

"You'll be gorgeous," Megan said.

"I hope so. Aunt Trudy wanted me to wear Mom's dress. I had to explain about Beatrice."

Megan murmured sympathetically. Trickiest part of getting married was trying to keep everyone happy. Megan had made so many compromises that by the time her wedding rolled around, she felt like she'd stepped into the middle of someone else's.

"Sugar break!" Ella rose gracefully from the couch, tall model's body virtually unchanged from her teenage years when it sent boys and men alike into a slack-jawed stupor.

"Bring me another pecan bar, would you?" Dorene patted her flat stomach. "I'll probably gain ten pounds, but I need to keep my strength up for all this knitting."

Ella snorted. "You haven't gained an ounce since puberty. Sally? Want anything?"

"I won't fit into my dress . . . but sure, I'll have another. A small one."

"Aw shoot, Megan, I messed up my cable," Dorene wailed. "Can you fix?"

"Too much wine, Dorene honey?" Ella loaded up her plate. Unlike the rest of them she could put away glass after glass and stay steady as a ledge. "Want anything, Megan?"

"No, I'm fine, thanks, Ella. Sure, I'll fix it, Dorene." Megan dug out her crochet hook, crossed to the ottoman next to Dorene, took her violet square and scanned the uneven stitches for the mistake. "Here. You got off one and started your cable too early."

"Oh, yes, I see." Dorene's eyes were already devouring the pecan bars.

Megan took two stitches off the needles, let them unravel down a few rows and used the crochet hook to weave them back up to the top. So simple. She'd been knitting cables by the time she was five, taught by her mom, who knitted to keep herself busy and to keep herself company—probably to keep herself sane. Megan had learned to do the same.

"Oh, there's my cell." Dorene dug it from her purse and squealed. "It's Cara! *Hey, girlfriend.* What are you doing? Tell us everything, especially about the bodybuilders. Leave nothing out, not a thing!"

Ella wiped her fingers on a napkin and picked up her red square again. "Especially not how many breaths they've taken since they arrived."

"Cara, honey, Ella wants to know how many breaths you've taken since you arrived." Dorene listened, then giggled. "Cara says you came back from Florida an old fart, Ella. She wants to know what happened to you."

"A divorce." Ella knitted peacefully, but her relaxed posture had stiffened. "I'm allowed to be cranky."

Sally looking up anxiously. "Aw, Cara doesn't mean it. You know her . . ."

"*Oh my Lord!*" Dorene lunged forward in her seat, as if the force of her laughter had knocked her over. "She says they haven't been sober for three days! Wait 'til you hear this . . ."

"Here you go, Dorene." Megan held out the repaired square, then put it down and got to her feet when Dorene made no move to take it. Megan wasn't at all sorry Cara and Jocelyn would be out of town for a while. Even coping with them on the phone wore her out.

She'd known the women of Purls Before Wine for over two decades, since Dad moved Mom and her yet again the summer before Megan's senior year, trading the Minnesota lakes for the North Carolina mountains. Time marched on, but the group didn't change. Shortly after Megan married Stanley, Ella had moved to Florida with her new husband, but Jocelyn, Cara, Dorene and Sally kept right on going to the Anchor Bar every Thursday night, to the nail salon every Wednesday morning, to the Chit Chat Café for coffee. They still kept in touch all day, notes in class and giggling conferences in the halls and during lunch evolving to phone calls, e-mails and text messages. As if they might cease to exist in any recognizable form if they reached beyond the social boundaries of Comfort High School.

Their daughters played together, joined cheerleading squads together, tried out makeup and hairstyles together, ensuring their mothers' immortality by repeating their lives. Hundreds of years from now there would still be descendants of Cara, Jocelyn, Dorene, Sally and Ella sitting at the Anchor Bar on Thursday nights, talking about clothes and children and husbands and other people's flaws.

As soon as it was polite, Megan took her glass and plate into the kitchen and laid them on the discolored counter next to the scratched metal sink. After good-byes all around, she stepped out of the house and down the front steps, careful not to stumble on the loose board at the bottom. Sally deserved the easy life she'd inherit by marrying into the Tucker family. She was a real sweetheart, the only one in Purls, in Megan's opinion. But without them, Megan would be home knitting on the front porch with her mother-in-law, as she was most every night, and so she kept coming.

Down the front walk, she stepped onto the cracked, uneven pavement. At this time of night North Carolina's July became a friend, free from vengeful sunlight, with crickets chirping and floral smells magnified by lack of daylight distraction.

Even after twenty years here, and after nearly another twenty moving around the country year after year whenever her father got restless, Megan couldn't get Newfoundland, her birthplace, out of her blood. When the thermometer reached toward a mild eighty degrees, natives glowed with languid enjoyment of the summer weather while she wilted and sweated and dripped dark stains through her clothes.

She strolled to the end of Snowden, turned left onto Wiggins, not letting herself hurry even though she needed to relieve her mother-in-law from kid duty. At fifteen, her eldest daughter, Lolly, was old enough to sit for the other kids, but Megan wouldn't bet on the younger two having a healthy or stimulating time in their sister's care. The thought made her smile and slow her steps further. On warm nights she could still believe in romance, still craved it. Dancing under the stars, necking on an old porch swing . . .

From David's darkened porch she heard the tinkle of ice against the side of a glass. "How was knitting class?"

Megan took a couple of steps, to the edge of his front walk. The lights were off in his house, but she could see his dark shape sprawled on the oak bench his great-aunt Delia Cooper had bought shortly before she died the previous spring.

"Fun." She wouldn't bother elaborating. He knew the cast of characters, knew the general drill. He'd come to Comfort only a couple of years before Megan, though with his great-aunt already here, he had more to root him in the community than she did.

His ice tinkled again. Bourbon tonight. He drank his martinis straight. "All that hard work to benefit those less fortunate. True nobility."

"Thank you." Megan didn't react to his sarcasm. She'd figured out that if you extended a hand to help David with his pain these days, he'd try to bite it off.

"Join me for a drink?"

The invitation startled her. "I don't—"

"I know you don't. I've got juice, water, milk, Sprite . . ."

She hated not being able to see his face. "No. Thanks. I have to get back to the kids."

"Ah, such a good mom, Megan."

She took a step back, unsure if he was being sincere or making fun. In high school she flattered herself that she'd gotten to know David better than anyone. Seemed a silly, romantic notion now, but the two of them, outsiders both, had been drawn to each other, eventually having a brief fling before he blew out of town for college and career.

On his subsequent visits to see his great-aunt, Megan had been half intimidated by the man he'd become, felt left behind and stagnant, especially when he showed up with his wife, Victoria, the type of glamorous intellectual who made Megan want to apologize for being born.

But when he came alone, increasingly in recent years, he'd seek her out when Stanley was out of town. They'd sit in her backyard late into the night—Vera hovering disapprovingly— and talk the way she hungered to. Books, culture, movies, politics . . .

"Any calls about your guesthouse?"

Megan breathed in the soft night air and sighed it out. Since David's marriage fell apart, she'd felt as if she had a target painted on her back. He kept calling the apartment over their garage a guesthouse, probably because he could tell it annoyed her.

Stanley hadn't liked the idea of renting the apartment out. Said he didn't want a stranger living in their backyard. Megan thought he hated more the public sign that he couldn't support his family. Bitten off more than he could chew, had her darling husband. But he wasn't the one home all four weeks of the month trying to juggle three kids, his mother, too many bills and not enough paychecks. "Not yet."

"After three weeks? Can't see why. That's prime real estate—Stanley Morgan's backyard. And with the steady flood of eager tourists coming weekly to view the fascinating non-sights of Comfort . . ."

"You never know." She turned and started walking, not in the mood for David to take out his failures on her. Life changed everyone. Sometimes for the better. Sometimes not. In David's case, she hoped one day it would change him back. "Good night, David."

"Leaving so soon?"

She kept walking. "Got to get home to my kids."

"Megan Morgan, devoted part-time wife and full-time mother."

"David Langley, bitter ex-husband and full-time boozer."

She could hear him laughing as she closed her front door. The sound hurt.

"I'm home." She called upstairs to her brood and got one weak "Hi Mom" in response, making her think back to not that long ago, when the sound of her voice catapulted the three of them downstairs in a thunderous tangle of eager legs.

Maybe it was that long ago. "Vera?"

"Watching TV." Her mother-in-law's deep voice sounded from the living room. Most warm nights they sat together on the front porch, but when Vera babysat, she'd knit in front of the set so she could hear better upstairs.

"Kids do okay?" Megan paused opposite the living room where Vera half-lay in Stanley's recliner wearing her purple flowered housecoat, thick needles predictably busy.

"Kids were fine." She didn't glance up from the log cabin pattern of dark blues she'd chosen for her last blanket square, speaking as if Megan worried way too much about a little thing like her children. Given how Vera still fussed over her forty-one-year-old son, Megan figured her mother-in-law shouldn't invest in any glass houses. "How was the group? Sally get her dress yet?"

"Great. Fun." She was suddenly exhausted, the anything-can-happen mystery and romance of a summer night sucked out of her by David and now Vera. "Sally hasn't, no, but she's picked out the one she wants."

"Nothing more exciting than getting married." Vera pulled at the dark blue acrylic-wool blend; the thick yarn waggled, snake-like, across her broad stomach. "Happiest day of my life. Everything about my wedding was magical. The weather, the food, the guests—all perfect. And what came after, forty-six years . . . Not an hour goes by that I don't miss Rocky."

Megan rubbed her hand across her forehead. Vera rewrote history, brushing aside facts like so much eraser dust. According to Stanley, at his parents' wedding a surprise storm had soaked the guests on the way to the reception, where the maid of honor got so drunk she hiked up her gown and propositioned the groom on the dance floor. Vera's marriage to Rocky Morgan had lived up to his first name, alternately sullen and tumultuous. Rocky finally died two years ago, after Vera had been wishing him gone several times that long; she'd moved into her son's house almost immediately. Apparently, that was how things were done in their family. Vera had hosted Rocky's mom for eight years after her husband died. Now Megan got Vera.

"I better get Jeffrey and Deena to bed." Megan climbed the stairs, stopping to pick up books meant for Lolly's room and drawings meant for Jeffrey's.

"Oh, Megan?"

She backtracked down half the flight and leaned over the worn banister. "Yes?"

"Some woman staying at the Quality Inn in Hendersonville called. She saw your ad at the Chit Chat Café. Wants to take a look at the apartment."

"Really?" Megan got that same hit of claustrophobic panic to her stomach as when Stanley announced his mother was moving in, only this time the intrusion had been her own idea. "Did you get her number?"

"Mo-o-om?" Her middle child, Deena, in that injured tone she'd perfected two years ago at eleven. "Will you *pleez* tell Jeffrey to stop—"

"Hold on, Deena. Sorry, yes Vera? The number?"

"By the phone in the kitchen. She wants you to call back tonight."

"Thank you."

"Jeffrey keeps singing another song while I'm trying to listen to this one."

Megan rolled her eyes and turned to her daughter, plump,

dark and introverted as her older sister was golden, outgoing and athletic. "And?"

"It's buggin' me. He won't stop."

"Boohoo, tattletale." Jeffrey stood defiantly in the hall, a skinny, rumple-headed nine-year-old, spitting image of his father's photos at that age.

Deena fisted her hands. "Try singin' on key and you won't be so annoying."

Megan sighed. "You're both annoying. It's late. Jeffrey, you're supposed to be in your pajamas, teeth brushed."

"You said I had to be ready to go to bed. I *am* ready. I just don't have my pajamas on or my teeth brushed."

Megan frowned hard so her smile wouldn't show. "When you're a famous lawyer, you can split those hairs, not while you're in my house."

"Famous lawyer ha, famous *barber* maybe. Split *those* hairs, Jeffrey."

"Deena . . ." Megan hauled out her I'm-losing-patience voice, which, she'd noticed, worked less and less the older her kids got. Maybe she wasn't tough enough. Maybe they needed their father around more. . .

Half an hour later, children nestled all snug in their beds, Megan went downstairs, trying not to count how many more days until school started again. Summer seemed to go on forever.

She bypassed Vera, yarn slack, nodding off over a rerun episode of *ER*, and stood by the phone staring at the number scrawled in Vera's sloppy hand on the pale yellow pad sprinkled with faint sunflowers.

Tidy up the kitchen first. She picked up a big plastic bowl

the kids must have used for popcorn, dumped the unpopped kernels into the trash and filled it with warm water bubbled up with Palmolive detergent. She had a perfectly good dishwasher but sometimes she needed to stand at the sink, gazing out into her garden, now dark and invisible, and gradually trade the chaos of used dishes for a neatly organized drain rack of clean ones.

Dishes done, she wiped the counters dreamily, passing over the burn scar where Stanley had dropped a pot he thought cool enough to carry from the stove with his bare hands, past the pitted surface caused by her youngest playing carpenter with one of Daddy's screwdrivers. By the time she'd wiped under the dish rack, put away the place mats and the butter and jelly left out, she wondered if it was too late to call, aware she'd been procrastinating all along.

But if she didn't call tonight, the thought of having to tomorrow would disturb her reading and her sleep, and she'd wake up dreading it.

She dialed. The phone made a loud jingly ring once, twice, then a pleasant woman answered and connected Megan to the room of her potential boarder.

Another ring, then another woman. "Yes? Hello?"

"This is Megan Morgan. You answered my ad at the Chit Chat Café about our garage apartment?" She wasn't going to call it a guesthouse.

"Yes, yes. Thanks for returning my call. I'm Elizabeth Detlaff." The voice was clear, young, confident, with a minor flavor of New York.

"I hope I'm not calling too late." Self-consciously, Megan tuned in to her own words and heard traces of her adopted Southern accent, which sprouted when she got nervous.

"No, not at all, I'm a night owl. I just finished my run and was about to do some yoga and meditate."

Megan had no idea what to say to that, but her stomach started feeling a bit sick. "Well, welcome to Comfort, Miss . . . Mrs.?"

"*Ms.* Call me Elizabeth, though. Can I come by tomorrow morning?"

"Yes, sure." She'd forgotten how Northeasterners attacked conversation as if it were a nuisance weed best gotten rid of quickly. "How about ten o'clock?"

"Perfect. Thirty-seven Wiggins Street? What does the house look like?"

"A white colonial with burgundy shutters." Which badly needed painting.

"Got it. I'm *so* looking forward to this. The last few days have been crazy, I still can't believe I'm here!" Elizabeth's enthusiasm was startling. "And *then* to find you have a one-bedroom to rent by the week . . . I can't get over it."

Megan had a stupid urge to giggle nervously, like she did when she was a girl. People always wanted to know what was so funny, which she hated, because there was nothing funny about being shy. "Well . . . good, then."

"See you tomorrow, ten o'clock."

"Yes. I'll be here." Megan hung up, feeling sicker, and went into the living room to wake Vera for bed. The rental announcement had been out for weeks in the *Comfort Gazette* and up at the Chit Chat Café. The family wasn't yet desperate, but having decided to rent, Megan couldn't bring herself to turn down money. If not this woman, then who?

"Vera." She shook Vera's soft shoulder.

Look how she'd made peace with her mother-in-law moving in, gradually getting over her horror at the thought of Vera underfoot every day. Given that Stanley was gone so much, having another adult body around wasn't so bad.

You adjusted. You got used to things. Overlooked what you could and bore what you couldn't. Most stopped hurting eventually.

Chapter Two

Elizabeth still couldn't believe she was doing this. Though sitting in the back of the taxi on her way to meet Megan, peering eagerly right and left, she was slowly being charmed out of her panic. Over the last two days everything had fallen into place in ways that still seemed eerie. Her late grandmother would have been thrilled. Emma Burschke believed strongly that God sent guiding signs to His people, and she'd carefully taught her dutiful daughter and rebellious granddaughter to watch for them. Okay. Whatever.

But . . . two mornings ago Elizabeth had woken abruptly from a dream in which her *babcia* had lectured her, somber as always in the black anachronism of a dress she insisted on wearing until her death, gray hair pulled back severely, impressive brows an awning for her still-vibrant blue eyes. *Elizabeth. You must go find comfort.*

The dream had been so vivid, her grandmother's voice so urgent, Elizabeth had lain there, alone in the Manhattan condo she shared with her chef boyfriend, Dominique, heart pounding while her brain produced a disturbing slide show of other "signs" from the previous days. At the coffee shop. The museum. The story on the radio about someone retreating to a small town in North Carolina that Elizabeth barely heard until the town's name jumped out at her.

Comfort.

Everything could have stopped there, been left with an uneasy shrug, if Dominique hadn't chosen that moment, while the dream was still fresh, to call her from England, where he was spending a month as a guest chef and pursuing summer truffles for a new fall menu. She'd e-mailed him impulsively the night before, asking if he'd consider using one of her fledgling fabric designs for his restaurant linens, since she hadn't managed to sell them anywhere else. Seemed a no-brainer to her. Original cloths and napkins for him, exposure for her.

His response was typically to the point. No. They were too *her* and not enough *him*. Not to mention she had no design or business experience, just a natural drawing talent that she'd never pursued seriously. *And* he had no time to hold her hand through yet another entrepreneurial idea she wouldn't stick with. If she wanted something to do, she shouldn't have quit her secretary job, blah blah blah.

The fight went south from there until anger released the ultimatum he'd been hinting at for months but not laid down, a less blunt version of "Marry me . . . or else."

She'd had to stifle panic. *Or else what?* He'd kick her out? Stop supporting her? She loved him, but marriage . . . Maybe she'd find out on this trip what was holding her back, maybe that was why she'd needed to leave New York so desperately.

Comfort. From her first glimpse of the rolling Blue Ridge Mountains out the plane window to today's drive over the picturesque winding roads and her eyeful of the quaint brick buildings that comprised the tiny downtown—still decorated for the Fourth of July celebration—she had a strange impression that she was coming home. Given that she'd never set foot in the area before, it made no sense, unless her grandmother's woo-woo theories had something to them after all. Regardless, she felt as tied to this lovely spot as she'd come to feel foreign and adrift in Manhattan.

Maybe Dominique felt this way each time he got off the plane in France, back on home soil where his DNA belonged. She'd never really thought about his status as an immigrant since he thrived so heartily in New York, and since to her he spoke mostly about food and wine . . . and Dominique. The good and bad of strong personality traits—confidence was the sexy yang, the trait that had drawn her to him, self-absorption its flipside yin.

Having seen Comfort, she wanted to stay the whole month he was away, who knew beyond that? After she'd secured the last seat on the last flight to Asheville, leaving half an hour after her impulsive arrival at LaGuardia, and after she'd walked into the Chit Chat Café and seen the ad for a room to let by the week, she'd been tempted to offer up a freaked-out but grateful prayer to *Babcia*, and felt renewed guilt that she hadn't visited her grandmother before her death, or her mom in the decade-plus since she'd fled Milwaukee. Stilted phone calls, birthday and Christmas cards—Mom didn't understand her life and its sudden changes; Elizabeth couldn't fathom Mom's stoic and static existence, decade after decade.

"How much farther?" She leaned forward, grasping the back

of the seat in front of her, tickled at the lack of bulletproof glass between her and the driver.

The pudgy blond cabbie gestured forward. "A few blocks is all."

"I'll walk the rest."

She paid and hoisted her overnight bag onto her shoulder. The day promised to be hot, though not humid-unbearable like New York—the mountains took care of that. Oaks and maples and other trees she couldn't identify lined streets and punctuated neat yards, providing shade and cool. Birds called, cicadas sang, a group of yelling kids charged around a plastic wading pool. How different from noisy, crowded, overstimulating New York, where only yesterday she'd felt she'd suffocate, mind full of her grandmother's urgent words, *you must go find comfort,* and Dominique's, *marry me now or admit you never will.*

Comfort.

She turned left on Wiggins Street, excitement rising. There would be nice people here—decent, honest and hardworking people who knew how to relax without spending thousands of dollars on therapy and prescriptions and spa visits.

There it was. She could see the house halfway down the street, white with burgundy shutters, exactly as Megan had described, flying an American flag. She quickened her steps, ready to start taking on this town, this neighborhood, this new life, try them on for size and see how they fit.

One house before Megan's, a sudden movement—the front door hurled open. A man stepped out, eyes circled and bleary with sleep, dark hair pointing in all directions, considerable stubble on his jaw, cheeks unhealthily pale, steaming mug in one hand. He was barefoot, shirtless, wearing boxers whose fly gaped to reveal darkness when he bent to scoop up a familiar copy of the *New York Times*, which seemed oddly out of place anywhere but in her city.

The man straightened and saw her, showed no embarrassment to be caught just out of bed at 10 A.M. on a Tuesday in his underwear. He tucked the paper under the arm with the mug and shielded his eyes with the other hand, squinting as if the warm sunlight pouring over the town was torture. "Who the hell are you?"

"Elizabeth Detlaff." She smiled graciously. "Who the hell are you?"

A flicker of amusement. "David Langley."

He looked as if he expected—no, dreaded—some reaction. The name sounded familiar, but she couldn't remember where she'd heard it. "Nice to meet you, David."

He slurped his coffee loudly. "Uh-huh."

Her city soul suggested she blow him a raspberry, which made her even more determined to be polite. "I'm meeting your neighbor Megan about renting her apartment next door."

"Yeah?" His stomach gurgled loudly; it was that quiet in this neighborhood. "Where'd you come from?"

"Manhattan."

"You know someone here? Have family nearby? Wedding? Funeral?"

"I came on my own."

"Because . . ."

"To experience the town."

He snorted. "That'll take a good bite out of half an hour. What, you're some kind of missionary?"

"No."

"Mary Kay?"

"Uh . . . no." She called his disdain and raised him.

"Don't tell me, let me guess." He rubbed his belly, snapped the waistband of his boxers with his thumb. "Ditched the boyfriend or he kicked you out."

"Nothing like that." She rushed her answer, sounding defensive and therefore guilty.

"No, of course, nothing like that." He took another slurp of coffee, staring at her over the rim. She waited him out. "Well, *welcome* to Comfort, Ms. Detlaff. If there's anything we colorful locals can do to make your stay more enjoyable, please let us know."

"Thank you." She ignored his sarcasm. If she wanted to indulge cranky cynics, she would have stayed in New York. "I'm sure I'll see you again if we're going to be neighbors."

"Oh absolutely. We'll do potlucks and Tupperware parties."

Elizabeth stalked next door, happily unable to hear whatever else he mumbled as he went back into his house. He didn't seem to belong here any more than she belonged in New York, though for a lot of years she thought she did. Too easy to fool yourself into thinking something was true just because you wanted to believe it.

Up the evocatively creaky front-porch steps, across the porch itself—with genuine rocking chair!—to the screen door, so picturesquely in need of painting she nearly got a lump in her throat. If she'd had to spend one more night in the soulless decorator-perfect condo she shared with Dominique, she would have gone over the edge. Hard to remember how thrilling it had been when his restaurant's success and subsequent cable-show stardom not only bought them the place, but gave them license to remodel it to their taste . . . to Dominique's taste.

She rang the doorbell, *ding-dong*, and waited breathlessly for a collie to start barking and Timmy to show. *Down, Lassie, it's that real nice lady I was tellin' you 'bout.*

Instead, a woman who must be Megan opened the door, pushed out the screen, making only brief eye contact but with a smile. Elizabeth did get a lump in her throat then, along with yet another shivery dose of woo-woo insight: She and this woman were going to be close friends.

Okay, Babcia. *Enough.*

Megan was older than she sounded on the phone, probably ten years older than Elizabeth's thirty, and beautiful—even if Elizabeth hadn't been in the mood to think everything in Comfort was beautiful. She had thick auburn hair pulled back in a short, low ponytail, greenish eyes set wide apart and slightly freckled skin, flawless without makeup. A few extra pounds softened her, partly camouflaged under an apricot scoop-neck tee and a chocolate brown jumper. She looked so casually cool and comfortable, Elizabeth felt self-conscious in her all-the-rage sleeveless tunic and cropped designer jeans, and promised herself she'd go shopping soon and find a new image to match her surroundings. When in Comfort . . .

"Hi Megan! I'm Elizabeth. It's really nice to meet you."

Megan nodded at her floor, still smiling. "Nice to meet you, too. I hope you had a good trip."

"I had a trip from hell."

"I'm sorry to hear that." Megan glanced up. "Did you drive or fly?"

"I flew. The flight was fine." She tapped her head. "The hell was in here."

"Oh . . ."

Elizabeth bunched her mouth. She'd probably just scared

the poor woman to death. "I'm fine, really. Just some upheaval. It's all behind me now."

Megan's brows rose. "Well good. The apartment is in the backyard. You can come through the house or go around, whichever you'd like."

Like David's, her accent wasn't quite Southern. Elizabeth hadn't been able to tell for sure on the phone, but she'd suspected not. Disappointing, since the lilting local language-tune made her want to lie down and be told stories past her bedtime.

"I'll come through." Who wouldn't want the chance to see part of someone's life? Megan nodded and moved aside so Elizabeth could step in.

Inside, a real home. Not the dreary European-widow look of Elizabeth's childhood in South Milwaukee, nor the sloppy college-kid apartment she'd shared with then-boyfriend Alan in Boston, nor the bonsai/exotic artwork/koi-pond artifice of her and Dominique's condo. Instead, a dark paneled living room—with genuine recliner!—and a TV that looked to be all of nineteen inches; a cross-stitch sampler in faded pastels, framed and hung on the wall: *Bless this house and all who live within its walls;* a shabby floral rug on scuffed plank floors; a coffee table covered with a lace cloth; more lace curtaining the windows. Exquisite lace, now that she looked harder, intricate and cobwebby soft.

"What gorgeous curtains."

"Thank you." Megan kept walking. "We enjoy them."

Elizabeth followed slowly, glancing around, taking in as much as possible, itching for her sketch pad to record what she saw. Some people kept journals with words; hers comprised pictures—most recently, failed fabric design ideas. To the left, a dining room with chubby-legged dining table and chairs and a matching sideboard. One of the chairs had been re-glued or repaired, ropes still holding the legs in place.

On the right, a family room, entrance under the stairs, games stacked haphazardly on shelves, worn and stained olive green carpet, an air hockey table and a fleet of metal vehicles jumbled in one corner—yellow backhoes and diggers and dump trucks. Megan did have children; Elizabeth couldn't wait to meet them. Husband too? She'd have to ask. To the left at the back, the kitchen—faded and cracked linoleum floor in a yellowing spotted pattern that had probably always been ugly; cheap table and chairs; dingy countertops.

But everything recently scrubbed and tidy, everything with character and probably a story, everything said family, home, warmth . . . and comfort.

"Your house is beautiful, Megan."

Megan glanced over her shoulder in surprise. "Well. Thank you."

Outside, down concrete steps into a garden—an entirely different story.

"Wow." Elizabeth turned slowly, savoring each sight, shape, color and scent. "Your yard is amazing."

Megan laughed abruptly, self-consciously. "Thank you."

"Did you do this all yourself?"

"Yes." She swung her sandaled foot to kick at scalloped black edging. "I enjoy it."

"Where I live, you could charge people a fortune to make their yards look like this."

Megan laughed again, still nervously. "Mostly I grow what we eat."

"Seriously, you should think about it." If Megan was taking

in boarders, she had to need the cash. "Dominique had someone design a garden on our building's roof, and the guy could buy a Hawaiian island on what we paid him. I can take pictures of your yard and show some people I know who've moved to North Carolina from—"

"Thank you, but no." Megan met Elizabeth's eyes then, expression calm but definite. "I just do it for our family."

"Okay." Had Elizabeth offended her? She hadn't meant to. "Where are you from originally, Megan?"

"Oh." She waved around her. "All over."

"Your accent . . ."

"I was born in Newfoundland, but we moved frequently."

"Newfoundland, how *cool*!"

Megan looked taken aback. "Oh. Thank you."

"So you moved a lot. Was your dad in the military?"

"He's an electrician." She took a step away, arms folded, each hand clutching the opposite elbow.

"His company kept transferring him?"

She pressed her lips together. "He just liked moving."

"I see." Elizabeth tried to look pensive while she wondered if there was anything Megan would talk about in longer sentences. "I grew up in Milwaukee, then I lived in Boston for a while, now New York City."

Megan nodded, head at an angle that made Elizabeth want to draw her. Madonna Among the Herbs. "How long do you think you'll be here?"

"I don't know." She turned her face blissfully up to the sun. "One month certainly."

"But it could be longer?"

"Mmm. I don't know."

"Ms. Detlaff—"

"Elizabeth."

"—I'm . . . curious. About why you chose Comfort."

Elizabeth opened her eyes. Megan was watching her a little anxiously. This would probably not be a good time to become *Babcia* and say Comfort had chosen *her*. At the same time, she didn't want to lie. Lies didn't belong in a place like Comfort. "I had a fight with my boyfriend and needed to get away for a while."

"Oh, I'm sorry."

"Thanks." Elizabeth did another visual sweep of the garden. Sage, thyme, lavender, tarragon, oregano, dill, rosemary, basil, vegetables Elizabeth recognized and a few she didn't.

"Dominique is a chef, so our garden has herbs and vegetables too. Here's his card." She dug in her purse and handed it over proudly. *Dominique!* in gold, the name of his restaurant, then underneath, his cable show: *French Food Fast.* "Are you the cook of the house?"

"Yes."

"Are you married?"

"Yes."

"With children? I saw the playroom . . ."

"Three. Two girls and a boy. My mother-in-law lives with us too."

Wow. Three answers to one question. "What does your husband do?"

"Stanley is a salesman." Megan looked back down at the brick path. "He sells physical therapy equipment."

"Does he travel a lot?"

"Two weeks out of the month."

"Ouch. That's hard, I know. My boyfriend not only travels, but when he's home, he's gone all day and way past midnight at his restaurant. It's that much harder to have any kind of relationship, isn't it?"

"I guess." Megan's cheeks flushed; she turned away. Obviously, Elizabeth shouldn't have said anything about relationships, though she'd only meant to show sympathy. "I'll show you the apartment now."

"That would be great." She followed Megan on the flagstone pathway to a side entrance in the garage, anticipating the sight of what she hoped would become her new home, up a flight of steep, musty stairs carpeted gray blue.

The place was small, two rooms and a bathroom, the bedroom in wall-to-wall dark, plush gray, a single bed covered by a quilt sprigged with tiny pink flowers over a rose-colored bedskirt, a mottled dark wood dresser with more of that intricate lace draped across the top, and a plain blue chair with a couple of white paint drips on its seat.

In the living room, a navy love seat with red-white-and-blue pillows, a bare coffee table, an eagle-emblazoned rocker by the window and an overstuffed chair in what looked like a home-made maroon slipcover. More lace curtains blew gently in the warm breeze. In one corner, a small brown refrigerator, a sink with two cabinets above, two below and a two-burner electric cooktop sitting on its tiny counter.

Elizabeth walked through, stood in the center of each room and felt an aura in the place. Honesty. Hard work. Pride.

"I'm sure it's not what you're used to."

"Oh, no, it's—"

"The kitchen's not much. Rent includes supper in the house

with the family every evening if you want. Or not, if you'd rather not." The last added somewhat hopefully.

"It's perfect." Hodgepodge, mismatched, and perfect.

"Really?" Megan was looking around as if Elizabeth were talking about some other apartment, and she'd like to know whose.

"Yes, really. And that lace . . ." She sighed rapturously, walked over and stretched the panel out into the room. Exquisite. *Handmade*. "Did you get it locally?"

"We—yes. Most of it."

"I'll want to buy tons to take home." Elizabeth dropped the curtain and turned in a complete circle, arms wide. Imagine waking up in that cute bed, hearing the birdies chirping a good-morning song worthy of a Disney movie. Drinking her coffee with a view of mountains, reading by the window in the rocking chair. She could picture the life so clearly it was almost as if she'd already lived here. "I'll take the place."

"Oh." Megan backed up a couple of steps. "When were you thinking of moving in?"

"Right away. Today. Right now." She couldn't believe the positive vibes she was getting from this whole experience. *You win*, Babcia. She was meant to be here, in this room, near this house, in this tiny town in a state she'd never visited before. And even if she never figured out why, the experience was already uplifting and healing. Her panic over the last few days had completely abated.

"The kids can be loud. You might not be used to that."

"I'll love it."

"They're around all day, not in camp or anything."

"It's not a problem."

"I . . . will need to make sure your check clears."

Elizabeth smiled. "I can pay cash if you point me to an ATM."

"Cash." Megan slid her eyes sideways, as if to consult the door. "Well."

"I have excellent credit. No criminal record. I'm quiet, neat and clean. I don't smoke or use drugs. I'm on a journey I don't understand yet, but I hope to soon. Maybe you're supposed to share it with me."

Megan looked slightly horrified at this last impulsive addition to Elizabeth's speech. Her lips parted, closed. Parted again. "I don't think I need to go on a . . . journey with anyone."

"Right. Okay." She rubbed her forehead. Too much too soon. "Then maybe I'm here to learn from you."

Megan laughed her nervous laugh and took another step back. "I have nothing to teach anybody."

"My grandmother used to say, 'Everyone can be a teacher, if only by example.'" Elizabeth smiled encouragingly. "Which would make me a student just being around you."

"Ah." She looked as if she wanted to step back farther, but she was nearly at the door and might topple down the stairs.

"I know this sounds crazy because you haven't lived through the past few days with me. Even I thought it was crazy at first. I still don't know why, but I need this time to be away from my life." Elizabeth moved toward her, eager to explain this much at least. "When I walked into the Chit Chat Café, the first thing I saw was your advertisement tacked to the community board. The breeze from the door blew it toward me. The fringe tags with your number tapped me on the shoulder, 'Hey, Elizabeth, check me out.' This apartment is *exactly* the type of arrangement I imagined when I flew down here, but I never dreamed

I'd find it. Now here it is. And here you are. And here I am."

Elizabeth waited anxiously, afraid she'd babbled on too long, willing Megan to understand how important this was to her, and who knew, maybe to both of them.

Megan took in a deep breath which pushed the slight bulge of her stomach against the knit fabric of her loose dress, then exhaled so the material deflated to hang straight again. "No one else has come asking about the place. I could use the money. If you want it, it's yours."

Chapter Three

*Fiona's love, Calum, lost his father to illness the previ-
ous year. He fishes alone in the* voes—*the small fjords of
the islands—or goes out farther with Fiona's father, Andrew. This week his mum has gone to Lerwick by horse
carriage to see a doctor for Calum's younger brother, who
is ill. Fiona's mother, Mary, and her father invite Calum
to share their Saturday dinner of* krappin—*a stuffed fish
dish—and oat bread Fiona baked herself, praying the
rounds would come out perfect and that Calum would
notice and think what a good wife she'd make.*

They have a merry time in the but *end of the house—
the main living area—while outside, rain pelts the
thatch and wind buffets the sheep and horses who roam
there, feeding and watering themselves. Calum has never
looked so handsome. He is tall, grown broad and muscu-*

lar with age, and fair-complected with lively brown eyes and boyish freckles, his short coffee-colored hair attempting as usual to escape its combing.

The talk is of fishing, of the storm that blew up from a beautiful calm and threatened the men and their catch, how they took down sails and rowed grimly over the writhing gray waves to a sheltered voe. How, while they waited out the gale, one man told a tale of his great-grandfather, approached during such a storm by a mermaid who tried to lure him into her arms with sweet songs and promises of safety. Had his friends not held him back he would have jumped overboard to have her. Legend has it that mermaids must bewitch humans into consummated marriage or suffer the loss of their beauty to unions with coarse, brutal finmen, amphibious creatures who have no love for the humans competing for their fish and women.

At the Tullochs' that night they talk further, about how the house next to Calum is empty, how Paul Halcrow and his wife and children left one night years back, taking nothing with them, and never returned.

Calum is thinking how pretty Fiona looks, firelight glinting in her eyes and off the fair strands of her hair. He feels the expectations of everyone around him that they will marry. His head tells him he won't find a prettier or harder working or more agreeable wife; his heart tells him she's loyal and good tempered; his loins tell him she's shaped to please and to bear him strong sons. But a voice coming from a place he doesn't understand tells him to be patient and wait. So he does, though Fiona is of marrying age and someone could steal her from him.

As the dinner breaks up, as he prepares to tramp over the wet and uneven land to his home, where he'll bank the fire, crawl into his enclosed wooden box bed and shut out the twenty-four-hour summer light, he finds himself asking if Fiona has seen where they're breaking ground for a lighthouse at Eshaness's highest cliff's edge, over by the broch—an ancient round stone ruin.

She says no, shyly, eyes shining, and right there in front of her parents he offers to take her to see. Fiona says yes, hardly able to control her joy. Her parents beam; they like this young man, trust him and want their daughter to be happy with him almost as much as she does.

As Calum says his thank-yous and good-byes, there is a knock at the door, always unlocked, always open to strangers and friends alike, as is the Shetland way. A beautiful woman stands outside. Green eyed, ruby lipped, she clutches a black cape around her tall, proud, slender body and greets them in the voice of an angel temptress. She is Paul Halcrow's niece, Gillian, moved here from Unst, the most northern of the Shetland Islands, into her family's house next door to Calum. Would he bring his tusker and help her cut and stock peat the next day after church? She will pay him for his trouble, though she hasn't much to offer.

Watching her full lips surrounded by alabaster skin speaking such unexpected words, and watching her loose black hair blowing wild, Calum suddenly understands, as well as he understands the wind and tides on the surrounding sea, why he needed to wait.

* * *

Megan took a sip of coffee and grimaced. Too watery. She didn't like the new machine, or maybe she hadn't yet figured a way to work out proportions and grind. Her old maker had lasted five years before it vanished. She was used to things developing legs around the house, though so far, nothing too personal had disappeared, like jewelry—she'd kill him—but she'd liked that coffeemaker. When replacing it, she should have known better than to go for the lowest price. You got what you paid for.

Another sip, sitting in the backyard on the worn green lawn furniture handed down from Vera and Rocky. Megan didn't need to be rich, but being able to own things she enjoyed rather than put up with would be nice. She and Stanley had had big plans when they moved in, to renovate floors and bathrooms and cabinetry first, then gradually replace the worn and ancient furniture and appliances with quality. But money had been tight at first; they waited to try for children, then her body took a while to catch on to the idea of pregnancy. Everything changed while she was carrying Lolly, when she discovered her husband's other life.

She'd married Stanley because she loved him, but also, with her family moving again, to embrace the luxury of stability, of staying in one place with a chance to put down roots, form relationships that didn't have to be cut short before they'd deepened enough to become comfortable and dependable. Megan had read that sometimes soldiers hesitated to form close friendships in combat situations to keep themselves safe from grief on top of the fear and stress. Moving became her combat situation. She'd learned to keep to herself, devouring books, playing alone, spending time in her head. The skills stood her in good stead in this town. Things hadn't turned out the way she expected, with her husband gone so often and with Comfort the way it was. Unless you were native, you didn't really belong.

The only deep friendship she'd developed in childhood was with her mother, Aileen, who stayed calm through the relentless upheavals, knitting the Shetland lace of her ancestors, passing along the craft and the stories to her daughter. Megan had wanted to pass the same along to Lolly and Deena, but she'd stopped knitting lace. She wasn't even sure they knew the curtains in their house had been made by Megan's mother and her grandmother Bridget. None of the lace her great-grandmother Fiona knit on Shetland had survived.

Megan settled back, adjusting her shoulder blades more comfortably against the chair's plastic slats. A cool breeze brought fresh herbal scents to mix with her coffee's too-weak aroma. This time of day was her favorite, early, just after dawn, before the kids got up, before Vera got up, when the only creatures sharing her day were birds and butterflies, none of whom asked or expected anything. The only time she could reliably be other than mother and wife except the precious hour before sleep when she escaped into a book.

Megan needed this morning more than most, having spent yesterday helping her new whirlwind move in. Taking her to Hendersonville to rent a car; giving her directions to the supermarket, then back home; in the middle of making oatmeal chocolate-chip cookies answering the phone to hear Elizabeth exclaim that there was so much pork in the meat section at the supermarket and hardly any chicken. Then calling Stanley with the news that she'd succeeded in finding a renter, and Stanley insisting he speak to Elizabeth, thereby giving the necessary head-of-the-household stamp of his approval.

At dinner, Elizabeth continued her examination, question-

ing the kids, what were their favorite toys, movies, subjects . . .
more questions than even Jeffrey asked, which was saying something.

This peaceful morning time gave Megan the energy she
needed, charged her batteries almost better than sleep could,
and good thing, because she hadn't slept well. All night long
she'd wakened, her subconscious aware of Elizabeth's new
presence as if she were sleeping right there on the floor in Megan's room.

The garage apartment window rattled up only yards from
where she sat, making her jump and grip her mug too tightly.
The screen grated up next and Elizabeth's blond head poked
out, straight hair falling neatly into its fashionably uneven
bob, even though she was still in her pajamas and probably
just out of bed. Her bright blue eyes were closed; she breathed
in the morning air as if it would save her life. Megan held
still, coffee clutched halfway between resting and her next
sip, memory bringing back New York's sounds and smells and
the lung-starving feeling that there wasn't enough space or
air. The move away from there was the only one she hadn't
objected to.

Elizabeth's eyes opened; she scanned the sky, David's trees
next door . . .

Maybe if Megan didn't move, she'd pull her head back in
without—

"Hey, good morning. It is so-o-o gorgeous here!"

Megan put her mug down, breathing through a wave of annoyance. Overreaction. Maybe her new housemate had woken
early just today. Maybe it wouldn't be a habit and Megan could
keep her sacred alone time for the next month—or however
long before Elizabeth left.

"Good morning. How did you sleep?" She kept her voice low to signal that the rest of the house wasn't awake yet.

"Like a *rock*." Elizabeth didn't take the hint. "I couldn't believe how quiet it was. No shouting, no sirens. No honking horns."

"Only birds." Megan smiled more warmly than she felt. *And now you.*

"They're wonderful." She took another rapturous breath. "I'll get dressed and be right down."

Megan picked up her mug again, wrapped both hands around its fading warmth. She'd do fine without her quiet time, even if Elizabeth did get up this early every day. For heaven's sake.

She got to her feet and wandered around her soothing garden. The tall okra plants were blooming well, unfurling yellow petals to show off deep purple inside. Some pods needed harvesting; if they grew bigger than three inches, they'd get tough enough to build with. Next to the okra, bees buzzed around the flowering mint. She brushed her hand over the rounded sage bush and pinched a rosemary needle to inhale its calming fragrance.

The side door to the garage opened and out stepped her tenant in another expensively casual outfit, a floral minidress that showed off her still-young cleavage and made Megan feel dowdy in her plain khaki shorts and pale olive T-shirt.

"Hi again!"

This time Megan put a finger to her carefully smiling lips. "Everyone's still asleep."

"Oops. Sorry. I assumed you were all up." She stretched her slender, muscular arms above her head. "Mmm, is that coffee?"

Megan's smile drooped. She thought she'd been clear about supper being the only meal she'd offer. "Would you like a cup?"

"I'd love it, thank you." She brought her arms down, smiling and more relaxed than the day before, when she'd been all nervous energy and draining excitement. "Just tell me where it is, I'll help myself."

Megan started toward the house, ashamed to have been so grudging about a cup of coffee. "It's in the kitchen. I'll show you."

"You don't have to—"

"It's no trouble. This way." Megan stepped into the house and into the kitchen.

"Good morning." Vera, up already, shuffling in her green flowered robe and pink terry mules, fissured heels slipping sideways off the soles.

Grand Central Station this morning.

"Did we wake you?" Megan reached into the cupboard for Stanley's favorite mug, the biggest one they had, to scold herself for feeling so inhospitable.

"No. I was up reading. I can't sleep worth a nickel anymore." She nodded to Elizabeth. "Getting old is not for sissies."

"Bette Davis."

Vera lowered herself stiffly into the chair, letting go the last few inches so she thumped down with her trademark loud sigh. "I'm sorry?"

"Bette Davis said that."

"That is such a pretty dress, Elizabeth. Megan, why don't you get something like that? It'd look real cute on you. Get Stanley to buy you a dress next time he comes home, he's always buying you things. Something with some color in it. You're always so drab."

"We have better things to spend our money on, Vera. Do you take anything in your coffee, Elizabeth?"

"Black is fine." Elizabeth walked around the kitchen touching everything in reach like a child—the china plate on the wall, Jeffrey's black and red drawing of a battleship, the basket of still-unripe peaches. "This house is so nice."

Vera raised her thin brows. "I'll show you the house *I* grew up in. Now that was a house. Built by a retired ship's captain who was sick of the sea in, oh, let's see, can't remember the date exactly . . ."

"Here's your coffee, Elizabeth." Megan thrust it out to her. "A little weak I'm afraid. New machine I'm getting used to."

"Thanks." She took a sip, looked surprised and set the mug down on the counter, went back to touching. The bunch of mint in the glass on the sill; the tile backsplash; the butcher-block holder for Megan's knives; the vase of peonies with a doily underneath, leaving her mark everywhere. "Okay, now you have to tell me exactly where you got this lace. I've never seen anything like it."

Megan set Vera's coffee down in front of her, then turned and began putting together plates of homemade biscuits, sliced plums and her own strawberry jam. All these questions. Let Vera answer how she would.

"I made that."

"*You* did? Wow!" Elizabeth gently pulled the doily out from under the vase and trailed a reverential finger around its edges. Her hands were smooth and elegant, not yet showing the tendons and veins that had turned Megan's middle aged. "Tatting? Is that what you call it?"

"Ah, no. No no. This is Shetland lace, it's knitted."

"Knitted!? You *knitted* this?"

"Yes, ma'am." Vera was practically floating out of her chair with pride.

"With what needles? Size zero?" Elizabeth laughed as if she thought she was making a hilarious joke, and held the lace up to the window for the light to come through its delicate design, transferring shadows of the trellis diamond center and wave edging onto her face.

"I used double zeros."

"*Double* zero needles?" She turned, mouth dropping comically wide.

"One-point-seven-five millimeters thick."

"Holy shi—" She stopped when she saw Vera's scowl. "Sorry, New York mouth."

"Do you knit, Elizabeth?" Megan spoke to give Vera time to recover, though she'd heard her mother-in-law swearing up a storm when she thought no one could hear.

"Yup. My grandmother taught me. She and my great-grandmother both worked for the National Knitting Company in Milwaukee when they were young, making gloves, mittens, sweaters . . . My mom knits too. How did you learn to do this?"

"Megan's great-grandmother grew up in the Shetland Islands, north of Scotland."

"Really! Wow! Where the ponies come from?" Elizabeth laid the delicate circle over her arm and stroked it admiringly. "So you taught Vera, Megan?"

"Yes." Megan spoke shortly, putting a loaded plate in front of Vera, praying no more questions would be hurled at her. Her relationship with lace was none of Elizabeth's business.

"It's *so* beautiful." Elizabeth held the doily back up to the light, then draped it onto her hair and preened, laughing.

Megan wanted to grab the lace and put it back under the vase where it belonged. "Have some breakfast, Elizabeth?"

"I don't eat breakfast." She saw Megan holding the plate and gasped. "Oh no! You shouldn't have gone to that trouble."

"It was no trouble. Someone else will eat it."

"Why don't you sit down here, Elizabeth, so we can chat." Vera patted the table beside her, Megan's place. "I still haven't heard how you came to Comfort. Megan was vague on answers."

Megan poured herself more coffee and put her plate at Jeffrey's spot.

"Well, it was funny." Elizabeth plunked herself down as if she'd lived with them all her life. "No, not funny. It's actually sort of weird."

"Weird how?" Vera asked.

"Kind of . . . message-from-beyond-the-grave weird."

"Mercy." Vera was all ears. "I've often thought I had psychic powers myself. Tell me."

"Two days ago my grandmother told me to go find 'comfort.'"

"The one who knits?"

"She's no longer alive."

"Well *my* goodness."

"It was in a dream. I had no idea what she meant at first, but then I remembered the day before in a coffee shop, I'd had *Comfort* tea."

Megan brought Stanley's mug to the table, then sat down to her breakfast. She didn't want to hear the rest of the story almost as much as Vera did. "Did you want your coffee, Elizabeth?"

"Oh, yes, thank you." Elizabeth took another tentative sip. "So *then* I remembered that after the coffee shop, I'd been at this antique store on Tenth Street that specializes in Biedermeier furniture, and the guy kept talking about the convenience and *comfort* of the furniture compared to the Empire style. I swear, he kept repeating this word. So I was actually standing there thinking of naming my first fabric line Comfort!"

"You're a designer?" Vera glanced at Megan, who didn't react.

"I'm *attempting* to be a designer. I brought my sketchbook and paints with me. I thought I could try the mountains and woods around here for inspiration. So far I haven't come up with any patterns I really love."

"You will." Vera attacked a biscuit, a crumb adhering to one of the fjords in her upper lip, dug by years of smoking, though she quit when Rocky was diagnosed with cancer.

"Anyway, *then*, on the radio in the cab coming home from the museum, I heard them say something about *Comfort*, North Carolina! I wasn't listening to the story, but the name jumped out because the word was so in my brain."

"Oh, yes. They'd have been talking about—" Vera caught Megan's look. "Something local."

"What?" Elizabeth looked eagerly between them, puppy hoping for a treat.

"We had a minor celebrity event. The news wires picked it up." Megan spread jam on her last bite of biscuit, not sure why she was bothering to protect David except that the ugliness had touched them all. "Go on, Elizabeth."

"Oh, so, well, *then* the next day, after *all* those signs pointing to Comfort, there came my dream about my *babcia*—my grandmother. I still didn't put it together until I had a fight with my boyfriend, and I was so upset and thinking if I didn't get out of the city, I'd totally lose it. It was like . . ." She beckoned with her hand, coaxing out the analogy. "Like being in a jar filled with stones that some giant was shaking, you know?"

"Well sure. I feel that way at least once a week. No offense to your children, Megan, they're fine children."

"Yes, they are." Megan finished her breakfast and took her plate back to the sink. Without the full measure of her quiet alone time the day already felt long.

"I knew I had to leave New York. I just didn't know where to go."

"You don't have family?" Vera asked.

"None I'm close to."

"So you came here."

"Yes." Elizabeth laughed uncomfortably. "Pretty wacked-out reason, huh?"

"No. Your grandmother meant you to come here. She's a wise woman." Vera held up a wise-woman finger. "This town does give comfort. And peace. Otherwise I couldn't have survived the death of my husband. Forty-six years we were married. Without him I'm like a sailboat with half an oar."

"Sailboats have sails, not oars." Megan's youngest, Jeffrey, from the hall outside the kitchen where he'd probably been eavesdropping for some time. He loved curling up small and silent—under a desk, on a closet floor—so no one knew he was there.

"I know boats that have both, young man."

"Jeffrey, come in and say hello to Elizabeth and have some breakfast."

"Yes, Mom. Okay, Mom. Hi Elizabeth." He dragged himself in, skinny legs emerging like knobbly sticks from his short pajamas. Megan ruffled his hair, bent to kiss his sleep-smelling skin, feeling love so deep she wanted to pull him back inside her body.

"This town will help calm you down, point you in the right direction. Make you feel God is on your side after all," Vera continued.

"That's exactly what I'm looking for." Elizabeth turned her delighted smile on Jeffrey. "Hi there. Did you sleep well?"

"Yes. You have weird dreams."

"Don't you?"

"Sure. Sometimes. Can I ask you a question?"

"O-kay." She grinned and touched his chin.

"If people were jelly beans, how many would you eat?"

"Jeffrey, that is not a question for guests."

"Sorry, Mom." He took his place at the table, next to Elizabeth, clearly not sorry at all. "I just think it's interesting. I'd make the good people into bad flavors so no one would touch them."

"Our family has been in Comfort for centuries," Vera went on, oblivious to interruptions. "In fact, my grandmother was best friends with one of the Vanderbilts, who used to summer in North Carolina. The town has everything you could want."

"Then why do you go to Hendersonville so often?" Jeffrey pushed a small truck around his place mat, using the border for a highway.

"It's a beautiful place for a child to grow up. It's safe . . ."

"What about the time Dad broke his leg?" Jeffrey ran his truck into the napkin holder and made an exploding sound. "You said the rocks he was climbing were dangerous."

". . . with good people. Stanley is still friends with childhood buddies, all fine men. One said Stanley had inspired him to give up drinking in high school. That he owed him his life. Remember that, Megan?"

"You told me, yes." Megan brought Jeffrey's breakfast over. Elizabeth was looking at her curiously. The story of Stanley's life became more impressive and more mangled every time his mother got hold of it, and Megan had probably been looking skeptical. She rearranged her face into a more wifely expression and was relieved when Elizabeth turned back to Vera.

"You must be so proud of your son."

"Oh, yes, I am. Of course what mother isn't proud of her child? But Stanley is special. He went to the University of North Carolina, and could have graduated, probably with honors, but he missed Megan and wanted to settle." She shook her head as if Megan were responsible for bringing Stanley down from a sure shot at the White House. Stanley had actually failed out of UNC all by himself. "He's a fine salesman, but he could have been a CEO if he'd set his sights that high. A Bill Gates or a Steve Jobs or a Jimmy Buffett."

"Warren Buffet, Vera. Jimmy is a singer." Megan put the plate she'd fixed for Elizabeth on the table for her son. "Jeffrey, put away the truck and eat."

"Yes, Mom, I will, Mom."

"Stanley is a fine singer too. You should hear him in church, Elizabeth."

Of course he was. A fine singer and brilliant scholar, exemplary friend—but a lousy swimmer because his feet stayed on top of the water and he had to walk it.

"G'morning." Lolly filed in sleepily, sexy in a worn, black Johnny Cash T-shirt of her father's, hair in a sloppy ponytail. At fifteen, girls could look sexy covered in garbage.

"Hi Lolly. Nice to see you." Elizabeth smiled at Megan's daughter, who nodded, giving Elizabeth's cute dress a covetous up-and-down.

"Deena up?" Megan opened the cookie tin where she stored her biscuits, and got down two more plates.

"She's reading." Lolly made it clear she thought this a completely lame way to spend time. "Some dumb science-fiction thing about shapeshifters from another galaxy."

"Tell her it's breakfast time."

"Knock knock!" Ella's voice, through the front door screen.

Megan sighed and pulled open the can of coffee to make more. "Door's open, Ella."

"Deena, get your lard-y butt down to breakfast!"

"Lolly, there are nicer ways to invite your sister."

"You keep your door *unlocked*?" Miss New Yorker was aghast. "At night?"

"Who's going to steal anything?" Vera started a chuckle and ended up coughing, thumping herself on the chest. "When Stanley was a boy, he and his friends returned a wallet with over three hundred dollars in it, which Mr. Clements had left in the—"

"Hi everyone." Ella's tall elegance made the kitchen seem smaller and shabbier. "Sally and I came to say hi to your new boarder."

"Come in, come in." Megan put on a big welcoming smile. "Lolly get your own juice. I'm making more coffee. Ella, Sally, this is Elizabeth Detlaff. Ella and Sally both grew up in Comfort. Sally is engaged to be married next month. Ella just moved back home in April."

"It's nice to meet you both. Sally, congratulations."

"Thank you." Sally beamed. "Nice to meet you, too."

"Very nice." Ella's eyes followed Lolly's path up and down Elizabeth. "So what brings someone like you to a place like Comfort?"

"'Someone like me'? What do you mean?" Elizabeth looked like a scrappy cat ready to pounce. Two beautiful, vivid women—some jostling for position was bound to happen. Just the thought of it made Megan want to shoo them out into the yard like she did to her kids.

Ella shrugged, giving that aloof stare she used to protect herself. "Nothing bad. You just don't look like—"

"Her dead grandmother told her to come." Vera leaned her enormous bosom forward, speaking in a hushed voice. "In a dream."

"Sally? Ella? Coffee?" Megan could hear desperation in her attempt to sound cheerful. She was not in the mood to listen to the weird story again. Nor was she anxious to watch Elizabeth attacked by Ella's divorcée bitterness, though Elizabeth could probably hold her own.

"Coffee'd be good, thanks." Ella drew Deena's chair out from the table and sank gracefully into it. "Your dead grandmother told you to come here?"

"In a dream."

"Yeah, thanks, Jeffrey, I heard that part."

Jeffrey sent Ella a look of jelly-smeared disdain. "*What*-ever."

"Manners, Jeffrey."

"Yes, Mom, okay, Mom."

"It's true." Elizabeth turned her chair to face Ella. "In my dream she told me to go find comfort."

"And that made you think of this town . . . how?"

"Signs." Vera nodded somberly, another crumb clinging to the corner of her mouth. "A powerful array, all pointing here."

"Really." Ella didn't stop her critical study of Elizabeth. "So . . . what, you'll stay until dead grannie tells you to go home?"

A snort of laughter from Lolly, abruptly snuffed, otherwise awkward silence during which Elizabeth's eyes narrowed, and Megan started to panic.

"Ignore her, she thinks she's being funny." Sally gave Ella an exasperated look, which on her sweet face barely registered, then jumped to help Megan distribute mugs of coffee. "It's real nice to have you here, Elizabeth. If you need anything, a tour or . . . well, anything, you let me know. Foster, my fiancé, owns the hardware store, so he can help if you need anything too."

"I thought his *hardware* was spoken for."

"Ella . . ." Sally smacked her friend on the shoulder, blushing sunburn red. "You are terrible."

"Good morn—" Deena looked around at the crowd in startled horror. "Whoa. What's going on?"

"Hi baby." Megan blew a frazzled kiss to her middle daughter. "We'll get some more chairs."

"I'll eat under the table."

"No you won't, Jeffrey. Help me, would you, Lolly?" Megan started toward the family room, counting down to the inevitable. *Three . . . two . . . one.*

"*Fine.*" Lolly said it in three syllables, fi-ee-*nuh*, and rolled her eyes.

"I'll help." Elizabeth jumped to her feet.

"No, Lolly should—"

"I don't mind."

Megan gave in with a sigh. She wasn't up to explaining how important it was that her daughter help. Not this morning. A we'll-talk-about-this-later stare at Lolly would have to do. "All right. Thank you."

She led the way, aware of Elizabeth's sweet floral scent behind her and how it made their family room seem dingy and stale. She opened a window, embarrassed by the smell, and headed for the folding chairs they kept stacked in the closet behind the stored winter coats.

"I *love* your house, Megan."

Megan handed her a chair, not sure what that was about. The house was a house, not much charm or character. "I'm glad, thank you."

"It has so much charm and character."

"Really?" She handed over another chair. "It's just a house. An ordinary one at that."

"I know, but it has . . . warmth. And people in it who love each other."

Megan closed the door to the closet, flushed from burrowing through sleeves and hoods and zippers to get to the chairs. What was she talking about? "We're family."

"Yes, and friends gathering for coffee to meet the newcomer. It's just so . . . perfect."

Perfect? What kind of life had this child-woman had if Stanley and Megan's house counted as perfect? "Well, thank you. That's very sweet."

"I don't know if I came here for a reason or not. But if I did, I think I'm figuring out what that reason is."

For a moment Megan considered ignoring her obvious cue and moving back into the kitchen, but she couldn't bring herself to be that rude. "What?"

"To show me what my life has been missing. I think I'm going to find it here."

A sharp laugh threatened to burst out of Megan. She gave in to the cliché and tried to make it sound like a cough.

"Well. That's very nice." She shut the closet door, bewildered. Maybe she should have known that someone from New York wanting to move into a garage apartment in a town like Comfort would be a little off. Stanley would say told-you-so, and then he'd imitate his grandmother's deep old-lady voice and tell Megan she'd pooped in her own bait bucket, which would make Megan laugh in spite of herself.

Maybe Megan needed more time than she expected to adjust to the newcomer, more time to adjust to having yet another body and mouth around, this one not part of her family or Stanley's.

Or maybe Megan would discover there were limits even to what she could cope with.

Chapter Four

Banana-cream pie!" Elizabeth couldn't stop beaming. Another great meal. Pork and beef meat loaf. Potatoes mashed with butter and milk. Green beans from the garden cooked until tender and served with lemon and salt. Tossed salad with bottled Italian dressing. Now pie, and she was pretty sure she saw an empty box of Jell-O pudding—a childhood favorite—though Megan had made her own crust. "I haven't eaten this well in way too long."

Lolly exchanged a what-is-*her*-problem look with her sister. "It's just normal food."

"It's Comfort food!" Elizabeth giggled at her own joke and got a chuckle from Vera.

"I thought you were married to a chef." Jeffrey, fast becoming Elizabeth's favorite, wrinkled his slightly upturned nose in comical curiosity. He was brown haired and brown eyed, as was his sister Deena, a contrast to strawberry-blond Lolly, who would probably end up auburn like Megan. "Can't he make meat loaf?"

"Well yes. But he'd make bison meatloaf with crimini mushrooms and sun-dried tomatoes, and mash his potatoes with fennel, garlic and imported goat-milk Parmesan."

"Mercy." Vera looked appalled. She had a great face: high forehead under old-lady white curls, sunken eyes and a ball at the end of her nose. Twin grooves extended outward from nostril to lip, two more from lip to chin, like the stacked roofs of Japanese temples. "What a fuss over meat and potatoes."

"I know! Then for salad he'd have organic *mâche* with—"

"Organic mash?"

Elizabeth laughed, then noticed no one else did and stopped abruptly. "*Mâche*. It's a kind of lettuce, also called lamb's tongue."

"Ewwww!"

"More milk, Jeffrey?"

"Yes, please, Mom, thank you, Mom."

Elizabeth got up to get herself more water while Meg poured milk for her son. She missed having wine with dinner, but that was the only criticism. With meals like this she'd have to keep up her running schedule or inflate like a balloon. "Can I get anyone anything?"

Megan looked up as if the question surprised her. "Oh, no. Thank you. We have everything."

"We're all fine here. Just fine," said Vera.

"Good. Okay." Elizabeth went back to the table. Apparently she'd managed to say the wrong thing. Again.

"Hey, Elizabeth."

Just the sound of Jeffrey's voice made her smile. "Yes, Jeffrey?"

"Do you think if you could fly, that painting your house would be fun?"

Elizabeth grinned and ruffled his short, enviably thick hair. "Has anyone ever told you that you have a very original mind?"

"Weird, more like it." Deena looked to her golden sister, who nodded confirmation.

"No kidding."

"Kids . . ." Megan spoke absently, cutting pie, as if she'd said the word so many times that K-I-D-S had become a meaningless four-letter assortment. "This piece is yours, Elizabeth."

"Oh boy." Elizabeth accepted the plate. "I love banana-cream pie. Can't remember the last one I had."

"Vera? Pie?"

"No, thank you. I'm trying to remember where I put my waist."

"What kind of food did you eat before you married the chef guy?" Lolly held out her hand for a plate, obviously used to being next in line.

"We're not married."

Megan's smooth serving motion faltered. Vera's eyes darted from Elizabeth to her daughter-in-law and back. Lolly and Deena exchanged wide-eyed looks of fascination.

Uh-oh. "So, um . . . I grew up with my mother and Polish grandmother in Milwaukee."

"That's in Wisconsin, right?"

"No, Deena, *Florida*." Lolly rolled her eyes.

"Milwaukee, Florida!" Jeffrey burst out laughing. "How about Milwaukee, *France*?"

"No, Milwaukee, *Africa*." Lolly giggled, losing several years along with the sneer.

"Milwaukee, *Jupiter!*"

"Yes, Deena, Wisconsin. This piece is for you." Megan transferred a third perfect piece of pie to the center of another white plate.

"Mmm, the pie is fabulous, thank you, Megan."

"Well. You're welcome." Compliments seemed to surprise her. Because she never got any or because she didn't think what she'd done deserved them?

"I had Polish friends before they moved away from Comfort, oh, I guess twenty years ago now." Vera stuck her fork in Lolly's pie and snuck away a bite. "Good sausage."

"A lot of good sausage. And sauerkraut, and cabbage. That's what my grandma made anyway. My mom was as bad a cook as I am. Overdone meat, watery soups, charred cookies . . . When I moved to Boston we lived on sandwiches and cheap takeout. That's why this is so good. Plain food done really well."

"I guess we're plain people." Vera was looking steadily at Megan now.

Elizabeth sighed. She'd done it again. "I didn't mean—"

"When did you leave home?" Lolly asked.

"Seventeen."

"Really?" Deena's eyes widened. "You didn't finish high school?"

"I left the day after graduation. I have an August birthday."

"You must've totally wanted out of there." Lolly looked wistful.

"My then-boyfriend Alan was leaving town for Boston. I went with him. We lived in a horrid basement in a great neighbor—"

"Another piece anyone? Vera? Deena?"

Elizabeth glanced at Megan in surprise.

"You were living in sin." Vera spoke quietly. "Around here that's not done."

Elizabeth let out a blast of laughter, then realized that was probably not the best reaction, though she couldn't tell if Vera was condemning her or explaining Megan's interruption. "Um, wow. Yes. I guess we were. I didn't think about it that way, I'm sorry if I offended anyone."

"It's okay, Elizabeth. Jeffrey, you look ready for more." Megan held out a hand toward Jeffrey, who passed his plate.

"Yes please, Mom, thank you, Mom."

"Fine by me, I wasn't born yesterday." Vera raided Jeffrey's plate with her thieving fork.

"No, definitely not." Elizabeth realized how that sounded and flushed. "I'm sure the world is a lot different, though, than when you were young. Not that it was that long ago. I meant that things change so fast."

"Well yes, they do."

Elizabeth sighed, worn out by her floundering. If there was a career path for people who had a gift for saying the wrong thing she'd be a billionaire. She finished her pie, listening to the children chatter and laugh, thinking they probably had no idea how special this was. Her childhood meals had been mostly quiet at the dark table in the dark dining room—lonely widowed grandma, lonely single mother exhausted from a day at work and lonely only child Elizabeth. Why hadn't they turned to each other in all that loneliness? They'd been too different. Ultra-conservative, iron-ruling grandma who lived in the past, grown-up ex-hippy mom waiting for rescue from the future and Generation-X daughter, concerned only with her present.

The phone rang. Lolly leaped for it.

"Oh, hey, Grandad." She sounded disappointed.

Elizabeth glanced at Megan, who froze for half a beat, then calmly—always calmly!—put a sliver of pie on her own plate, rinsed her hands in the sink and waited for the phone, on which Lolly was speaking monosyllabically. "Yes. No. Okay. Yeah, here she is."

"Hi Dad." Megan walked to the kitchen doorway and stood with her back to the room.

"That's Megan's daddy."

Elizabeth nodded to Vera. She got that.

"He's a widower. Aileen died a couple of years after Megan and Stanley got married."

"Oh, I'm sorry."

"She was a lovely person." Vera folded her hands with the quiet superiority of someone enjoying spreading tragic news. "Megan had a terrible time. She and her mama were very close."

"Her mom—Aileen—taught her the lace."

"Yes ma'am." Vera sighed heavily. "Megan has a gift passed down through generations. It's a terrible shame she doesn't knit it anymore."

"She stopped? Why? Because her mom died?"

Vera looked uncomfortable, then surprised, then nodded gravely. "Yes. That's why."

Elizabeth's instinct kicked in. That wasn't why.

"Can I have s'more pie, Grandma?"

"It's not *s'more* pie, it's *banana-cream* pie."

Deena stuck her tongue out at her brother.

"I think you've had plenty, Deena."

"*Again?*" Megan took another step out of the kitchen. Elizabeth smiled sympathetically at chubby Deena, wishing she could hear more of Megan's conversation.

"Hey, Elizabeth." Jeffrey put his fork down. "Do you know what gas makes Neptune look blue?"

"Swamp gas?" suggested Lolly not-helpfully.

"*Poo* gas?" Deena giggled like mad and earned a scowl from Vera.

Jeffrey ignored his sisters. "Do you know, Elizabeth? Take a guess."

"All right, then, Dad." Megan sounded impatient to be off the phone. "Yes, okay. Thanks for letting me know."

"I can't even guess."

"Methane!" he announced triumphantly."

Lolly choked on a swig of milk. "That *is* poo gas!"

"Ha!" Deena turned on her brother, barely able to speak through her giggles. "I was *right*."

"Okay, kids, enough." Vera watched Megan coming into the room. "Everything okay?"

"Yes, fine." Megan spoke brightly, but put her piece of pie back into the serving dish, which she took to the counter. "Dad is moving again. To New Jersey this time. That's all."

"Good heavens. No moss on that man." Vera pushed her chair back. "I'm going to get my knitting and sit on the porch."

"I'll help you with the dishes, Megan." Elizabeth stood to clear her plate.

"Ooh, good idea." Lolly nodded enthusiastically.

"You will not, that's Lolly's job. Deena and Jeffrey help too. Go out on the porch and talk to Vera. She likes company."

"I can at least do something."

"We've got it covered. You go have fun."

"If you're sure." She backed up a few reluctant steps. "I can take a walk, I guess."

"Good idea. It's beautiful out tonight. Today wasn't too hot." She all but made shooing motions with her hands.

Elizabeth hesitated in the doorway, on the verge of asking if Jeffrey wanted to come with her, then stopped at the sight of the kids all chipping in, like something out of a perfect-family TV show, Jeffrey clearing plates, Deena scraping them and Lolly wrapping up leftovers to put away.

She turned and left the room, nostalgic for her childhood fantasies of belonging to a family like this one. Not that she hadn't spent time with her mom and grandmother—she had, but grudgingly, with an eye toward getting out to meet this or that boyfriend, sneak into this or that bar, get naked in the back of this or that car. Vera would love those stories. Next dinner Elizabeth would toss out a few and get herself recommended for exorcism.

Out on the porch Vera's sturdy rocking chair waited in the soft evening air, which smelled of mowed lawns, flowers and mountain wind. Elizabeth pushed the smooth wood gently, imagining the chair starting to rock impatiently at this time every night, anticipating its occupant's arrival.

Elizabeth would be different if she'd grown up in a house like this, warm, homey, fresh and uncomplicated. She'd be stable and peaceful like Megan, raising her children uncomplainingly while her husband was out hunting the bacon he'd eventually bring home. Maybe she'd already have married Dominique and be happily settled.

Or maybe she was doomed to be a restless soul regardless. In which case she'd turned her blame and her back on a family that didn't deserve either. And maybe on Dominique too.

She stepped off the porch, then impulsively returned through the house to get her sketchbook. Two steps from the back door, a nearby male voice exploded in hoarse shouts and furious curses.

Elizabeth spun around, staring into the kitchen, where Megan and Lolly were still cleaning up, though the raging was clearly audible through the window.

"I . . . don't you hear that? Shouldn't we do something?"

Lolly chortled; Megan turned back to her sink, smiling. "That's David."

"Well what's . . . what's it about?"

Lolly cracked up again. "Believe it or not, squirrels."

"*Squirrels?*"

"They get into his bird feeders. Drives him crazy." Megan braced her hands on the edge of the sink, gazing out toward his yard. "He loves birds."

"He's been through like three different feeders in the last month, all supposed to be squirrel-proof." Lolly shoved the foil-covered pan of meat loaf into the refrigerator and closed the door. "The squirrels got into all of them."

"Is he always so angry?"

"He's really nice when he wants to be." Lolly moved toward the kitchen door. "Mom, Sarah and I are going to a party at Chuck's tonight, okay? His parents are home. Sarah's mom is driving us."

"Back by ten."

"I kno-o-w," she sang. "Bye Elizabeth."

"Have a good time." She watched the teenager hurry out of the room, remembering how thrilling it had been to get away from Mom and *Babcia* and go out with friends at that age. Contrasted with how often she was home alone now, wishing for quiet time with Dominique. "She's lovely."

Megan pursed her lips. "She's starting to realize that."

"Ah. Yeah." She had no idea what else to say, because the things she did at Lolly's age Megan undoubtedly didn't want to know. "Is everything really okay with your father?"

Megan pinched her lips together.

Elizabeth wanted to smack herself. Why had she bothered asking? "I'm sorry. I speak before I think. None of my business."

Megan glanced at her, then hung the kitchen towel carefully back on a rack under the sink. "He's moving again and called to tell me. That's all."

"Okay." An agonizing moment of awkwardness while Elizabeth thought of a million more questions she couldn't ask. "So . . . what's up with David? Why is he so cranky?"

"Why don't you ask him?"

"Because he doesn't seem real cuddly?"

Megan actually grinned. "Classic case of bark worse than bite. Though he does both."

"I gathered." Elizabeth traced the edges of the beautiful lace doily under the peonies. She'd have to see someone knitting this stuff before she believed it possible. "He seems out of place here."

"He grew up next door from teenager on. Raised by his great-aunt."

"No parents?"

"His mother . . . couldn't handle him. I don't think his father was around much. You'll have to ask him the rest. If he wants you to know he'll tell you."

"If not, he'll tell me where to go."

"Undoubtedly." Megan pulled the elastic from her hair and re-formed her ponytail. "If you talk to him, tell him hello. I'm going to see what Jeffrey and Deena are up to."

"Sure. Okay. Thanks again for dinner." Elizabeth let Megan precede her out of the kitchen before she allowed her smile to droop. Progress, but not much. Megan's barriers were mighty.

In the backyard, on her way again to get the sketchbook, she peered over the fence and saw David in the middle of his yard on one of two chairs with a table between, the rest of the patio set incomplete on the flagstone terrace next to the house. He wore a red T-shirt and black shorts and was scowling—the only way she'd seen him—a drink clutched in his hand. His shadow made an elongated human stripe across the ragged, patchy lawn, a study in spareness compared to Megan's lush garden.

"Hello?" She spoke impulsively. "You okay?"

"Ms. *Det*-laff." He turned and said her name slowly, savoring the syllables. "Nice to see you again."

"I heard you shouting."

"And?"

"I thought you might need help."

He laughed bitterly. "The amount of help I need is beyond your ability."

"Squirrel issues?"

"Rat bastards." He twisted to glare at the bird feeder on a pole next to the patio. "Outwit me every time. No one should have to feel inferior to a rodent. Join me in a cocktail?"

His invitation took her aback; he positively radiated charm compared to their first meeting. "What are you drinking?"

"Ah." He raised his glass to the setting sun, which sparkled appetizingly through the clear liquid. "'The proper union of gin and vermouth is a great and sudden glory; it is one of the happiest marriages on earth, and one of the shortest lived.'"

"Yours?"

"Bernard DeVoto, American historian and author. Have one with me?"

"Will you be nice to me this time?"

"Cross my heart."

"Then yes, I will. Thank you."

"I'll meet you inside." He got up and strode steadily enough toward his back door.

Elizabeth hurried through Megan's house, relieved when she didn't see anyone. She felt guilty and surreptitious, as if she were about to consort with the enemy.

Still no sign of Vera outside, so Elizabeth gave the rocker another push and headed to David's bungalow. Maybe he was meant to teach her something too.

She mounted the steps to his porch and peered through the screen door into the dim interior. "Knock knock."

"Back here, come on in."

She wandered through the small dusty living room, furnished in Bland American Drab, the stone mantel strewn with those porcelain figures Dominique made so much fun of. Then through the dining room, past a sturdy wood table and beautiful built-in china cabinets she restrained herself from peeking into. Then the kitchen, probably remodeled in the fifties, yellow metal cabinets, green formica counters, and, incongruously, a new enormous black refrigerator, futuristic in context.

"Poor Elizabeth, stuck with teetotalers next door." David opened the freezer door and pulled out Bombay Sapphire gin, a shaker, a glass, and a small pitcher.

"I'll manage."

"No, you'll suffer. But you can always come here." He poured an enormous amount of gin into the shaker, sloshed in vermouth and dispensed crushed ice from the door of the Darth

Vader refrigerator. "'One martini is all right. Two are too many, and three are not enough.' James Thurber."

Elizabeth laughed and ran her hand over the faded counter. "I know one too. Dorothy Parker . . . Give me a second, I can't remember it all."

"Take all the time you need. I'm going nowhere."

She moved toward the back door, frowning in concentration. It was the kind of oh-so-witty quote Dominique's friends were fond of outdoing each other with. "It's a little poem, very funny. Something about being under the table."

"Don't know that one."

"It'll come to me." She examined a wall hanging, a linen tea towel with pictures of wooden-clog-wearing Dutch children holding hands. "What do you do, David?"

"Besides plot against squirrels and mix pitchers of martinis?"

"Besides that."

"I'm a professor of English at Boston University."

"Impressive." She prowled further. A few old-lady-type decorative items, a glass apple, a dusty arrangement of dried flowers in a pewter vase. Not much she'd equate with David's personality. Weaponry and poison would be more fitting, maybe S&M gear. "So you live here in the summer?"

"You're such a Northeasterner."

She walked back and leaned on the counter next to him, seeing up close that he was older than she thought. Maybe late thirties or early forties. Touch of gray at his temples, lines at the corners of his eyes, the faintest loosening of the skin on his stubbled jaw and long, masculine neck. "What do you mean?"

"Northeasterners don't chat, they interrogate, without compunction or introduction." He tumbled the gin and vermouth; condensation on the shaker turned to frost. "Olives? Lemon? Onion?"

"Lemon. Like yours. But I'm a transplanted Midwesterner, so your theory doesn't work."

"Learned behavior." He bent to get a nearly zestless lemon from an otherwise empty vegetable bin and pared off the last strip, squeezed the peel, then ran it around the rim and the inside of the glass before he let it drop. "My great-aunt lived in this house."

"I knew that. I asked you if you live here every summer."

"No, I don't." He poured the drink expertly into the fresh glass, topped his off, then drained the rest into the pitcher. "I'm here for the same reason you are. To escape life."

"I'm not escaping." She took the lid off a cookie jar in the shape of a chicken and peered inside. A tiny dead bug, otherwise empty. "Escaping is a looking-back thing. I'm doing a looking-forward thing."

"Ah, right. Completely different. Here you go, Queen Elizabeth." He handed her the drink and picked up the pitcher. "Come outside with me and we'll get smashed."

She followed him out, peering at a pile of mail on her way. David Langley. Where had she heard that name? "Megan says hi."

"Which necessitates a 'hi' back?"

"If it's that much strain, don't bother."

He turned to grin at her, light brown eyes doing this incredibly sexy Paul Newman down-at-the-corners thing. The transformation made her want to gape. "I like you, Elizabeth. Have a seat."

"Thank you." She sat on the surprisingly comfortable wooden chair, a little flustered.

"Welcome to my nightmare." He clinked his glass with hers, then drank and closed his eyes. "Mmm, that virgin sip is always the best."

"Cheers." At her first taste of the fragrant icy liquid the Dorothy Parker quote popped. "'I love to drink martinis, two at the very most. Three I'm under the table. Four I'm under the host.'"

He actually laughed that time, and Elizabeth felt another quick shock of attraction. "Shall we get you to four and see what happens?"

"Um . . . no?" She took a larger swallow, feeling a dopey blush coming on. "What's your nightmare, gin? Squirrels? Your backyard? Comfort? Life?"

"I'm surprised no one has rushed to fill you in."

"Megan said I should ask you."

"Really." He ran his finger around the rim of his glass. A musical note rang out from contact with the wet crystal. "That was fine of her."

"Will you tell me?"

"You're probably the only person in the country who doesn't know." He shifted down in the chair, butt nearly at the edge of the seat, shoulders hunched, muscled legs stretched long. "My wife wrote a book called *When Women Rule*, the premise of which was that war-making men have freed women throughout centuries to take charge, and that when each war was over, they'd cede some authority, but not all. Her theory is that we're heading gradually toward a world in which women will rule."

Elizabeth gasped. David Langley. The story on the cab radio must have been the latest on his wife, Victoria something. "Yes, yes, I haven't read it, but heard of it, of course, who hasn't?"

"Exactly. All the world loves a scandal. And there is such

a lovely headline-grabbing irony in the fact that for her *New York Times* best seller, she ripped off her theories and roughly an eighth of her prose from an obscure book written during the Depression."

"By a man."

"By a man." He laughed; the sound was painful.

"I heard a story on the radio only recently . . ." The reporter had mentioned David. Was Victoria being prosecuted now? Was their divorce being finalized? Elizabeth hadn't listened that closely. "I knew your name was familiar. I just didn't put it together."

"Well now you have, and congratulations."

"I'm sorry. Really, David. That must have been awful."

"It still is." The beginnings of a slur made her wonder how many martinis he'd had before she showed up. "My Vicky flew too high with wings of wax, if I might borrow a tired mythical metaphor."

"Beats feet of clay."

"I suppose." He glared murderously at a squirrel perched on the fence between his and Megan's yard. "She not only broke our marriage, but sacrificed scholarship in pursuit of celebrity. That, I've had the harder time forgiving her for."

"Then maybe it wasn't much of a marriage to begin—" She smacked her hand over her mouth, then lifted her fingers. "Sorry, David. Note to self, engage brain *before* speech."

"Yes, it was an average marriage. But it was *my* average marriage, Elizabeth, and therefore painful to lose." He watched the squirrel disappear over into Megan's garden. "Love is the great ruination of our species. Tennyson got it all wrong."

"Tennyson . . ."

"'Tis better to have loved and lost than never to have loved at all.'" He gulped the rest of his drink, poured out another from the pitcher. "Tennyson never got divorced."

Elizabeth frowned at her martini. Everyone she knew whose marriage failed went through temporary insanity. People like her mother never recovered, to the degree where their ongoing misery became a point of pride. "But he must have experienced *some* loss."

"A friend of his died. It's not the same."

"Grief is grief."

He turned toward her, eyelids drooping slightly. "Ever been dumped on your ass, Elizabeth?"

She rolled her eyes. He wanted her to feel guilty for not being in the club. "I hate suffering contests."

"I didn't think so."

She laughed. No, she hadn't been dumped on her ass. She always evolved out of relationships before the man did, was always ready first to move on to the next experience, the next adventure. Not therapy-textbook healthy, but she didn't know how to adjust wiring that ran so deep.

"Because if you had been, you'd understand how much more peaceful and healthy it is to keep your pride and your heart intact, your sanity whole and vigorous, your faculties untarnished by the corrosion of anger, pain, jealousy, regret."

"Therefore welcome to your nightmare. I get it."

"What's yours?" He quirked an eyebrow when she looked surprised. "C'mon. Everyone has one."

"Well . . . I guess mine got to be New York." She drew her finger around the rim of the glass, but couldn't get it to sing for her. "Somewhere along the way I stopped existing. Or maybe I finally want to start."

"So you're here to *f-i-i-ind* yourself."

She grimaced at his TV-psychologist imitation. "Yes, ew, cliché. But the shoe fits."

"Boyfriend left behind?"

"He's in England."

Again the eyebrow.

Elizabeth took a deep breath. "He doesn't know I'm here. We'll put it that way."

"You ran away behind his back. We'll put it *that* way."

"You ran away too." She gestured to the sunlit mountains in the distance. "To drink yourself into regular stupors."

"I say go with your strengths."

She grinned at him and blushed when he winked. The yard seemed suddenly warmer and smaller, lengthened shadows promising intimate darkness. Romance was not what she had come over for.

"The radio said you left your job at Boston U?" She shook her head, answering her own divert-the-tension question. "No, I must have misheard. You wouldn't quit."

"You think not?"

"I'd bet the rest of my gin." She took another sip of the drink, which was going down more and more easily. "Work is your ultimate squirrel-proof bird feeder."

He chuckled. "You're right. I'm taking a sabbatical to escape my wife's very public humiliation and our therefore very public divorce. While I'm here, I'm writing a novel, every word of which is my own. The book will be published and sell twenty-one copies, ten to me, ten to Megan, one to Ella."

"Twenty-two." She waved her hand. "I want one."

"And one to you." He shoved his hand through his dark hair, rumpling it further. "Inconceivable, how the reading public survives without my brilliance, but apparently it does."

While the same public had gobbled up his wife's cheating. "So make this an absolutely amazing book no one can put down. It'll become a best seller, and on a book tour you can meet a sexy, brilliant woman and not only believe in love again but live happily ever after, while your ex-wife dines alone on her own manuscript. How does that sound?

"Like bad movie dialogue?"

"I *think* I remember something about the 'ruination of our species' . . ."

"Touché." He grinned, turning into a brown-eyed Paul Newman again. "I'm just old and bitter."

"Right, and wrinkled and gray and impotent."

"Lest we forget." He rolled his eyes. "Now tell me what you think of Comfort and your new family."

"I love it, and them, especially the kids. I love Megan, too, except sometimes I think she's either unhappy or doesn't like me."

"Mmm."

"Which?"

David put his drink down and clasped his hands behind his head, gazing off toward the glowing mountains. "You'd better ask her."

"You protect each other."

"Friends do. Tell me what you love so deeply about Comfort."

"Its beauty. Its peace. Its purity, and innocence. Its unspoiled Norman Rockwell family values that—" She scowled at him, hearing the slurring starting in her own voice. "What'so funny?"

"*Things are seldom what they seem.*" He sang the words in a surprisingly smooth baritone, picking up his drink again. "*Skim* milk masquerades as cream. *Highlows pass as patent leathers; jack-daws strut in peacock feathers.*"

"Um . . ."

"Gilbert and Sullivan, *H.M.S. Pinafore.* My mother sang professionally in Chicago, before alcohol ruined her voice."

"So you were brought up in the Midwest too, on opera." She could sort of picture it, but only sort of.

"Until age fourteen, when I was sent here."

"Because your mother was too busy performing?"

"Because my mother was too busy drinking." He gestured; gin overshot the rim of his glass and ran down his arm. "Off I went, over the river and through the woods, to be raised by Great-Aunt Delia, who trusted nothing but God and Lemon Pledge.

"Here's to Aunt Delia." Elizabeth toasted and drank. "I was raised by fat Polish women who feared everything but sausage and misery."

"Here's to fat Poles." He raised his drink more carefully this time.

"To them!" She hoisted hers, only half gone and she was looped already. And enjoying herself. David was a challenge, but not, as she first suspected, a threat. And he was sexy in that brooding, tortured-artist way, and he made her feel witty, smart and interesting.

Did she mention she loved Comfort? Maybe she really did belong here. Of course, right now she loved everything. Even David. Especially David.

"Tell me what you have against—"

"Hi there." A throaty female voice behind them. Ella appeared from the shadows of a tree near the back door, tall and sexy in a tight fuchsia top and cropped pants that left her stunning figure with no secrets. She sauntered up next to Elizabeth and gave her yet another once-over, as if she hadn't already examined every pore. Then she flicked a pointed glance over to David and back. "Well. Elizabeth. You work fast."

"Nice to see you again, Ella." She kept her tone pleasant, wondering how Ella would look with a martini dripping off her face.

"You two stunning women have already met?"

"This morning at Megan's."

"Ah." He looked back and forth between them, then settled on Elizabeth. "Ella is my favorite drinking partner, and the only other person in Comfort who doesn't bother."

"Bother . . ."

"With Comfort."

Ella gave a laugh that excluded Elizabeth from the joke, then adopted a model-like pose, one foot pointed forward, hand on her hip clutching a pack of Marlboro cigarettes and a lighter. "Any gin for me?"

"There's always gin for you." David got up, a little less than steady by then, and gestured gallantly. "Take my seat, martini pitcher's here, I'll get you a glass."

"Thanks, darlin'." Ella sank onto the just-vacated chair, tapped out a cigarette and lit it, drawing in the smoke with such elegant pleasure that Elizabeth had to picture her in a cancer ward or be envious. "So. Elizabeth."

"Ye-e-es?"

Ella arranged herself, legs slanted in a beautiful diagonal, torso languorously applied to the back of her seat. "How are you liking our town?"

"Very much."

"We don't get many Yankees down here in li'l ol' Comfort."

Elizabeth ignored the über-Southerner act. "How long have you lived here?"

"For all eternity." She tipped her head back and blew out a stream of smoke. "Minus seventeen years in Florida."

"What were you doing there?"

"Rotting."

"Sounds fun. Are you married?"

"Divorced."

"Children?"

"No." She spoke flatly; Elizabeth sensed pain in the answer. What a pair she and David made, hiding hurt, nursing bitterness over gin. Were they lovers, too?

Some of the blissful shine dulled from her buzz. "What do you do?"

"I have a job at the Comfort Public Library, Elizabeth. I live with my parents. I wear a size eight shoe and thirty-four C-cup bra, and I—"

"Good to know, thanks."

"What do *you* do?"

"When I'm not trying to be polite to rude strangers?"

Ella laughed unexpectedly. "Yes."

"I live in Manhattan with my chef boyfriend, and I'm starting my own design business. Fabrics, mostly."

"Interesting." She picked up a lock of hair and started toying with it, long fuschia-polished nails flipping the dark chin-length strands over and over. "Do you knit?"

"Yes, why?"

"Our group has temporarily lost two members to the lure of

Vegas. Quaint as it will sound to your big-city ears, we need more hands to get our blanket project finished in time for the local craft fair."

"Oh, wow." Elizabeth's mood perked up again. What could be more small-town perfect than getting involved in a knitting club and craft fair? She knew women in New York who knitted, but it seemed more like a genuine way of life here, less like a trendy diversion. "Thank you, that sounds totally fun."

"Really." Ella took another hit from her cigarette and twisted her mouth to blow the smoke away. "You need to get out more."

"Here y'go." David made it to the table, brandished a fresh frosted glass and poured generously from the pitcher. "If martinis be the food of oblivion, drink on."

"Oblivion is where I do my best work." Ella reached for hers. "What shall we drink to tonight?"

"Elizabeth and I were talking about love."

"Then here's to love." She took a blissful swallow. "May it rest in peace."

"Careful." David turned to Elizabeth, which put his face half in rosy light and half in shadow. "This sweet young thing still believes."

"Break her, Brother David. Pain now spares her later."

He reached and let his hand hover over Elizabeth's wrist. "Listen and learn, child. Love is a dangerous trap set by human nature, toothed metal jaws hidden on the forest's leafy floor."

Ella snorted. "You are *such* an author."

"You can't get caught without being hurt. *Snap.*" He grabbed Elizabeth's wrist and held it tightly, his compelling eyes lit by the fading sunlight. "Were you about to get caught, up there in New York?"

Elizabeth recoiled, then set her drink down on the table holding the now-sweating pitcher and tried to pull her wrist out of his grasp. "Who's spouting bad movie dialogue now?"

"Uh-oh." He grinned, let her struggle another second, then let go. "I think I struck paydirt."

"Looks like." Ella was smiling too, not unkindly. They were teasing her. There was no reason for Elizabeth to be this upset.

She stood up. "I do believe in love. It's not an easy thing to say, but it takes more courage than rejecting it."

"Sweet Jesus, it's Pollyanna. And all this time yer pa 'n' I thought you was dead."

"Down, girl." David spoke quietly, watching Elizabeth.

"Thanks for the drink." She stepped away from the chair. "I'll leave you two to enjoy your despair."

"Oh, ouch." Ella laughed good-humoredly. "Good night, Elizabeth. Don't forget your rose-colored glasses on the way out."

"Not a chance." She managed a smile back. "I see so much more clearly with them."

"Elizabeth, you are a gem." David stood and took her shoulders, kissed her on both cheeks, closer to her mouth than was purely friendly. In spite of the drinking he managed to smell good. "The gin of oblivion is always flowing here in hell. Stop by anytime."

"I'll stick to the milk of human kindness. But thanks, Lucifer."

"Lucifer!" He laughed, deliberately demonic, bent to pick up his drink, and toasted her with drunken affection. "Call me a sadist, Ms. Detlaff, but I look forward to watching you get to know Comfort."

Chapter Five

The day Fiona is to see the new lighthouse site with Calum dawns drizzly and gray, but nothing can dampen her mood. She helps her mother prepare breakfast oatmeal, milks the placid cow and feeds the busy chickens, waves to her favorite horse, Vogue, who tosses his chestnut head, turns his back and trots over the hill behind their house. Inside she dresses in a straight gray skirt she's sewn herself and a sweater knitted from her own carefully spun wool, with a gray, blue and cream pattern of eight-pointed stars. The blue catches her eyes, her mother says, and smooths her daughter's bobbed curls proudly, wishes her a good time.

Just before Fiona is to leave, the rain stops, the sun breaks through, making drops glisten on the heather-strewn hills. She smiles at the sky and hurries to Calum's, *where he'll be waiting to walk with her to Eshaness's highest cliffs. As she descends the slope to his house she sees him coming around the corner and waves, quickening her steps. He raises his hand, dark hair curling in the wet, tall and solid in his charcoal sweater. As Fiona is about to call out a cheerful hello, Gillian appears in a flowing black skirt and a sweater like nothing Fiona has ever seen. Reds, blues, oranges, greens, buds and blooms and vines and butterflies. Her hair is long and free, blowing in slow graceful waves as if it's underwater, making her look like a wild tangle of the world's most beautiful garden.*

She says hello to Fiona and smiles a smile that keeps part of her to herself, quiet with deep secrets. Fiona nods, shy with sudden uncertainty and looks to Calum. Is Gillian to come with them? Calum cannot meet her eyes beyond a glance and she has her answer. Disappointment is hot and hard, but she will not let it show.

As they walk, with her musical voice and gracious manner, Gillian tells stories of her life on Unst, of meeting her husband, of their life together, of watching him waste slowly toward death until there was scarcely enough flesh to keep his bones together. Calum listens, Fiona listens, the tale seems to weave a spell over them so that the long walk is swift and barely noticed.

They reach the site past the mysterious circular ruin of the broch *and walk the outline of the lighthouse foundation, a smaller building and a larger one that will house the light in one corner, both atop a cruel jagged cliff that could be the very edge of the world, two hundred feet above the cobalt sea. Gillian stands facing the salty*

Atlantic, endless to the horizon, and her face transforms into such fierce longing that Fiona is frightened and Calum lunges to grab her. She breaks free and runs to the edge, stopping as Fiona screams, Calum goes white. Gillian throws her arms wide, tips her head back and laughs. Twenty yards offshore an orca breaks the surface of the water as if summoned by her wild joy.

Fiona calls for her to come back, not to stand so near the edge with the wind lashing. Calum strides toward her. When he is near, she turns and he stops as if she has put up a wall. Fiona holds her breath while Calum walks gently, tenderly, the way he'd approach a wounded animal, closer and closer until he's through the wall, takes Gillian's hand and they are together, brown and white-winged skuas swirling around them, with Fiona still on the outside.

It begins to rain again.

Megan sat on the front porch with Vera, working on her Acre lace pattern blanket square. Two-row repeats of ten-stitch segments over and over. Knit, knit, knit two together, yarn-over, knit, knit, yarn-over, knit two together, knit, knit, knit. The only excitement: changing colors every twenty rows to progressively greener shades of blue.

Beside her, Vera's needles clicked over and around, forming the stockinette rectangles she'd join for her fifth indigo square. Her rocker moved forward, back, forward, back, at the apex of each rock, a tiny creak that was getting on Megan's nerves.

No reason to be so tense. Around them were the sounds and smells of summer, kids playing, sprinklers hissing, crickets discussing the latest insect news. Over at David's house, occasional laughter. He and Elizabeth must be enjoying each other.

A plain knitted row. Knit, knit, knit. Megan's great-grandmother, Fiona Tulloch, and her cronies could knit up to a mind-boggling two hundred stitches a minutes, could finish a lace shawl in six weeks.

Knit, knit, knit.

Laughter boomed again next door. David's this time. Megan lost thirty years and became a lonely adolescent home with her mother instead of part of the boisterous gang.

"Sounds like a party," Vera said.

"Sounds like."

"I saw Ella heading around back next door too. With Stanley yours, there aren't many men around Comfort who can handle her. David must have his hands full."

"I'm sure he does." Knit, knit, knit, row's end and turn.

"Bless Ella's heart." Vera shook her head, smug amusement showing through her sympathy. "I'll never forget the look on her face when she found out Stanley asked you to marry him so soon after you started dating, and she'd been with him what, four years? Dorene said Ella thought she and Stanley'd get back together after he had his 'little fling' with you. She had her sights set on him from the time—"

"Yes." Megan put her blanket square down on the rickety table Stanley had made at her request and stood. The air on the porch had gone; she didn't know where. "I know."

"Of course, then she married Don, the first man who'd take her away from Comfort. What a mistake that was. A passionate woman is a dangerous thing, but men don't find out 'til it's too late." Vera looked up from her knitting over bright red magnifying half-glasses bought at Hansen's Drug. "Good Lord, Megan, you look like you've seen Elvis."

"I'm . . ." She gestured vaguely. "I'm just—"

"Don't you start worrying about Ella. My Stanley's still as crazy about you as the day he married you. He tells me every time on the phone how he can't wait to come home to you and the—"

"I'm thirsty is all. You want some water? Juice? Ginger ale?"

"I'll take a ginger, but only if it's diet. Doctor Helverson keeps telling me I'm close to diabetic. Too many years of too much—"

"I always buy diet, Vera. I always *have* bought diet."

"Yes. Yes, you have."

"I'll get one for you." Megan fled to her kitchen, leaned on the sink, looking out at her garden. Vera would be wondering what was wrong with her. She'd tell Stanley. *Something's not right with that wife of yours.* He'd want to know what.

How could she tell him when she wasn't sure herself? Adjusting to the new stranger had been more difficult than she imagined, that was certainly true. If she could, Megan would take back Elizabeth's standing invitation to dinner with the family. But that perk was the only way she could set the rent so high for the area. And in Elizabeth's place, Megan wouldn't want to have to cook dinner on two cheap burners in the corner of a living room.

She pulled a diet ginger ale from the refrigerator and twisted an ice cube tray to fill a glass for Vera, then filled another glass with tap water for herself.

Outside she heard Vera's voice again, Elizabeth's answering; she'd come back from David's. Was it too much to ask that she'd go to her apartment and stay there until morning?

Megan grabbed another soda just in case, filled another glass with ice, put it all on a blue-and-white striped tray she'd salvaged from a garage sale, and carried it out, heart sinking when she saw Elizabeth sprawled comfortably in the chair next to Vera's rocker.

Apparently, yes, it was too much to ask.

"Here's your ginger ale, Vera. I brought one for you, too, if you want it, Elizabeth."

"Thanks, Megan. That was really nice." She turned from watching Vera knit and smiled wide, eyes droopy, cheeks and nose flushed. She'd been drinking. Megan wasn't surprised. That seemed to be all that went on next door since David's marriage had collapsed.

"You're welcome."

Elizabeth went back to being mesmerized by the rhythm of needles expertly thrusting through stitches. "Ella invited me to the next Purls meeting. She said you'd tell me when it was, Megan."

Megan sat again, took her knitting into her lap, feeling sick. When she'd advertised for a boarder she'd imagined someone who'd want to live her *own* life. "Of course."

The ice cubes adjusted in Elizabeth's glass as she took her next sip, staring now at Megan's busy fingers. "What's that pattern?"

"Acre. An old lace pattern."

"Will you or Vera teach me to knit lace?"

Vera's hands stilled. She turned questioningly toward Megan. "Well, now."

Megan made herself smile, shocked at the burn of anger in her chest. She'd taught Vera after Mom died, probably in a futile attempt to fill some of the emptiness. When Megan stopped knitting lace, the day she canceled her and Stanley's vow-renewal ceremony, Vera had stopped too. Neither of them had mentioned the day since.

"Well." She struggled for a way to stay gracious. "There's an idea."

Elizabeth didn't have the right personality. She was too impatient, wanted gratification too instantly. The work would suffer under her hands, be uneven and slapdash.

Megan had spent hours watching at her mother's side, then hours, weeks, months learning until the knitting wasn't about stitches but whole rows, entire patterns internalized, the way eyes read words, not individual letters. In all the cities they lived in—different climates, different states, different schools, different friends—the only constant was Mom, the lace, and the stories of Fiona and her Shetland community, embroidered with Mom's flourishes—superstitions of the time or fairy tale plots or lessons she wanted to teach her daughter. Megan had one favorite story, one she used to ask for above all the others, and which she'd dream herself into most nights before she went to sleep.

"I'll teach her. I have the supplies in my room." Vera made a big show of preparing to hoist herself out of the rocker.

Megan's cue to jump up and volunteer instead. For a moment she couldn't bring herself to. But there was no reason not to let Elizabeth learn except Megan's territorial nature when it came to lace. And that wasn't reason enough. "I'll get what she needs."

"Thank you. These old bones get tired more easily than they used to. Larger needles for her first time, number twos. And some of that two-ply yarn, she'll do better with that. And the Cat's Paw chart. Not too hard for a beginner. And stitch mark—"

"Yes, I know." Megan escaped again into the house. Vera had sounded so excited babbling instructions she knew Megan didn't need to hear. Maybe it had been hard for her to give up lace when Megan did. Megan had been so miserable with shock and grief she hadn't considered anything but her own sudden distaste for the craft she'd loved her whole life.

Through the living room, to the back room they'd converted into a bedroom when Vera moved in, a room that smelled of stale mother-in-law. Vera hated open windows in her room. Megan hated to think how much they paid to have the ceiling fan going day and night.

She opened the top drawer of the old sewing chest that had belonged to Vera's mother and rummaged for number two needles and a box of the tiny plastic rings for marking sections of stitches. From the bottom largest drawer she pulled a small ball she'd wound herself a thousand years ago it seemed, cream-colored two-ply Shetland wool, soft, spongy, warm and familiar in her hand. Emotion thickened her throat, bitter and sweet.

In the middle drawer she leafed through beginner patterns she'd used to teach Vera and which her mother had used to teach her, pausing over the directions for a simple doily, her first completed project, aged twelve. Where was the family living then? She couldn't remember that, only the smile on her mother's tired face when Megan showed off her work. *Your great-grandmother Fiona would have been proud*, she'd said. Highest praise.

Megan pulled out the Cat's Paw chart and shut the drawer firmly.

Back on the porch, she handed the supplies to Vera and sat, watching uneasily while Vera cast on, only enough for a few repeats of the pattern. Elizabeth dragged her chair to Vera's side and peered with tipsy concentration as Vera demonstrated—yarn-over; make one; knit two together; slip one, knit two together, pass slipped stitch over—and explained how the stitches worked together to create the empty spaces necessary for lace.

"I'll do the first couple of rows and put in the markers. You'll be doing lace knitting, which is different from knitted lace."

"How?"

Next door, Ella laughed, then laughed again, low and throaty.

"Knitted lace is when you advance the pattern on every row. Lace knitting is when you advance the pattern on one row, then do a plain knit row on the way back. The angles are sharper, and the patterns are larger."

"I'll see if I can remember that." Elizabeth giggled. "I probably can't."

"Here's the chart you'll be using. Each row of the grid corresponds to a knitted row, each little box equals one stitch. Here's the key to the symbols. Blank square means knit, empty circle in the square means yarn-over, forward slash means knit two together, etc. Got it?"

"Oof. Sort of."

"Just do." Vera held out the piece. "No better way to learn. Right, Megan?"

Megan wanted to yank the needles and yarn out of Vera's hands, throw a tantrum worthy of Lolly when she was two, *I don't want you to do it. Lace is* mine; *my Mom gave it to* me. "Yes. That's right."

"Okay." Elizabeth took over the needles and painstakingly started on the first patterned row. Music came on in David's yard. Ella Fitzgerald with the world on a string. Megan fidgeted, breathing the night air, wanting to escape inside but not able to bear the airless house or being alone.

Got the string around my finger/What a world, what a life—I'm in love.

"I don't have the right number of stitches in this part, what did I do?" Elizabeth handed over her beginner's attempt to Vera like a child holding out a broken toy, please-fix-it, to Mama.

"In Shetland, girls learned by doing the plain return rows on their mother's lace-knit patterns. You're diving into the hard part right away. Mistakes are normal at the beginning."

Maybe Megan could check on Deena and Jeffrey. But they were no longer the ages for drawing on walls and sticking fingers in sockets, so if they were quiet they were happy. She needed to get over her silly jealousy, her anger at Vera for taking over as if the lace was in her heritage, anger at herself because it was her fault she hadn't offered to teach Elizabeth, anger at grave robber Elizabeth for digging up and pillaging Megan's past.

I can make the rain go/Any time I move my finger/Lucky me, can't you see—I'm in love.

"Argh! I think I've made about twenty mistakes already." Elizabeth put the tiny swatch down and laughed, face red.

"Maybe next time you can try when you haven't been" —Vera cleared her throat meaningfully— "to David's."

"Is it that obvious? You know, I couldn't even finish *one* drink." She hunched and let go her shoulders. "He pours a lethal one."

"Yes, well." Vera snorted. "Practice makes perfect."

"His drinking or my knitting?"

"Both."

Elizabeth laughed and looked dubiously at her not-yet-lace. "I don't know if I have the patience for this."

"Just you wait." Vera regarded her new pupil with the seriousness of a missionary. "The work will take you over before you know it. You'll start to feel the patterns rather than read them. You'll start to connect to all the women who have knit this lace before, and all those who will knit it after you."

"Wow, really?" Elizabeth's eyes went wide. Vera couldn't have hooked her more completely if she'd started her on heroin.

Life's a wonderful thing/As long as I hold the string/I'd be a silly so-and-so/If I should ever let go.

Vera nodded solemnly. "Yes, indeed. Right, Megan?"

Megan watched the delicate white thread wind around Elizabeth's finger, remembering the sensuous softness of the Shetland wool, the powerful feeling that she wasn't so alone when she was knitting with her mother, a feeling that carried over even after Mom died. "That's what my mother always said, yes."

Elizabeth bent over her effort. Megan went back to her blanket square. Knit, knit, knit two together, yarn-over, knit, knit, yarn-over, knit two together, knit, knit, knit.

St. Louis. That was where they'd been living when Mom invented Megan's favorite story and her favorite character. She remembered because there had been a girl in her class, Jill, tall, dark and beautiful, who'd chosen for her project at the start of the school year to make life unbearable for once again "new girl" Megan. Mom had come up with Gillian soon after.

"So, Megan, tell me more about—argh, I've dropped a stitch here."

"Pick it up and keep going," Vera said.

"I can't even *find* it." She started giggling again.

Ella Fitzgerald began a new song, which Megan recognized as "Witchcraft" because of her mother's passion for Sinatra. David started singing loudly, drunkenly, not his usual fine voice but just under the pitch and behind the beat. She wanted to be there, laughing with him, sharing pain and dissecting the world the way they used to. And to prevent any mistake he was going to make—or had already made—with Ella. Ella would eat him alive.

But it wasn't Megan's place to go over there or to interfere. Not as a neighbor, not even as a friend. And certainly not as Stanley's wife. Her place was to sit here on her damn porch with her intrusive boarder and mother-in-law, overhearing the fun.

Those fingers in my hair/That sly come-hither stare/That strips my conscience bare/It's witch—

"*Elizabeth.*" Megan spoke too forcefully; Elizabeth and Vera's heads jerked up in surprise.

"Yes?"

Megan didn't know what to say; she'd had to break the music's hold. "Why don't you . . . tell us about your Polish relatives?"

Elizabeth blinked. "Tell you what about them?"

"What brought them over to this country and . . . so on."

Vera lifted her brows and went back to her knitting.

"Oh. Sure. Okay." Elizabeth peered at her chart. "My great-grandfather came over from Kaszuby, northern Poland, on the Baltic. He and my grandmother settled on Jones Island in Lake Michigan with a bunch of other Kaszub immigrants."

And I've got no defense for it/The heat is too intense for it/What good would common sense—

"*Really?* What did they do there?" She was losing it. No way to drown out the music or her imagination about what was going on next door. No way to block out the emotions the lace brought on again. So? So she sat, polite, restrained, knitting her part of a blanket that was going to be artless and clumsy.

"Most of the Kazubs were fishermen, so being on the lake in Milwaukee meant they could keep right on fishing. Then in the 1920s the government kicked everyone off the island to build a sewage treatment plant."

"Where did they all go?" Her voice sounded shrill and forced. She felt like Augustus Gloop from the *Charlie and the Chocolate Factory* movie she and her kids watched last month, stuck halfway up the vacuum pipe, pressure building all around, something having to give eventually.

"South Milwaukee, where I grew up with my widowed grandmother and my mom. My dad left when I was five."

And although I know it's strictly taboo/When you arouse the need in me/My heart says yes indeed in me/Proceed with—

"Oh, I'm sorry. That must have been hard." Megan put on a sympathetic face, feeling as if she were going to throw up or laugh or scream or all three. Knit, knit, knit two together, yarn-over, knit, knit, yarn-over, knit two together, knit, knit, knit.

"Thanks. I was young . . ." Elizabeth looked at Megan curiously before she bent over the chart again. "If we're talking relatives, Megan, I really want to hear about yours on Shetland."

"Oh. Well." Megan smiled at her knitting this time because she didn't want to smile at Elizabeth. "My great-grandmother grew up there. She moved, though, to the Scottish mainland, when she was eighteen. But she brought her lace-knitting skill with her."

That wouldn't be enough. She knew it wouldn't be enough. Why had she brought up ancestor stories? Dig, dig, dig. Like a dog searching for its bone, holes all over the yard, never giving up.

"Wow. This is so fascinating. Tell me more, I want to know everything. What was her life like when she was—"

"Hi y'all." Sally, approaching.

"Hey there." Megan put her knitting aside, nearly ecstatic over the interruption. "Join us."

"Thanks." She climbed the first step to the porch; up close it was obvious, even through cosmetic attempts to conceal it, that she'd been crying. "I'm looking for Ella."

"Ella won't be any good to you right now." Vera peered at her with maternal concern. No one could know Sally without wanting to take care of her. "You stay here with us. Megan'll get you something cool to drink."

"Lemonade? Diet ginger?"

"No, nothing. Thanks."

Elizabeth frowned at her. "Are you okay?"

Megan sat again, picked up her blue square. Honestly. Not even giving the poor woman time to get settled, to chat about nothing and ease into her troubles *if* she wanted to talk about them. "Sally, we were just talking about—"

"You look like you've been crying. What's the matter?"

"Sally honey, have a seat." Vera patted the chair next to her. "You sure you don't want any ginger? It's diet. My doctor says—"

"Vera, let Sally tell us."

Vera was so shocked by Elizabeth's calm interruption she subsided, muttering.

"Oh. Well. My dress came today." Sally dug a tissue from her pocket. "Beatrice ordered the one I didn't want. The one she liked. I know I'm being a spoiled brat, but it's so . . . *plain*. I loved that other one."

"Oh, Sally, honey." Megan's stomach sank in dismay. Sally had been through so much. She deserved a perfect wedding. "I'm so sorry."

"Send it back." Elizabeth shrugged. "Tell her you want the one *you* picked out."

"I can't do that. She's paying for it." Sally dissolved again. "It'd be so ungrateful."

"Pfft." Elizabeth scoffed. "It's *your* wedding."

"Elizabeth." Megan managed to keep her voice gentle. "I don't think she wants to start out married life antagonizing her mother-in-law. You sure about the drink, Sally? I've got cookies too, oatmeal raisin."

"You need to draw the line now," Elizabeth announced. "Or you'll be catering to this woman the rest of your marriage. If you don't believe me, Dear Abby says so only every other week."

Megan frowned a warning, which Elizabeth didn't see. "Sally, what does Foster say?"

"He says I'll be beautiful to him no matter what." She sniffled, wiped her eyes, erasing the camouflaging concealer. "He doesn't want to take sides."

"Keep the dress." Vera harrumphed. "You don't want to pit your husband against his mother."

"She needs her husband on *her* side."

Megan stood. "I'll get those cookies."

"And because it's strapless I'll have to find some way to hide the scars on my shoulder from the accident." She looked toward Elizabeth. "I was in a car wreck when I was a girl. I *told* Beatrice I can't wear strapless."

"Maybe she thought you meant you didn't look good in that style," Vera said. "Like how people say, 'I can't wear orange.'"

"What did the dress you wanted look like?" Elizabeth asked.

"I'll show you both of them."

Megan went inside while Sally pulled out two folded pictures and passed them to Elizabeth. In the kitchen, she clunked ice into another glass and took another soda out of the fridge, put the cookies she'd intended for the kids onto a plate and loaded her tray again. Poor Sally. As the years passed the wedding faded in importance, but brides deserved the day they wanted. Especially Sally, who was cheated out of her dream ceremony the first time by eloping.

At her own wedding, Megan was so happy not to have to move again, so astonished by the intensity of Stanley's love, that she cared less about the trappings than most. She'd worn her mother's dress, decorated with Grandma Bridget's lace.

Back on the porch the women were studying the pictures.

"Here, Sally, honey." Megan put the tray down. "Have something to drink and a cookie. They'll make the problem seem less horrible."

"Megan, you are a doll, thank you." Sally took a cookie, opened the soda and started pouring.

"Okay." Elizabeth passed the pictures back to Sally, then put them down on an empty chair when she saw her hands full. "What can we do to fix the problem?"

"Oh." Sally laughed uncomfortably. "You're sweet, Elizabeth, but you don't need to worry about my problems."

"Don't be silly. I'd like to help. There must be something we can do." She looked to Vera and Megan, clearly expecting an immediate rush of ideas. "We could maybe talk to Beatrice for you, or—"

"*No.*" Megan and Vera objected simultaneously.

"Thank you, Elizabeth, but don't worry." Sally was blushing now. "I just needed someone to sympathize . . . and give me cookies. These are so delicious, Megan. Is this the recipe from the—"

"Maybe we can fix up the dress you don't like. Put sleeves on it. You have a seamstress here in town, don't you?"

"Beatrice would be furious," Vera said. "I remember—"

"So what?" Elizabeth blew a raspberry.

Megan glanced at Sally's stricken face and wanted to drop-kick Elizabeth back to New York. "I don't think that's what Sally—"

"I know!" Elizabeth held up her infant lace, barely three rows. "The proverbial answer staring us in the face! Vera and Megan can knit lace to decorate the dress you didn't like."

The porch grew silent. Even next door had gone quiet. Elizabeth of course picked up on nothing.

"I can help, a little anyway. The others in your knitting group can learn too. We can use small pieces to decorate the bodice and skirt, and Vera and Megan can make sleeves or a shawl to cover your shoulders."

"Elizabeth, I don't think this—"

"It'll be our wedding gift to you." Elizabeth cut Vera off without appearing to notice. "So your mother-in-law can't object, because you had nothing to do with it. Do we have time? When are you getting married?"

Sally was frozen holding a glass of soda in midair. "I don't— In five weeks. August fourteenth. Could . . . do you think you could?"

Megan and Vera exchanged glances.

"I am sure they could." Elizabeth grinned, triumphant in her own brilliance.

"That would be so amazing." Sally's eyes filled with tears. "It wouldn't be the Cinderella dress, but in a way it'd be better because my best friends would be making it beautiful for me."

"Well, I certainly . . ." Vera looked helplessly at Megan.

Megan sat like a brainless lump, horrified at her hesitation. Sally was a friend in need. Megan could help her. It shouldn't be more complicated than that. But it was. Upstairs in her room was the wedding shawl she'd made for the vow renewal ceremony with Stanley, when she was newly pregnant with Lolly, radiant still with the joy of having a permanent home, a wonderful husband she adored, a house of her own. Then that day digging through their files for the answer to a tax question, finding the mortgage statement for his other house. Such a small mistake he'd made, misfiling that statement. The only one. But it had been enough.

Megan smiled, she always smiled, panic welling, tears rising that she hoped the girls would think were from the warmth of her generous heart. "Of course we can help, Sally. We'll make that dress into your dream come true."

Sally got to her feet, hand to her chest as if her joy were too intense to be borne sitting. "Oh, Megan. Oh wow. This is so fantastic. I don't know how I could *ever* thank you."

Megan stood and hugged her, lingered long enough to look as if she were enjoying Sally's excitement, then excused herself and went into their downstairs bathroom to get herself back under control. Inside, door locked, standing at the sink, tears running down her face, a thought started her laughing.

She was beginning to understand David's fury at squirrels.

Chapter Six

*E*lizabeth sat in the eagle-decorated rocker by her afternoon view of the mountains, window curtained with the lace she was struggling to knit. Behind her the air conditioner near her bed hummed a monotone serenade. She'd woken relaxed, focused and centered; the mood had stayed with her all day. A week in North Carolina and she hadn't once felt the need to meditate to lift her mood and/or soothe the chaos of her thoughts. As if she needed any more proof that Comfort was good for her.

Another knit, another yarn-over. She still made mistakes and dropped stitches, still had to stop frequently to peer at the chart, but not as often as when she started. The inch or so hanging from her needles didn't look like what Vera and Megan made, but . . . miracle of miracles, her clumsy holes had assumed a regular pattern. Unmistakably. She felt as if she'd created a new wonder of the world. Enough practice and once Megan designed the additions to Sally's dress, Elizabeth should be able to contribute, which made her ridiculously pleased.

Sometime soon she hoped to internalize the pattern, as Vera promised would happen, instead of having to follow the chart. Then maybe less frustration and eventually, the hoped-for connection to the women of Shetland. Maybe she'd learn something from them.

Since Elizabeth had quit her secretary job to start her own business, first as an interior decorator, then event planner, then wedding consultant, now fabric designer, she'd tried hard to feel that sense of purpose, of proprietary pride, the drive of doing what needed to be done to succeed and to flourish. Instead, in each case she'd felt like a fake. Maybe all her businesses had failed so far because she knew deep down she wasn't doing what she was meant to do. Maybe lace knitting would turn out to be the reason her *babcia* sent her here.

Elizabeth grinned ruefully. Apparently, she was now buying into the signs-from-the-universe philosophy she'd scorned so insistently as a girl.

An odd metallic chirping sounded outside, growing louder, accompanied by the noise of a car engine pulling into the driveway.

"*Dad's home!*"

Stanley! Elizabeth half rose, then forced herself to knit to the next marker so she wouldn't lose her place. Outside, feet pounded; the back door slammed. Stanley was home! Megan had mentioned he was arriving, but later tonight. Elizabeth couldn't wait to meet the *pater* of this idyllic family.

Knit two together, yarn-over, knit, knit, knit. Done. She

jammed point protectors on the needles, stuffed the soft wool into the Ingles Market plastic bag Megan found for her, ran to the window and peered out.

A large man, very tall, lean and handsome, medium brunet, like Jeffrey and Deena, with his mother's high forehead and a less pronounced version of her bulbed nose, under which sat a full, neat mustache. He was grinning, holding squealing Lolly in one arm, laughing Deena in the other, and whirling them around so hard their legs flung out. Jeffrey danced nearby on his skinny limbs, unsteady from what must have already been his turn in Dad's arms. How often had Elizabeth fantasized about her own father coming back exactly like this?

Megan stepped out of the house, gathering her hair into a fresh ponytail, welcoming smile making her face glow. Stanley stopped spinning and met her eyes over the heads of their children, in that split second ceasing to be Father and becoming Husband.

Every woman in the world wanted to be looked at like that.

The scene blurred. Elizabeth impatiently wiped the moisture from her eyes. Megan approached; the children receded so their parents could greet one another.

A tear trickled down Elizabeth's cheek. Another one. Stanley took Megan's face in his hands and kissed her reverently, then enveloped her in a long, rocking hug.

The trickles became downspouts. Elizabeth backed away from the window and sank numbly into the rocker. What the hell was the matter with her?

"Elizabeth!" Stanley's rich tenor voice. "Hey, *Elizabeth!*"

She took a long, shaky breath, grabbed a tissue to wipe eyes and blow nose, then checked out her slightly damp appearance in the mirror. Pleading an allergy attack was always an option.

"C'mon down and say hello!"

"Coming!" Down the stairs into Megan's hot, peaceful garden, then around to the driveway where Vera stood in front of her son, hands reaching up to his shoulders, beaming into his face.

"Here's Elizabeth, Dad!"

"Hey there!" He broke away from his mother and strode to meet her, hand confidently outstretched, unusual gold eyes brimming with warmth and humor. "Glad to meet you. Megan says you're a regular part of the family by now."

Elizabeth took his hand, as happy as she'd been miserable moments ago. Sadness couldn't exist around this life force of a man gripping her hand, grinning as if meeting her was the highlight of his week.

"Only because this family is the best anyone could have." She looked past him to include Megan in the compliment and saw her smile tighten.

How could Elizabeth have said the wrong thing this time?

"I couldn't agree more." Stanley dropped her hand and walked back to his wife. "A wonderful family."

Instead of comforting her, his words seemed to make Megan stiffer. "Come on in, Stanley. I wasn't expecting you before dinner, but there's plenty. Lolly can quick help make some more—"

"No!" He held up his hand. "No cooking for you tonight. I've brought dinner, which we are all taking . . ."

The silence stretched, kids breathlessly waiting for whatever was coming.

" . . . to Lake Lure for a picnic."

Shouts of delight, arms thrust into the air, legs sashaying.

Elizabeth pressed her hands together in front of her mouth, a grateful happy prayer. They'd have such a good time. She wished she could be a fly on the—

"You too, Elizabeth."

"Oh, no." She turned her hands palms out. "You've just come home. I'm not *that* much a part of the family."

"Aw, c'mon, Elizabeth." From Jeffrey. "We want you there."

"Sure, sure, come along." Vera beckoned toward the blue minivan in the driveway. "But don't bring knitting, you'll never get the sand out. I'm teaching her lace, Stanley."

"Really." Stanley glanced at his wife before nodding approvingly at Elizabeth. He stood solidly planted, a natural part of Megan's backyard landscape. "That's wonderful. It's a beautiful talent."

"Not the way I do it."

A hearty laugh, as if he thought she'd made a really fabulous joke, which made Elizabeth laugh too. The man could probably sell you your own teeth. He reminded her of Dominique, joyful, indomitable, with that magnetic and very sexy intensity.

"So, my beautiful cook." He squeezed Megan to him, making her shoulder hunch to her ear. "Am I ruining your dinner plans?"

"Not at all." Megan laid her hand on his chest and pushed gently away. "Since it's hot, I was just going to have a big salad with grilled cheese sandwiches. Nothing that can't keep until tomorrow. Elizabeth, you should come with us. You'll enjoy the lake. It's beautiful, and only about a twenty-minute drive."

"The lake! The lake! Woohoo!" Deena and Lolly were doing a do-si-do swing in the driveway while Jeffrey waggled his arms and knees in his own private chicken dance.

"If you're sure . . ." Who knew whether she was? Megan would probably be polite to a mugger. But Elizabeth really wanted to go, so she would.

"Bring your suit, we'll swim! I'll show you my weird frog kick." Jeffrey dropped to a crouch. "Ribbit, ribbit."

"Jeffrey, go get ready. Girls, you'll need suits, towels—"

"We kno-o-w," Lolly sang.

The kids jostled into the house; Elizabeth scurried up to her rooms and changed into her Comfort-purchased demure navy and white swimsuit, glad she had something to replace her plunging black one with side cutouts, which would undoubtedly have scandalized Vera.

Last time she'd been on a country picnic was three—or four?—years ago, with Dominique in the South of France, a basket of pâté and a baguette, heavenly cheeses, wild strawberries and local wine. They'd sat on a rocky outcropping among hills and fragrances of lavender and thyme. He'd told her his dreams for his new restaurant, the menu, the decor, the clientele he hoped to attract, then his dreams of translating that success into an international food empire. She'd been so overwhelmed by this cosmopolitan man who wanted the world on his half shell, and so turned on by his confidence and determination, she'd seduced him right there under the hot Provençal sun. Afterward he'd proposed, the first time, and bliss had fled from pursuing panic.

But she'd loved France. Finally she understood why Dominique complained about the lack of aesthetics in American lives. Elizabeth had wanted to return to that purity of experience, to dive into the *S'il vous plait, Madame* and *Il n'y a pas de quoi, Monsieur*, to have butter so good the always freshly baked bread was an excuse, to walk down a street and be able to look into shop windows with the appreciation of someone taking in an art gallery. But after that trip Dominique had always gone alone.

Here in Comfort, she had a variation of that purity of experience. The trip to Lake Lure through the green hills was like something out of a Hollywood family road-trip movie. Stanley bellowed out songs, "Oh! Susanna" and "Over the Rainbow"; the kids joined in with enthusiasm from the third row of seats, Lolly in a pop-influenced nasal croon, Jeffrey in a surprisingly sweet soprano, and Deena with spirit but not much sense of pitch. Vera, next to Stanley in the front, would once in a while turn and smile at him. Behind them Megan sat next to Elizabeth; she laughed sometimes, but didn't join in the singing. The joy in the car was palpable. How the kids must miss their dad when he was gone, and vice versa, to unleash this much happiness at the reunion.

At the lake Stanley paid the beach fee, waving off Elizabeth's attempt to take care of it, "When I'm staying at your house, you can pay."

The area was gorgeous, the long narrow Lake Lure manmade by damming the Rocky Broad River. Around it, forested hills bent thirstily to the water or stood proudly, green tops balding here and there to gray ledges. A breeze blew away some of the heat, though just the sight of the lake made Elizabeth feel cooler. The kids ran shrieking toward the water while the grown-ups trudged to a likely picnic spot, carrying coolers of soda and of food Stanley had bought from Kentucky Fried Chicken.

Stanley spread the blanket, Megan unpacked non-perishables and a few cans of soda; Vera unfolded a chair and swung up an awning from its back to protect herself from the sun. Peace and cooperation. In Elizabeth's family, there had always been bickering, always disagreement—where should we eat, how long should we stay, what SPF sunscreen is the right one—Mom and *Babcia* quarreling in rapid Polish, Mom and Elizabeth in shrill English. When it was Elizabeth and Dominique, he decided and she chose: fight or fall in line.

Stanley wiped his forehead with his sleeve. "Elizabeth, there's another chair in the car . . ."

His thoughtfulness touched her. "I'm okay on the blanket, thanks."

"Shouldn't we eat before the food spoils in this weather?"

"It'll be fine, hon." Stanley dropped onto the blanket next to his wife and kissed her bare shoulder, his reassurance dismissing even the idea of food poisoning. "I only just picked it up in Hendersonville on the way home."

"If you're sure." Megan passed out diet root beer and flavored sparkling water, diet ginger ale for Vera. The heat flushed her face, brought out the hazel beauty of her eyes. She was obviously so happy to have her husband home, her family complete.

Elizabeth turned away and scanned the idyllic scenery, trying to picture Dominique here with them. He'd enjoy the lake, complain that it was too hot, take one look at the food and go off on one of his lectures about how Americans had become so accustomed to boxed, chemical-laden, processed, mass-produced food that they'd lost their taste for real ingredients. He was undoubtedly right, but Elizabeth was relieved not having to hear about it.

"So you're from Manhattan, Elizabeth?" Stanley turned toward her on his elbow, head and shoulders visible behind Megan's torso, long legs stretched on her other side.

"Most recently, yes. Before that, Boston, before that, Milwaukee."

"And your boyfriend is a chef. How did you meet him?"

"At a friend's party. In Manhattan." She was ridiculously pleased Stanley seemed so interested and wished she had one of Dominique's cards with her. "My then-boyfriend and I were on our last legs in Boston, so I went to New York to visit my friend alone. Dominique was celebrating his graduation from the CIA—"

"Mercy." Vera put down *People* magazine.

"No, no, the Culinary Institute of America."

People went back up.

"He said he picked me out because I looked like I needed cheering up."

"And he did the job?" Stanley winked, which made Elizabeth blush stupidly.

"I wasn't that interested at first, but he was—*is* very magnetic, very charming and very persuasive when he wants something."

"And he wanted you," Stanley said.

Elizabeth dug her fingers into the soft white sand. "I didn't stand a chance."

"Sounds familiar."

Elizabeth peered back at Vera. "How so?"

"That's how it was with them." She gestured to Stanley and Megan. "She didn't stand a chance."

"I think we should eat. I'll call the kids to dinner." Megan stood and walked toward the shore, feminine and curvy in a green one-piece under khaki shorts.

Elizabeth turned to Stanley, caught by the passion he felt for his wife. "Tell me how you met Megan."

"Ho, let's see. I was—"

"I'll tell this one, Stanley. Megan came to Comfort their senior year. Stanley was dating—"

"Someone else."

"—someone else, but he noticed her right away and thought to himself, 'There's the woman I'm going to marry.'"

Stanley frowned comically and shook his head. Elizabeth hid a giggle behind a sip of sparkling water.

"So he lost no time ending that relationship and pursuing Megan."

Stanley rolled his eyes. "A year later."

"At the time Megan was dating—"

"Someone else."

"—someone else. But he left town, and finally, Stanley—"

"Got it right."

"—went to a party where he knew she'd be. She was all dressed up, a black short skirt and high heels."

Stanley held his fingers close together to show the actual height of her heel.

"He took just one look at her. Just one—"

Stanley held up two, then three fingers.

"—and knew he'd propose that night."

"Did you?"

Stanley nodded.

Elizabeth looked down at the sand, drew a circle with her finger, feeling that same shaky longing she'd had when Stanley embraced his wife in their driveway. Which made no sense given her skittishness about marriage.

"It took Megan a few weeks to say yes, but Stanley swore he'd keep after her until she gave in, and he did, didn't you, son?"

"That is actually the truth. I did, and I thank God every day."

Elizabeth punched the sand circle, obliterating it. "Dominique's been asking me to marry him for four years."

"Four years!" *People* was slapped emphatically against Vera's thighs. "Good Lord, child, what are you waiting for, tablets from God?"

"I don't really know."

"Well you better find out. He's not going to wait around forever."

"So he said." She fisted sand and let it run out between her fingers.

"You girls today think you have all the time in the world to get married and have your babies." Her voice rose, became quavery with emotion. "That's not something you can take for granted. Not ever."

Elizabeth froze, fingers splayed, sand grains sparkling on her fingers. "I don't take it for granted. I'm just not ready."

"Ready? What do you have to be *ready* for? If you can take care of yourself, you can get married and take care of a man." She made a sound of derision. "Ready. Honestly."

"Okay, Mama." Stanley shook his head at Elizabeth, closing his eyes wearily.

"I married Rocky barely knowing him. You've been living with this man for years without the benefit of mar—"

"I think what Mom is trying to say is that while committing to marriage is risky, because you can't know how it's going to be in advance . . ." For the first time since she'd met him, Stanley's face lost its assurance. "If you wait forever, then all you know for sure is that you'll end up alone."

"True." She dug her hand in hard enough to reach dampness underground. "It's good I came here. I needed space to think this all out."

"You've got that. *Uh-oh*, watch out." The beginning of laughter in Stanley's voice. "Incoming."

"*Starving* . . ." Jeffrey threw himself down on his towel, dripping, hair in wet spikes over his head. His sisters and mother were close behind. "Must . . . have . . . chicken."

"All right, Jeffrey. Here it is." Megan patiently dug out the containers and plates from their cooler and passed around the food.

Elizabeth looked at her meal without much appetite, not just because of the heat. Around her the family chatted and ate, laughed and teased. Stanley took every opportunity to touch, kissing his wife, patting Jeffrey's head, tickling Deena, pulling grimacing Lolly close for a hug before he'd give her more food.

Elizabeth needed to get Dominique away from the artifice of New York, away from his addictive ambition and bring him here to Comfort. She needed him to sit by the lake with her, with Stanley and Megan and their children, show him something even more perfect than impressive menus and meticulously arranged store windows of pastry and cheeses. Maybe this family did eat artificially flavored mass-processed food, but when it came to the things that mattered, they were all about beautiful, pure, honest living. Here in North Carolina she and Dominique might be able to recapture the essence of why they were together—and then she could make her marriage decision based on something other than gut feeling.

The thought cheered her up enough to stick her spork into dinner and renew her love affair with KFC. The food was still as good as ever, coleslaw just the right amount of vinegar-sweet, slightly blank mashed potatoes hot and comforting, biscuits salty and rich, chicken tender, juicy and peppery. She felt like an adolescent indulging a parentally forbidden treat in their absence, then chided herself. Nothing to stop her buying fried chicken during all the meals she ate alone in their condo. Dominique hadn't forced her to adopt his values, she'd done it—or tried to—happily.

When she went back to Manhattan—even the thought depressed her now—she'd make it a point to eat more "Comfort" food, and to get outdoors more, to Central Park or away from the city to the Jersey Shore, Long Island or Maine. She could entice a girlfriend or two into leaving jobs and/or families to come with her, since Dominique would rarely have time. That would help. Some.

The light grew tired; the carbohydrate orgy waned. Vera dozed in her chair. The kids wandered off to play in the sand. Megan and Stanley sat close, talking quietly, Stanley occasionally stroking his wife's arm.

Elizabeth got up and retrieved her sketchbook and pencils, strolled restlessly to the lake, then along its edge for several yards before she stopped and gazed into the hills. Clouds made moving shadows that turned the trees dark then golden green again. A hawk flew in circles, riding the breeze that ruffled her hair. She held her pad, inhaling the fresh, natural air, cooling as the evening waned toward night.

Where to start? The lines of the hills? She selected a dark green pencil, took another look, squinting when the breeze blew stronger . . . and suddenly saw past the view.

She sketched furiously before her brain could forget a single detail: tree lines arching and flowing; fluid, varying patches of green; dark, child-drawn bird squiggles. This was good.

"Elizabeth?"

She jumped at Stanley's voice. He was standing right next to her and she hadn't heard him approach. "Hi."

"Drawing?"

She gestured at the view, laughed for pure pleasure. Before this she'd always worked at a table, straining, stretching, sketching whatever came to her. Bits. Shapes. Motifs. Okay in themselves, but never coalescing into a design that reflected her ideas or style. This was different. This felt right. "I just thought of a pattern."

"Lace?"

"Oh, no. Fabric." She laughed self-consciously. "I'm a . . . that is, I'd *like* to be a fabric designer."

"That's a fine thing to want to be." He spoke seriously, feeding her excitement. "To make beautiful things people will love to use or wear."

"That is such a nice thing to say."

"I wasn't saying it to be nice. I meant it. You and Megan can talk design."

"Oh . . ." She couldn't quite imagine Megan into fashion. "Clothes?"

"Not clothes . . ." He was looking at her curiously. Cautiously.

"D'oh!" She smacked her forehead. "You mean the lace! And her garden!"

"She's very talented, but she has so much to do with the kids and with me gone so much, that she neglects her creative side." He touched Elizabeth's shoulder. "Maybe you can inspire her to start again."

She gazed up at him, noticing the sun highlighting the dark gold in his eyes and occasional strands of his hair, noticing the fullness of his lower lip, the faint lines crossing his forehead. She wanted to draw him: brother, father and lover all at once. "I already volunteered her to design lace for Sally's wedding gown."

His surprise told her Megan hadn't mentioned it yet. "And she agreed?"

"I didn't give her much chance to refuse. I get sort of enthusiastic when I'm excited about an idea."

"You are a miracle, Elizabeth." He chuckled and the power of his confidence seemed to flow right into her. "I had a feeling."

"Thank you." She felt herself blushing again, wondering how Megan could stand having him gone, wondering if he'd let her sketch him sometime.

"Thank *you*." He gestured back toward the car. "We're on our way. Kids are getting tired . . ."

Elizabeth started, as if she'd had to wake suddenly from a delicious dream. "Oh. Yes, sure. I'm ready."

He waited until she pulled alongside him, then fell into step with her, his long stride a contrast to Dominique's small, hurried steps.

"How long have you wanted to be a designer?"

"Not long." She forced herself to be honest, bracing for his disappointment. "I've tried a lot of things. But this one feels good."

"Then it's right."

"Dominique says I have too many dreams too often."

"No one can have too many dreams."

She wasn't sure about that, but the words sounded wonderful, and she loved hearing them from him. "Are you living yours?"

"Yes. Not that I've always wanted to sell physical therapy

equipment, but I love working with people, I love what I do, it's good honest work that helps people get better, and my family life is incredibly important to me."

"That's obvious. Your kids adore you. Megan, too."

"I don't get to see them enough, but it makes the time we do have together special."

"I can see that." She tried to imagine Dominique saying any of those things and failed. He was always about wanting more than he had, complaining about how long it was taking him to get it. She stopped impulsively, before they got within earshot of the rest of the family. Stanley turned questioningly and she laid her hand on his arm. "Megan is a lucky woman, Stanley."

He smiled, though not naturally that time. "Well. Thank you."

"C'mon, Dad!" Jeffrey yelled. "Race me to the car."

"Excuse me. I'm being paged." He squeezed Elizabeth's shoulder, then turned to his son. "Watch out, here I come!"

Father and son raced to the minivan, Jeffrey winning but only by a fingertip. Elizabeth went to help Megan lug the picnic things, still feeling as if she was part of something sleepy and golden and not quite real. "Your husband is amazing."

"Thank you. He's . . . remarkable." Her tone suggested maybe she didn't know what she had. Or maybe she was one of those annoying happily married women who complained about their husbands for something to do.

The trip home through the oncoming twilight was quiet, but once the car stopped in the driveway, the kids sprang into action as if they'd been released from hypnosis, tumbling out of the car and racing into the house, arguing about who got to use the computer first. Elizabeth unloaded the minivan with Megan and Stanley and insisted she help clean up and put things away.

Afterward, though she knew she should go back to her rooms and leave the family alone, she joined them on the porch, where Vera sat finishing her final blanket square. Just a few minutes, then she'd climb up to her little apartment and refine her pattern before she painted it. With luck she could get the colors right, the shapes the way she envisioned them. With even more luck she wouldn't wake up tomorrow and realize her beautiful vision was a piece of crap. She'd done that plenty of times.

"That was a really lovely trip today. Thank you for including me."

"You're welcome, Elizabeth. The lake is special, we always enjoy going." Stanley rubbed the nape of his wife's neck, fingers tangling in the rich auburn strands. Megan's eyes half closed in pleasure. Elizabeth stretched, wanting that sweet touch herself. She'd need to call her masseuse when she got back.

"Good evening Morgan family, good evening Ms. Elizabeth." David and Ella strolled over from a path in the woods, up to the front of the house.

Stanley's fingers stilled. Megan's eyes shot open. Vera stopped knitting.

"David." Stanley nodded briefly. "Hello Ella."

"Stanley. Welcome home." Ella must practice making her voice as sexually charged as possible. Elizabeth wanted to smack her. Right in front of Megan!

Stanley rose, his size advantage bolstered by his position on the porch of his home territory. "You two taking a walk?"

Below him David stood solidly, hands on his hips, chest lifted. "Looks that way, doesn't it."

"David." Ella giggled, not taking her eyes off Stanley. She looked so beautiful in the soft evening light, younger, and more vulnerable. Elizabeth wanted to shoo her away, not that Megan had anything to worry about. Stanley, obviously, wouldn't even glance at another woman.

"It's a beautiful night for a walk." Megan sounded so unlike herself that Elizabeth snuck a peek, surprised to find her looking agitated.

"Yes. It is." Vera glared at the intruders. "So keep walking."

"Mom . . ." Stanley warned.

Elizabeth glanced sharply at Vera, shocked by the venom in her voice. Who was her target? Ella for being attracted to Stanley? David for drinking? The two of them for the sin of taking a walk when they weren't married? Or for doing a lot more than that? Though if they were lovers, why was Ella looking at Stanley like he was her first meal in a week?

"Elizabeth."

Elizabeth turned to David, confused by too many undercurrents. "Yes?"

"I'm going to pour some bourbon next door. I know you've been seriously deprived here—"

"I wouldn't say that." Stanley's voice was overly hearty. "Elizabeth? Have we deprived you?"

"Oh. No. Of course not." She shook her head too many times, feeling sick.

David smiled, dark-eyed Paul Newman in the warm night. "I hope you'll join me."

"Us," Ella said.

Megan made a small sound. Surprise? Disapproval? What the hell was going on?

"You told me you were going home, Ella," David said.

"Did I?" Her smile was artificially sweetened. "I guess I changed my mind. Woman's prerogative."

Elizabeth hated this. After such a beautiful, simple day be-

ing able to share the family's happiness, and with her first decent design idea making her so excited and proud, the Twins of
Doom had to show up and complicate everything in ways she
didn't understand, and what's more, didn't want to. Comfort
wasn't supposed to be like this.

She stood up next to Stanley in a show of solidarity. Her
motion turned the porch light on, flooding the group of tense
faces. "Thanks for the invite, but I'm staying here."

Stanley's arm landed strong and warm around Elizabeth's
shoulders. "She's with the family tonight. You two enjoy yourselves."

"Actually." Ella edged toward the porch. "I think I'll visit
here. I haven't seen Stanley in a while, and Megan and I have
to talk knitting and Sally's wedding plans."

"*Et tu*, Ella?"

"Sorry, sweetie." Ella mounted the steps, pushed past Elizabeth and stood on Stanley's other side. "I changed my mind
again."

David nodded, hands shoved into his pockets. He glanced
at Megan and for a brief, shocking second the cynical sneer
dropped and he looked like the kid last picked in gym class.
"I'll be going home, then. Good night all."

Megan made a quick movement in her seat, then got up and
went into the house. Ella still hovered hopefully behind Stanley, who was staring murderously after the retreating David
and didn't see Megan's face, which was just as well. One look
would have made it obvious his wife was about to cry.

Chapter Seven

In Eshaness over the next weeks there is constant talk of
Gillian. Of her chanting to the sky at sundown. Of her
bewitching birds to eat from her hand. Of her swimming
nude every morning and every evening—she has been
seen coming back from the cliffs with her hair wet and
clothes dry. Boys and men, young and old, start scanning
the shores, morning and evening. There is talk that Alban
Tait spotted her, but when he called, she dove and resurfaced as a seal, letting out a mocking bark. Others swear
she is no selkie, but a mermaid after a mortal husband.
Still others confirm she is a witch brought to curse them
all. Their crops will fail, their animals will die, many
will be lost at sea. All murmur that nothing good will
come of having her there.

Fiona says nothing; she merely listens. One evening as

she and her mum, her Aunt Charlotte and her Granny Nessa knit by the peat fire, a recently completed shawl stretched on a frame behind their bench, father's fiddle hanging next to the hearth, mutton and fish drying in the rafters, there is a knock at the door. Fiona opens to Gillian. Her house is lonely, she says, she needs the companionship of women. Fiona longs to shut her out, but that is not the Shetland way. She draws back, lets in Gillian's beautiful colors, her flowery sweater, her green eyes and red-plum lips, welcomes her and fetches a chair, in which Gillian sits as if she's been there every night of her life and pulls out her knitting.

The women dart glances first, then longer looks, then finally give in to their longing and stare. This is lace such as they have never seen before, finer than theirs, more intricate, with patterns new to Eshaness, maybe new to Shetland, maybe new to their world. The chatter stops and they watch, spellbound by her needles working, by the cobweb lace falling in cascades like mermaid's hair onto her lap.

Gillian tells them in her lovely lilting voice how she was orphaned by the sea and by disease, taken in by an old woman the rest of her village distrusted, who taught Gillian how to pluck the finest hair from the necks of her sheep, how to spin so that a spider would envy her, nine thousand yards from a single ounce, taught her to look for patterns, not from other women or from tradition, but in the foam of waves, in the branches of trees, in the arrangements of stars, in her mind's eye and most of all in her heart.

Fiona and her mother and aunt and grandmother lis-

ten and it seems their own knitting goes more quickly, their stitches are more even, their backs not so stiff and their hands not so tired.

When her story is done Gillian admires Fiona's lace, clumsy in comparison to her own, and asks where she learned, did her mother or granny teach her? In Fiona's heart the black snake of jealousy thrashes. She says she learned from a woman who appeared only at night—dripping wet from the sea, where she'd swim naked every day—who would sit with Fiona and teach her 'til just before dawn, when she'd disappear back into the darkness.

Fiona's mother and grandmother laugh and tease her for the story. Gillian nods in peaceful acknowledgment and Fiona bends over her knitting again, angry and ashamed of her lies. In the ensuing silence, she looks up to find Gillian watching with her green gaze full of wisdom and understanding.

The talk turns idle, the needles fly. Gillian rises to go. Fiona sees her to the door and Gillian presses her hand, said she was privileged to hear the story of Fiona's mysterious teacher. Then she leans in and whispers that Calum has spoken highly of Fiona in all ways a man can speak about a woman, and that if Calum truly belongs to Fiona, Gillian will not be an obstacle to their happiness.

She smiles her sad, private smile and goes off into the night, leaving Fiona to think on what she's just heard and wish she had not so many doubts about the word if.

Megan shifted in the lawn chair, unable to get comfortable. She'd made the coffee too strong this morning, still trying to get the proportion right, and it was burning a hole in her stomach, making her jittery and headachy. Or maybe it wasn't the coffee.

Last night she'd dreamed of Shetland, of the wide, moody ocean and walks along the cliffs. Of knitting lace next to the fire with her extended female family, of riding Shetland ponies over the heather, of fog and storms and moon paths on the water.

She'd woken this morning, body next to Stanley, mind still in the dream, except the dream seemed more like a memory, of her rising early to see her father off in his boat, helping prepare his breakfast and packing his lunch. While she listened, her dream dad had talked winds and tides, fogs and seagulls, how fishing wasn't what it used to be, how other fisherman were doing—well, poorly, retired, injured, ill. A hard life. A frowning, tight, cold life.

Around her now, North Carolina smiled warmly, drowsy with laziness and conceit. Homesickness pierced her for a place she'd never been. The freedom of the sea. The battle to survive, keeping one close to the edge, open and alive. Was the dream about Shetland? Or a mishmash of memories and remembered stories of her seaside birthplace, Newfoundland, where Fiona's daughter, Bridget, emigrated to from Scotland?

The window of the garage apartment went up with its distinctive grating rattle. The screen raised next, got stuck halfway, lowered. Elizabeth would try again, then her blond head would poke out to greet the morning and her landlord.

Megan grabbed her coffee, jumped up and rushed into the house. The second she crossed the threshold, she started laughing. What was she running from? Crazy woman.

From Vera's room, the sound of scuffing slippers. Another morning. Another breakfast to get. Another day to spend with her children and half-husband, getting meals, organizing, listening, refereeing, offering support and validation. The life she'd embraced for so many years threatened to overwhelm her with its insignificance.

She stepped into the kitchen, grabbed the sunflower-strewn notepad and wrote briskly, "Gone for a walk," left the note on her chair pulled into the middle of the room and let herself out the front door, giggling again, this time from nerves.

A grown woman running away from responsibility like an adolescent playing hooky from school. At the bottom of the porch steps, she stopped. This was silly. She was perfectly up to the task of having coffee with Elizabeth and Vera again this morning.

She just didn't want to.

Her dream of Shetland had changed right before she woke up. The low rocky coast had raised itself into high black cliffs teeming with birds, nesting and wheeling in the salty air. Stanley had been there next to Megan, his plain-as-toast wife, but with eyes only for the dark beauty who dominated the other half of his life.

Her giggles faded. She'd found the picture in Stanley's wallet years ago when she'd been short of cash for groceries and hadn't wanted to waken him after a late night. She'd known immediately it was Genevieve. That beautiful face staring at her, dark exotic eyes, wavy thick dark hair, full lips, high cheekbones . . . The physical manifestation of what had hurt plenty as a concept nearly knocked the wind out of her. Megan had put the picture back in his wallet and had taken more cash than she needed, a petty gesture she still didn't regret.

She headed past David's quiet house, where he'd be asleep or nursing yet another hangover. The dream was a dream, brought on by her return to lace knitting, by her daydreaming ideas for Sally's dress. The Shetland story of Gillian was a fabrication of her mother's and had nothing to do with her adult life.

"Hey."

Megan turned. David, stepping out on his porch in jogging shorts and a T-shirt, holding a mug of coffee.

"Hello." She crossed her arms over her chest.

"Where are you headed this fine morning?"

Megan retraced a few steps. His color was good, eyes clear. He didn't look hungover, just morning-rumpled. "I'm taking a walk."

"At this hour?"

"Obviously."

"Hmm." He peered up at the sky. "Any pigs flying today? Usually you're out in the garden by yourself."

"How do you know that?"

"I'm up early too, Megan."

"Oh." She hovered, embarrassed and pleased to think of him watching her, wanting to keep moving, wanting to stay. "I didn't know that."

"Why would you?"

She felt herself blushing. "Did you drink bourbon by yourself last night after Ella ditched you?"

"Nope." He took the last gulp of coffee. "Did my brain cells a favor and skipped it."

"Good idea."

"I have them occasionally."

She took another step toward him, then right up to his porch. He wasn't scowling, his tone was light. A little more like the old David, which gave her courage. "I'm reading Hemingway.

A Farewell to Arms. I thought maybe we could talk about it sometime . . . If you wanted to."

His eyebrow lifted; lips curled; Mr. Sardonic was back. "Are you asking me for a date, Mrs. Morgan?"

She clenched her fists, face burning. "Stop it. What's the matter with you? We used to be able to talk like normal people. Now you act as if it's my fault Victoria left you."

David looked startled. "I wasn't trying to make you feel that way."

"Well you have."

He laughed humorlessly, rubbing the back of his neck. "So you want to dissect Hemingway?"

She lifted her hands, let them fall. "I miss talking to you, is all."

"I miss you, too, Megan." His eyes were calm and direct, staring down at her from his porch. Not a trace of sarcasm.

She felt a burst of familiar adrenaline. "Then why do you keep pushing me away?"

"Because I'm single now. You're not."

"What difference does that make?" She asked before she thought, then couldn't look up at him anymore. "It shouldn't make any difference."

"But it does."

"You're afraid people will talk?"

"Ha! After what's been published about my wife, my marriage and me, I no longer give a crap what other people think."

"Then what? The truth, David. No more cute lines."

"Okay." He put his cup down on the porch railing and braced his hands on it. "I'm afraid I won't be able to keep quiet anymore about what Stanley is doing to you. I'm afraid I'll spend every minute of my time with you showing how little he deserves you, trying to get you to stand up for yourself and tell him where to go. And I'm afraid in the midst of this noble attempt at helping you, I will find I have selfish motives for trying to get you to leave him because of what we were to each other a million years ago and probably still could be if we got the chance."

His words rose up and came at her like a too-big ocean wave. She spun around and walked away, fast at first, then broke into a jog, then a sprint, wishing Wiggins Street was a runway and she was an airbus with a flight plan to Anywhere But Here.

A few houses later she veered off the road, dropped back to a walk on a familiar path through the woods, climbed up Gambler's Hill to her favorite spot, a stream which had found an assortment of flat, tilted rocks and fashioned itself a gently cascading waterfall. She used to come here often after she first found out about Stanley's other family. It was a place to escape to while the kids were in school, when the four walls of her life had been too oppressive. And she'd had some idea that if she left all her tears here there wouldn't be so many to poison the atmosphere in the house.

Under and around a tree branch, she found her favorite rock, perched on it, breathing too hard and not just because she was out of shape. She didn't want to hear or understand or think about what David had just said. Forget talking to him about Hemingway. She'd Google information she needed to know. Someone—many someones—would have written articles on *A Farewell to Arms*. She didn't need David for that.

The water slid, splashing and rushing importantly over the arrangement of mossy rocks for a short way before disappearing again underground. Morning sun caught flung drops and made them sparkle before they fell, watering ferns on the leafy forest floor or rejoining the flow. Rhododendrons grew; saplings in the shade of their older siblings tried their best to become trees as well. Why had she stayed away from this place for so long?

"Megan."

She jumped, not having heard his footsteps. David found a rock close to hers and sat, gazing around him.

"You followed me here?"

"Sure, why not? I love this place."

She stared at him as evenly as she could with her heart refusing its regular rhythm. "I come here when I want to be alone."

"I know."

"Then why would you—"

"I want to talk to you." He turned his lazy grin on her, but his hands stretched taut and clawlike on the rock behind him. "And as usual, you run away from anything that doesn't feel good."

"Unlike you coming back to Comfort."

"Touché." He leaned down, dipped his hand in the water, let drops drip off the ends of his fingers.

"What did you want to talk about?"

He glanced at her. "Not going to make this easy, are you?"

"About as easy as you've made it for me the last three months."

"Fair enough." He shook his hand dry, leaned back again. "I bought a recording recently. Gundula Janowitz, singing Strauss's *Four Last Songs*, do you know it?"

"The piece or the recording?" She stopped him from answering. "Never mind. No to either."

"The songs are Strauss's last, written when he was eighty-four to poetry about facing death. Beautiful poems, not railing against the dying of the light, but accepting it. *Now that day wearies me, my ardent desires will receive more kindly, like a tired child, the starry night.* There's a moment in the third song when the soprano comes in after a violin solo that made me think of you."

"Why?" She was afraid of his answer, afraid to discover she hadn't shoved her feelings for him as neatly away as she thought.

"Because when you're listening, the rest of the world stops, and the physical response to that aural beauty is so intense you can literally feel something lifting you up." He stared into the woods, face in perfect profile, body still. "You want the sensation to go on and on, but you can't capture it; you have to accept that it's going to slip out of your grasp every time. Even knowing that, you keep wanting it back, keep trying to make the impossible happen."

Megan's heart swelled and opened, a peculiar breathless sensation. She stood, every muscle wanting to run away again. "What am I supposed to say to that?"

"Whatever comes into your head."

"Okay. Those were beautiful words. But you're also flirting with Elizabeth and probably sleeping with Ella."

He burst out laughing, making her want to sock him, the way she once socked a female tormentor at another new school, pow, in the solar plexus. "You jealous?"

She was. "Get over yourself, David."

"Believe it or not, I'm trying to get over myself."

"With alcohol and anger? By sleeping with someone who—"

"I'm not sleeping with Ella. I'm flirting with Elizabeth, but we both know it's harmless. Alcohol and anger . . . at least they're real."

"Not real. They're escapes. Easier."

"Than telling yourself nothing's wrong?"

"Than doing the hard work of confronting what's hurting you and keeping on in spite of it."

"And you're doing the hard work of confronting Stanley how?"

She sucked in a breath, suddenly annoyed by having to talk over the constant chattering of water. "That's not what I meant. I'm still living. I'm not trying to destroy myself."

"Not trying, maybe, but you are. Shut into the house, serving children and your mother-in-law and your part-time husband. That's your chosen life?"

"And you're *not* shutting yourself away?"

"I am shutting myself away. So is Ella. We're deep in anger and depression, playing them both to the hilt. She's good company when I need to dive into the bitterness, and vice versa for her. Because there's no avoiding the pain, just postponing it. Grief will have its day one way or other." He picked up a rock, flung it toward the water; it hit a stone with a sharp crack. "Both of us are still counting the pain in months. How long have you known about Stanley, fifteen years?"

"What do you want from me, David?"

"I thought I told you."

"You want me to leave Stanley."

"Yes."

"So you can have me."

"Not for that reason." He looked away to pick up another rock. "But that summer we were together . . . it ended because of circumstances, not emotion."

She fisted her hands, ready to tackle him to the ground. "You never told me that. Just that it was over."

"I thought I was doing you a favor."

"Some favor, breaking my heart for no reason."

He threw the second stone into the woods, probably wishing he could have aimed it at her, got up and brushed his hands together. "You married Stanley about ten seconds later."

She was nearly panting with rage. She wanted to find the rock he'd thrown and hurl it at his head. "I married him because my father was moving the family again. Because I was eighteen and finally old enough to fight being dragged all over the country in a futile search for enough success to satisfy my father's black-hole ego. Do you think if I'd known how you felt I would have made the same—"

"Megan?"

Stanley. Tramping through the woods on his big feet, lips smiling under his sienna mustache, gold eyes taking in the situation, judging, no verdict yet.

"Hi." She took a guilty step toward him, trying to control her shaking. "We were—"

"Hi, David. The kids wanted their breakfasts, Megan. I gave them cereal, wasn't sure if there was anything else."

"Cereal is fine." She wondered if he could see her tears, knew it would give her away to wipe them now.

"Everything okay here?"

"Yes. Fine." She walked to him, zombie on the outside, cement mixer on the inside. "I'm coming home."

He put his arm around her when she stood next to him. "Hey, you have designs on my wife, David?"

David didn't respond to his laughter, stood quietly watching Megan. "Why shouldn't she have as good a deal as you do?"

Beside her, Stanley's body went still. "I'm going to pretend you didn't say that."

"Fair enough. For what it's worth, her virtue is intact. But I probably didn't need to say that either."

"No, I trust her completely." He hugged Megan to him. "Oh, meant to ask the other night, David, how's your book coming? Think it'll outsell your wife's?"

David smiled grimly, a boy lost in the woods next to Stanley's huge and commanding presence. "Undoubtedly not."

"Stanley." She tugged him toward the path. "Let's go."

"I'm ready." He swung around, keeping her next to him, though there was scarcely room on the path for two. "See ya, David."

Megan's tears rose again; she stumbled on a root. Stanley's powerful arm tightened to keep her from falling. On the road she pulled out of his embrace, squeezing him first so he wouldn't take offense.

"What was all that about, Megan? He giving you trouble?"

"Not really. He makes me tired is all."

"He's so miserable, he wants everyone around him to suffer too." Stanley made a sound of disgust. "First rule of sales, never surround yourself with negative people. They suck the positive energy out of you."

"So you've said." Over and over.

She made herself breathe normally. Stanley didn't deserve her delayed rebellion. If she were going to take a stand, fifteen years ago was the time. Not now, when he had every reason to believe they were settled, and so had she.

"He's always had an attitude, like he's better than everyone around here. His dad was nowhere, his mom was a drunk, but you'd think he was Prince of England the way he acted. Well, what goes around comes around." He stopped outside their house. "People get what they deserve."

It was on the tip of her tongue to say, *I don't deserve what you did to me.* But maybe she did. She'd gotten herself engaged after an absurdly short time, and then put blinders on and let life happen. Even the day she found among their papers the misplaced mortgage statement for his other house. Mr. and Mrs. Stanley Morgan, 110 Allgood Street, Roxboro, North Carolina. Everything changed, except . . . David was right. Nothing really had. She'd just put on bigger blinders.

"So I must deserve you, my beautiful one." Stanley glanced down the street, then smiled lovingly into her eyes and bent down, insisted on a longer kiss when she tried to pull back. She complied, responding with obedience, then enjoyment, then passion, the familiar touch of his lips safe and reassuring after her emotional bruising in the woods.

A noise behind her, footsteps climbing to the porch next door, and she realized, sickeningly, why Stanley had kissed her out in the street like this, with so much love and so much possession.

Her brilliant salesman husband had just closed another deal.

Chapter Eight

On a warm night in late June, a month after Gillian showed up in Eshaness, Fiona; her mother, Mary; Aunt Charlotte; Granny Nessa and two neighbor women, Aileen Thomson and Kenna Mouat; sit outside the Tulloch house to do their knitting. After a brief chat about the upcoming midsummer dance at the laird's house, talk turns predictably to Calum. The women are worried. The day before, the sailboat he's tied every day as firmly and securely as the last was found drifting, nearly out to sea. His catch has been low on recent trips and the previous week he lost a precious net overboard. The older women, Granny Nessa and Kenna Mouat, repeat legends of finmen causing mischief for the human men their women are pursuing and say Calum must take care. The next generation, Mary and Aunt Charlotte, scoff. Finmen!

The old ones probably believe Gillian is a witch, too! Nessa and Kenna mutter and make signs of the cross.

Aileen, a pretty girl of nearly twenty with dark hair and a limp from a leg broken in childhood says Fiona can't sit idle and watch this creature bewitch Calum out from under her nose. She says sometimes men need a push in the right direction. When her Bill started hemming and hawing over their future, she lost no time showing him how much he needed her. She made him the world's tastiest meat pies, the lightest loaves of bread, the warmest sweaters, then ignored him for two weeks, panicking him into a proposal.

Fiona smiles peacefully, looping her wool up and down and over and around, though her insides are raging with doubt. Calum has never been careless with his boats or fish. Did Gillian inspire this new distracted state? Can he be in love with her so quickly, when he was on the brink of declaring himself to Fiona?

The next day she's as forgetful as Calum over her chores, switching the chicken and cow feeds, forgetting to close the garden gate against the horses or to bring in the day's supply of peat, and she scorches the breakfast porridge. Maybe Granny and Kenna are right, and evil spirits are wreaking havoc all over town.

She throws up her hands and takes a walk along the sea to discuss with her late brother what to do. At the edge of a voe, she comes across Calum, halfway down the slope, obviously waiting for someone. Fiona makes herself walk to him calmly, thinking of Aileen's words about fighting for the man she wants.

At his side, she greets him cheerfully, comments on

the fine day, then, keeping her voice light in spite of her pounding heart, asks if he'd like to escort her to the dance the next week.

He hesitates. Gillian appears at the top of the cliff. Fiona lifts her chin and acts as if she sees nothing, as if Calum still belongs entirely to her and marriage plans are in their inevitable near future. Gillian calls out and starts toward them, hair and skirts undulating. A flock of skuas startles from the cliffside and wheels into the skies, calling loudly, diving close to Calum and Fiona, as if commanded by a green-eyed enchantress.

The birds' behavior bewilders Calum, but when he looks to Gillian, she smiles with deeply red lips that distract him more than the birds. She is everything his heart has yearned for. Guiltily he turns back to Fiona, a proud, strong Shetland girl deserving of a man who loves her more than he does. He asks for forgiveness with his eyes, unable to be heard over the bonxies' screaming laughter.

Fiona acknowledges his answer with a nod, then turns and strides away without once looking back.

Megan pulled the pie pan of oatmeal shortbread from the oven. The cookie was plain, like her mother, Aileen, used to make, and its nutty fragrance took her straight back to their kitchen in Memphis, where the treat had been Megan's first experience baking. Instantly she'd been hooked. The second time, she'd changed the recipe, added a touch of cinnamon, which her mother agreed was an improvement. After that triumph, the dessert became her signature experiment: cinnamon, nutmeg, allspice, clove, ginger or cardamom, alone or in combination, different every time depending on her mood.

Tonight when the dishes were done, kids dispersed—Lolly upstairs, Deena and Jeffrey to play with the neighbor twins just back from an Orlando vacation—and Stanley off getting ready to spend the evening with one of his high-school friends, she'd lingered in the kitchen, postponing getting ready to go to Dorene's for the next Purls Before Wine meeting. She wasn't sure what had possessed her to dig so deeply into her mother's old recipe file, or why she chose to honor Mom by making the shortbread without spice. As it turned out, she still had the ingredients memorized, though she hadn't trusted she did. *One cup butter, one half cup brown sugar, two and one half cups oats, one cup flour*, written on a stained card in Grandma Bridget's careful hand.

She put the plate on a hot pad, scored the cookie with one of the knives Sally's late mother gave her and Stanley for their wedding, and cut small, neat wedges, then left the pan on a rack to cool. At the sink she washed the knife, gazing out at the mountains beyond her garden that seemed higher tonight, starker, more confining.

"I'm off." Stanley strode into the kitchen, put his arms around her and pressed her against the sink, burying his face in her neck. "Will you miss me?"

"Not a chance." She laughed to take away the sting, burdened by his constant need for reassurance that she loved him, needed him, wanted him still.

"I'll miss you." He moved back a few inches, slid exploring fingers down her hips. "I'll miss you a *lot*."

"*Stanley*." She bucked to free herself, glancing toward the hall. "Someone might come by."

"Maybe I shouldn't go tonight at all, since you were so upset last night." He murmured suggestively in her ear, arms tightening to keep her in place, rocking against her. "I still owe you."

"Nonsense. You go have fun." She twisted and pushed playfully against his chest, anxious now to get him out of the house, away from the memory that she hadn't been able to climax last night, afraid he'd start asking why. What could she say? *Because after fifteen years of tolerating the situation, I suddenly can't bear that when you're away, you're with her?*

"I'll come back early, how's that?"

"I've got a Purls meeting tonight." She saw him to the door, let him kiss her good night. He wouldn't come back early even if she was staying in. She knew him better than that.

The minivan started, revved, drove away chirping—he still hadn't taken it to Valyne Service to have Dick look at it—and Megan's muscles relaxed. Usually Stanley's being around was a relief, a break from being in charge of everything. Maybe her turmoil was from watching Elizabeth judge their marriage on appearances, admiring Stanley, eating up his admiration of her—the way he got people on his side. He was a good salesman, her husband. If all his successes came home to Comfort instead of half, they'd be doing fine.

She climbed to the second floor, step by step, using the bannister to help haul herself up, feeling older, heavier, burdened by her own body. A hot bath with Hemingway would be a slice of heaven. But the Purls couldn't be put off, they had the blanket to finish, and Sally would want ideas for her dress. Megan had a few, but nothing worth sharing yet.

In her room, she balked at getting ready, even knowing she'd be late, wandered to the window. Down in the yard, her garden was enjoying the summer, plants stretching for the sun, bean vines tangling across the trellis. A breeze blew, fluttering heart-shaped leaves surrounding the delicate pink-white blossoms.

Megan caught her breath. Into her head popped a lace design, better than any she'd tried to force, spiderwebs, diamonds, fans, some opaque, some cobwebby and indistinct. An edging of ring lace. A lace holes border.

Her hands itched for needles, for the warm, soft slide of wool. This hadn't happened in years, designs coming to her this way, like visions. Not in years. She turned away from the window as if in a trance. The clear picture of the lace stayed in her mind, now clean cream against the green backdrop of her garden, now flying to a mountaintop, interwoven threads fanning the firs. Beautiful lace, wafting on the wind over the treeless expanse of Shetland, fixing itself onto Sally's plain dress, decorating the bodice and skirt, ornamenting the hem.

And to cover her shoulders . . .

Megan closed the door to her and Stanley's room, crossed to their closet, feet directing her path. In the back of the highest shelf lay a flat box where she'd shelved it fifteen years earlier, loathing everything it stood for but unable to throw it away.

On their bed she now sat, box balanced on her thighs, lifted the cover and pulled back the tissue paper, tears obscuring the details of the lace. A Shetland wedding shawl she'd designed herself, tree-and-diamond center, a shell border and clematis edging, gossamer weight, light and delicate enough to pass through a wedding ring. Mom had taught her the craft, Megan had inherited the art.

Her last lace project, the shawl was supposed to have been a surprise for Stanley at their fifth-anniversary vow-renewal ceremony. A month before the event, on the eve of sending out invitations to most of Comfort, Megan had found out about Genevieve. She'd canceled the church, put the veil away and told Vera they had better things to do with their money than throw parties, that she'd lost interest in knitting, that she was a one-shawl wonder.

Vera hadn't believed her. Megan hadn't expected her to. But Vera's capacity for denial had worked in Megan's favor. Nothing had been said; Vera had asked no questions, though Megan had spent the next fifteen years under a smog of disapproval for rejecting lace and the ceremony rebinding her to Stanley. Ironic, since Megan had spent those same fifteen years protecting her mother-in-law from the truth of her son's life.

Out of the box, the fine threads of the shawl caught on her work-roughened hands. She'd never been as proud of anything in her life as she was of this, except for her children. Few things had hurt more than stuffing it away to be forgotten.

Soft shawl pressed to her cheek, she imagined Fiona knitting lace in anticipation of a wedding to Calum. Imagined her doing so with as much love and care as Megan had knitted this, before Gillian's arrival made Fiona's heart turn to stone, before Genevieve's had done the same to Megan's.

She gave a short laugh. Ridiculous to be so caught up in her mother's invented triangle, though the similarities were eerie. Megan had wondered about Stanley's other wife in the early dark days when she still let herself wonder, before she found the picture in Stanley's wallet that confirmed her fears. What kind of other woman did Stanley need? A woman with everything Megan was missing. Tall and dark with a toned, lean body, a loud contagious laugh, an overtly sexual nature. Ginger to Megan's Mary Anne. Gillian to her Fiona. A woman so sure of herself and her place in the world that sharing a man fit right into her independent life. Who maybe had a lover of her own for the weeks Stanley was gone. Another Ella. How Stanley must have missed her once he found himself tied to Megan.

Megan took the comforting wool away from her cheek. As divorce rates soared, as people sought more and more sophisticated forms of self-actualization, the notion of a one man-one woman family might become quaintly old-fashioned and die out, leaving a tangled civilization of beings striving to be "completed." Maybe Stanley wasn't a self-indulgent egoist, but a man on the cutting edge of social change.

Maybe.

She refolded the lace into the tissue paper, thrust the box back onto the shelf and banged the door closed with her hip to get it to latch. Useless to torture herself like this. She changed into a light green cotton sweater, frowning at the neckline, which had started to unravel and would need mending. Deep rose lipstick on, she gathered up her finished blanket squares, which she'd joined with the other four into a row a few days earlier, and put them in a plastic shopping bag.

On her way out of the room, the phone rang. Wearily, she turned back and picked up the receiver on her night table. "Hello?"

"Meg, it's your father."

Megan closed her eyes and leaned back against the bed. "Hi Dad."

"You busy?"

"Always am."

He cleared his throat, henh-henh-*henh*. Megan stiffened in Pavlovian response. Dad's warning system for bad news: *Henh-henh*-henh. *I hear the jobs are better in fill-in-the-blank-city* . . .

"I told you I was moving to New Jersey."

"Yes."

"There's a woman involved."

She tried to be happy for him. He'd run her mother into

the ground, ignored her worsening symptoms as isolation, depression and stress exacerbated her diabetes and sucked away her will to take care of herself. After they'd left Comfort her weight had ballooned. She'd ended up in the hospital, pieces of her regularly amputated to try and save what was left. Dad never did make the connection to the life he'd made them all live. Or maybe he couldn't face the truth. Or maybe that was just the way the world worked—men did what they wanted and women followed along. For Victoria's *When Women Rule* book to become reality, widespread social deconditioning would have to take place. "That's great, Daddy."

"We're moving into a retirement community near where her children live."

Megan tightened her lips. Typical Dad, dropping the news in pieces. Not just moving to New Jersey. Moving in with a woman. Moving into an independent living community. "Wow, Dad. Aren't those places . . . I mean, people don't really . . . leave."

"This is my last move, Megan."

She pushed herself away from the bed. He was only sixty-seven. "You're not ill, are you?"

"Just ready to stay put. Tricia isn't one to move around."

"Neither was Mom." The dig came out before she realized it was going to. Her father didn't respond. She wandered to the window, gazed out at the mountains, early evening light sharpening their colors in anticipation of sunset. "Well that'll be nice, then."

"Maybe you can visit sometime?"

"Sure, Dad."

"It's a smaller place, I'll have to downsize. I'll be going through my things here."

"Okay." She didn't understand why he was telling her this. She sensed he wanted something from her. Permission? Forgiveness? He didn't need her permission. He didn't deserve her forgiveness. "Did you need help?"

"Tricia will help me."

"Is there . . . anything of Mom's still?" She didn't like the idea of this new woman picking through her mother's things.

"I doubt it. You and I went through everything after she died. If I come across anything else, I'll send it to you."

"Thanks." She turned away from the window. More should be said; she wasn't sure what.

"So . . . I'll let you go now."

Megan sighed. She hated the ploy that made her out to be the one wanting to end the call. Even though she was. "Bye Dad. Good luck with the move."

"I'll be in touch soon."

"Okay." She hung up, experiencing as always the complicated wave of resentment and sadness that dealing with her father engendered.

"*Megan?*" Vera, downstairs. "You ready? Elizabeth's waiting."

"Just about." She brushed her hair, even more tired now, tucked it behind her ears, tried to perk herself up with a rare squirt of her mother's favorite *eau de cologne*, 4711.

"Lolly, Deena, Jeffrey—Elizabeth and I are off to Dorene's. Grandma will be here."

"Hey, Mom?" Jeffrey wandered out into the hall for a hug. "Would you be okay if you could only eat foods with the letter B in them?"

She laughed with a mixture of enjoyment and exasperation. "I guess so, maybe. Bananas and peanut butter on bread anyway. Be good tonight, and if you can't manage to be good, at least stay away from your sisters so you don't drive Grandma crazy."

"Yes, Mom, bye Mom."

The girls shouted good-byes over whatever boy-band garbage they were listening to in the room they shared.

Downstairs, Megan put the still-warm shortbread into a waiting tin. Dorene hated cooking, baking in particular, so Megan always offered to bring something. Yes, she was being nice, but she also loathed the store-brand boxed cookies Dorene adored and served every time.

"I'm ready. Bye Vera."

"Have fun." Vera handed over her finished blanket squares. "I've joined these already, Megan."

"Why don't you come with us, Vera?"

Megan stiffened. Could Elizabeth leave nothing the way it was?

"Go on, go on." Vera waved her away. "You don't want some old woman intruding on your fun."

"No, we don't. But we do want you."

Vera's offended look barely had time to get started before she laughed in delight, cheeks coloring pink. "You are something else, Elizabeth."

"Megan, make her come with us. Lolly's old enough to watch the others and we won't stay long. I'm sure Dorene wouldn't mind one more, and Vera can help sew up the blanket."

If people only had the muscle to support a certain number of faked smiles in their lives, Megan must be nearing the end of her ration. "The kids will be fine. Feel like it, Vera?"

"Well." Vera hauled herself out of her rocker. "I guess I'll go. A nice change to the evening. Thank you, Elizabeth. You two go on ahead, I'll freshen up and be right there."

"We'll wait." Megan stood, feeling like her parents had just volunteered to chaperone her senior dance.

"Don't wait. Go. I'll catch up. Go, go, go."

"We'll take your row." Megan led Elizabeth down the steps and they started out on Wiggins, past David's house.

"Here, let me carry that." Elizabeth took the blanket squares, leaving Megan with the shortbread.

They turned the corner onto Snowden. Hot tonight, probably rain on the way. Perspiration dampened Megan's skin. She imagined herself in Shetland, walking the cliffs like Great-Grandma Fiona in the stories. The air there must always be cool and fresh, alive with grassy, salty-ocean scents. Next time Stanley was away Megan should pack up the kids for a trip to the Carolina coast so she could see the ocean again. If Elizabeth stayed and paid rent next month, and if Megan saved carefully, it might be possible.

"Have you had any ideas for Sally's dress?"

"A few." She wiped the sweat from around her hairline where it always started, enjoying the familiar simmer of creative excitement beginning again. "I'm thinking of a panel, neck to floor, wide at the top, tapering to her waist, then widening again to the floor, and a border of lace around the hem."

"Oh Megan! That sounds gorgeous! I was thinking little patches all over, like daisies in a field. But your idea is better." She swung the bags of knit squares, bumping them against her knees as she walked. "Wait, what about Sally's shoulders, though? They still wouldn't be covered."

"I have something she can use."

"Ooh, what? Something you made already?"

"A Shetland wedding shawl."

"From your wedding?"

"No." All these questions. How much farther to Dorene's? They should have waited for Vera. "It was just a project."

"Have you ever been to Shetland?"

"No." Megan transferred the shortbread to her other hand and walked faster in spite of the heat. "It's too expensive to get there."

"Oh, that's such a *shame!*"

Megan still couldn't understand Elizabeth's emotional intensity; she reacted as if everything she heard about was happening to her. "It is what it is."

"Sally's dress will be gorgeous. Did you ever study design?"

"With my mother."

"Did she have a degree?"

"No." They were turning up Dorene's front walk. Not a moment too soon.

"What did she die of?"

"Sweet Jesus, Elizabeth." At the bottom of Dorene's front steps, a second away from entering and safety, Megan lost it. "Do you *ever* stop asking questions?"

Elizabeth's mouth dropped; her eyebrows rose, then she surprised Megan by giggling. "I know. I'm sorry. I drive Dominique crazy too. Ignore me."

Her grace in the face of Megan's rudeness made tears of shame rise. "I'm sorry for snapping. Elizabeth. I don't know what came over me. It's the heat or something."

She dug in her shorts pocket, came up empty, crossed hands and tried the other pocket, sniffling. Damn it. This was not a good time to fall apart.

Elizabeth slipped a tissue into her hand, grabbed the shortbread as Dorene opened the screen. "Hey, Dorene, good to see you again. Thank you *so* much for including me tonight.

Here are Megan and Vera's rows for the blanket, and Megan baked this incredible shortbread, which you need to take *now* because otherwise I'm eating it all on the spot. Doesn't it smell incredible?"

Dorene took the shortbread, looking slightly stunned at the full conversational attack. But Megan, able to sneak in a careful eye-wipe and silent nose blow, was grateful. And even more ashamed of losing her temper.

"It's beautiful. Come on in, Elizabeth, welcome to the Purls. Megan hey, c'mon in. Leave the bugs outside, though." Dorene laughed heartily and led the way into her living room, hodge-podge and angular as she was, upholstered here, modern metal there. Black and white rug, dark red walls in the living room, burnt yellow in the dining room, no pictures on three walls, then on the fourth a huge print of the Seurat painting of people enjoying the banks of the Seine. Ella and Sally were already seated, Ella on a blue couch, Sally on a black leather chair.

"Here they come." Sally beamed. "We're ready for your rows. Look in the dining room."

Megan peeked and couldn't help smiling. Laid out on Dorene's dining-room table, the blanket was pure, cheerful fun, missing only the blue and indigo above the violet to weight it at the bottom.

"It's gorgeous!" Elizabeth stepped into the room and drew her hand over the arranged rows. "You guys should totally win."

"Not in this town." Ella snorted. "Unless you want to spread for Roy. Dorene, you need help opening the wine?"

"Thanks." Dorene stopped tugging on the corkscrew and handed the bottle to Ella.

"What do winners get?"

"Cheesy plaque." Ella popped the cork with ease and started pouring red table wine into the mismatched stemware on the coffee table. "And five thousand dollars."

"*Wow.*" Elizabeth accepted a silver-rimmed glass. "That is pretty nice."

"Megan, I have juice for you." Dorene started for the kitchen.

"Actually." Megan cleared her throat, startled by her immediate objection. She hadn't planned this. "I think I'll have wine tonight."

"Well, well." Ella poured her a generous glass and lifted it in salute before she passed it to Megan. "Welcome to the dark side."

"Let's get started." Dorene crunched a handful of peanuts from a wobbly clay dish her nephew, Clara's son, had made. "We should be able to finish tonight."

"Then we'll want to get started on Sally's dress!" Elizabeth said. "Oh, Dorene, Vera's coming. I thought we could use an extra pair of hands."

"Perfect." Dorene led the way into the dining room. "Seven colors, six seams, one for each of us. You know how to crochet, Elizabeth?"

"Yup. My grandmother taught me that, too."

"*Before* she died?" Ella asked archly.

"Ha ha." Elizabeth grinned. Apparently she wasn't letting Ella get to her tonight. Maybe they'd bonded over martinis at David's. Megan sipped her wine, found it biting and rich. Stanley didn't drink because of his father's overindulgence, and she'd gradually given it up when pregnancies and kids came along. Not that she ever drank much, except the summer she dated David. They'd get together at nighttime, sneak out to sit in the woods, tie one on and talk and talk and talk. He'd rant about how small Comfort was, how frozen—*congealed* was the word he'd used—how he'd bust out and make a name for himself somewhere, somehow, with his writing or with his passion for education. She'd talk about her lonely roaming life, about her lace, about her mother and about Shetland. They'd make love, then talk some more and finally sneak home in the middle of the night.

"I thought we could sit opposite, on alternating rows so we don't tug the material away from each other." Dorene hovered nervously.

"Good thinking." Megan opened the shopping bags and laid blue and indigo in their proper places.

"I bought black yarn to join the rows as we agreed. Everyone brought a crochet hook?"

"Ye-e-s, Dorene." Ella rolled her eyes. "Drink your wine and calm down."

"Hey, anyone heard from Cara and Jocelyn?" Sally asked.

"I got an e-mail from Cara." Dorene fussed with the blue and indigo rows. "She said they have slept an average of three hours a night."

"Why does that not surprise me?" Ella moved into place by her red row. "Any sugar-daddy cosmetic surgeons or what-stays-in-Vegas encounters with bodybuilders?"

"If there was, they're not telling me. Ella, you join red and orange on this side. Elizabeth, you join orange and yellow over there."

"Knock, knock, I'm coming in." Vera came into view in the living room and ambled over to join them. "Megan, the kids have strict instructions to stay in the house."

"Thanks, Vera." Megan had the absurd impulse to hide her wine; her hand actually darted to cover up.

"Welcome, Vera, nice to see you." Sally stood by her green row as instructed.

"It's nice to be here. Elizabeth wouldn't let me stay home." A glance at Megan implying she should have been the one to invite her. Another glance, taking in her wineglass. "Well."

Megan sighed. So shoot her.

"Megan green to blue over there. Vera blue to indigo on this side and I'll do violet over there. Everyone know the stitches?"

"Ye-e-es, Dorene."

"Remind me," Elizabeth said.

"Pick up one loop from each side, slide the hook through, wrap with yarn, bring back and pull one loop inside the other."

"Got it."

"She's very good." Vera walked toward her row, giving Megan's wineglass another measuring glance. "I'm already teaching her lace knitting."

"You must be a fast learner, Elizabeth!" Sally beamed. "My dress already thanks you."

"Vera's a good teacher."

"Nonsense." Vera put her authoritative stamp on the conversation. "Anyone could have put the chart in front of you and you would have picked it right up. You have knitting in your blood, going back generations. Like Megan."

Dorene chortled. "So when you cut yourselves, *wool* comes out?"

"Vera?" Ella pointed to the last glass on the coffee table. "Glass of wine?"

"Well . . ." Vera shifted in her chair.

"Come on, Vera, live a little," Elizabeth said.

"I suppose one glass couldn't hurt."

Megan nearly dropped hers. Vera hadn't touched a drop in years. At least not in front of Megan. Who knew what she did on her card-playing afternoons?

"Woohoo!" Ella set her glass down and pumped her fist. "The dark one is converting them in droves tonight."

"Really, Ella." Vera shook her head, scowling, but reached eagerly for her glass.

"Okay, battle stations." Dorene made sure the women were armed with crochet hooks and the small balls of black yarn she'd wound for each of them. Megan made sure Elizabeth was started off properly before she made her way back to her blue row.

"What about the cookies?" Sally asked. "Or will our hands get greasy?"

"Who cares?" Ella stood and brought the bag of ghastly frosted-pink cookies Dorene loved, and the tin of Megan's shortbread, then went back for the peanuts, plunking all three in the center of the blanket, on Sally's green row. "Helps absorb the wine."

Five arms shot out for shortbread, one for the frosted atrocities. Cookies were munched, wine sipped. Megan tuned out the chatter automatically, as she nearly always did, and concentrated on the project. Pick up two loops, yarn-over, pull through, pull through again, pick up two loops, yarn-over, pull through, pull through again, the rhythm was hypnotic.

"I know a great party game for this type of gathering."

"Oh, God." Ella glared at Elizabeth, who blinked back sweetly.

"It's fun. Everyone takes a turn, and has to tell the others something they don't already know about her."

"Ooh, what fun. I'll go first. Here's mine: I hate party games."

Dorene snorted. "We knew that already, Ella, it doesn't count."

"Who's first?" Elizabeth looked around speculatively.

Uncomfortable silence.

"Sally?"

Vera glanced up over her red half-glasses. "Elizabeth, maybe you should *ask* first, if people *want* to play the—"

"No, no, it's okay." Sweet Sally, always trying to please everyone. "I'm just thinking, that's all. Y'all know most of my life already."

"If you don't have any secrets, Sally, you can disqualify yourself." Vera looked severely at Elizabeth, who was bent over her part of the blanket and missed it.

Sally laughed nervously. "I don't think I've told anyone the truth about the accident."

"Sally, you don't have to—"

"I know, but it doesn't matter now with my parents gone. Mom was an alcoholic. In public she was fine, but things were bad at home. That day she was about at her worst. Our dog, Godfrey, had died, and Mom had another fight with her brother. She drank to feel better, which then made her feel worse, so she drank to feel better and on and on. We'd gone late to the mall in Hendersonville for new ballet slippers for me, and stayed for dinner and more drinks. On the way home she passed out for just a second and drove off the road. I think we told people there was a deer." Sally's voice thickened; she kept her eyes on her green row, black yarn twisting and looping. "I'll never forget her face when she turned around in the front seat and realized I was injured badly, and that it was her fault."

Shocked murmurs.

Megan gripped her crochet hook, imagining being responsible for hurting Lolly or Deena. "Sally, I'm so sorry."

Sally shrugged and brightened. "The good news is that Mom didn't drink after that day. So I'm almost glad it happened. I'm sure she lived years longer because she stopped."

"Wow, that is *so* intense." Elizabeth gulped more wine. "Your poor mom. And poor you, Sally. That would leave more than just physical scars."

Megan went back to work on her row, hurting for Sally's suffering, embarrassed for Elizabeth, hoping she'd see now how some things were best left to lie undisturbed in people's pasts.

"As I said, good things came out of it." Sally gestured to the women gathered around the blanket. "And now partly because of those scars, you got the idea for making my dress work, Elizabeth."

"True! It's going to be gorgeous. Megan told me some of her ideas."

Sally's gaze zoomed in on Megan like a giant spotlight.

"I'm . . . I haven't finalized them yet." She took a nervous sip of wine, already feeling it warming her body and interfering in her head. "I'll do a sketch for you by the next meeting."

"Oh my gosh, I can't wait! And I'm so grateful, Megan."

Megan nodded, emotions mixed—still guilty for not having thought of the idea herself, still anxious about starting lace again.

"Okay, ladies, back to my game. Dorene, you're next."

"Elizabeth." Megan couldn't bear the mortification any longer. "I'm not sure this—"

"*Well.*" Dorene made the rounds of the table with triumphant eyes. "In high school I slept with Jess Banks."

"Jess *Banks*?" Ella gaped in exaggerated astonishment.

Megan stared, along with the rest of the women. Jess was the class heartthrob, swarmed by girls wherever he went, honey to their bees, dating only the perkiest, blondest and boobiest among them.

"My word, Dorene," Vera said. "What would your mother say?"

"She'd say, 'Jess Banks? What would a boy like that ever see in a flat-chested big-mouth like *you*?'"

Elizabeth winced. "Ouch. That would hurt."

"Are you kidding me?" Ella burst out laughing. "You slept with *Jess Banks*?"

"Just once." She grinned at Elizabeth. "He was the male god of our class. Hell, of the whole school. Not in my league. Not even close."

"Oh my Lord!" Sally finally appeared recovered. "Cara and Jocelyn are going to have a *fit* when they find out they missed this."

"How did it happen?"

Megan opened her mouth to tell Elizabeth that Dorene's sex life was none of her business, when she realized she really wanted to know too.

"Well." Dorene stopped crocheting and clasped her hands, clearly adoring this moment in the spotlight. "I was crazy about him. I guess you knew that."

"You might have mentioned it," Ella said drily. "Maybe three or four thousand times."

"The Bankses lived next door to us, Elizabeth. I knew his parents were out of town one weekend, and I just decided to see if I had a chance. So I went over there."

"*You* seduced *him*?" Ella shook her head as if she were trying to put her version of the universe back into focus. "Dorene! You've put me in the chair of shame. I tried once and he said brunettes weren't his thing."

"Well this brunette was. I told him I wanted to lose my virginity, and that if he didn't do it, I was going to ask Ted Sparrow."

"Oh, Dorene." Megan shuddered, and started giggling. "Not Ted."

"No, no." Dorene cheerfully fluttered Ted away with her long knobby fingers. "That was just a threat because they were so competitive."

"Why you little manipulator." Vera drank more wine, cheeks flushing. Megan couldn't tell if she was condemning or admiring Dorene and had the oddest feeling it was the latter. Maybe she and Vera should drink wine more often.

"Who's Ted?"

"Ted Sparrow. Bad boy, punk rocker, generally scary in a totally sexy way." Ella smirked. "I did him a few times."

"Good God, Ella." Vera turned on her. "What about Stanley?"

"Oh, don't worry, I did him too."

Raucous laughter, even from Megan, because Vera's face was priceless.

"I wasn't *with* him then, Vera." Ella touched the old woman's arm affectionately. "I would never have cheated on Stanley."

"I can't believe you girls. In my day women picked one man and married him."

"Oh come on, Vera, not all women. Human nature hasn't

changed that much in the last . . ." Elizabeth started looking panicked. "Years."

"Wow, Jess Banks." Sally shook her head admiringly. "I was too shy even to talk to him."

"I was too. Until that night." Dorene's face softened wistfully. "For a few hours I was dating the hottest guy in school."

"And it's been all downhill ever since." Ella ducked when Dorene mimed throwing her ball of black wool.

"Nonsense." Elizabeth brandished her wine. "The best is yet to come, Dorene. Ella, for that comment you're next."

"Umm . . . No thanks."

"Aw, c'mon, Ella," Dorene said. "I did it. So did Sally."

"Sorry, not my thing."

"Okay, Ella, you tremendous wimp. Then . . ." Elizabeth pointed to Vera. "Your turn."

Vera gave her a sour look. "What about *you*?"

"I'll go after you. Come on, something none of us knows about you."

Vera concentrated on her row so long Megan began to worry she was furious and that Megan should jump in and make excuses for her.

"Well. Since we're telling private things, there is something I'm sure none of you knows."

Irrational dread began turning over in Megan's stomach. Irrational because, even if Vera knew about Stanley, she'd never admit it to anyone. But the fear was always there that someone might find out, the fallout of carrying a shameful secret.

"No fair telling how your grandmother knew the Vanderbilts," Dorene said. "We know that one."

"I lost seven babies before I had Stanley." She kept her gaze on the wool in her hands, seemingly peaceful except that the crochet hook was shaking a little. "Rocky wouldn't let me stop trying even though I begged him. Even though Dr. Hanson told him to. I lost them all, two in the seventh month."

Megan gasped, trying to wrap her mind around that much grief over that many children, understanding a little better why her mother-in-law worshipped her son. "Vera. I'm so sorry. I had no idea."

"Oh honey." Sally's eyes filled with tears.

"Vera . . ." Dorene stared helplessly.

Elizabeth got up and gave Vera a tipsy hug. Vera squeezed her arm awkwardly before going back to her crocheting.

Megan bit her lip. Why hadn't she gotten up to hug her own mother-in-law?

"That is just cruel," Ella said.

"The cruelest part was that the first pregnancy was the reason I married Rocky to begin with." Vera shoved the crochet hook into her blanket square, split the yarn and had to back out and do it again. "I lost that baby. Didn't have to marry him after all."

"But since you had such a wonderful marriage . . ." Elizabeth rubbed Vera's back. "You had a silver lining too."

"Right." Vera shrugged to get Elizabeth's arm off her. "Now back to your seat and keep working. It's your turn."

"Why yes, ma'am." Elizabeth did a fair imitation of a North Carolinian accent, plopping into her seat. "But it's easy for me since you don't know much. I could say I like banana-peanut butter sandwiches and technically that would count."

"No way. We gave real dirt, you have to also." Dorene lifted her side of the blanket. "Hey, we're halfway."

"It's going to be beautiful," Sally said.

"Tell us your biggest regret, Elizabeth." Megan spoke impulsively.

"Ah." Elizabeth frowned. "I guess . . . not being born into a family like yours."

Megan recoiled involuntarily. She wouldn't wish her situation on anyone.

"Biggest regret? That's boring." Dorene gulped down more wine. "We want something juicy."

"Hmm." Elizabeth crocheted on, mouth twisted to one side while she thought some more. "I've never really had close girl-friends. Not like you all have here. It's always been about men for me, one after the other. Starting at age fifteen, when quantity was more important than quality."

"Good heavens!" Vera half laughed with the rest of them. "What is your generation coming to?"

"You wanted my secret, Vera." Elizabeth waggled her eyebrows. "You got it."

"That's actually kind of sad, Elizabeth," Dorene said. "I mean poignant sad, not pathetic sad."

"No strong father figure," Vera announced.

"Maybe it's that simple. But I won't ever be sure. None of us can really be sure why we do what we do. Whether we're born the way we are or made that way by—"

"Oh, please, Freudina."

"Okay, okay." Elizabeth laughed and pointed to Megan. "Your turn."

Megan kept crocheting, wondering what they'd do if she stood up and screamed that her husband had another house and another wife and other kids not two hundred miles away, that David was the best lover she'd had in her life, that she blamed her father for her mother's death, that once, briefly, she'd thought about killing herself.

Then it occurred to her that they'd probably come through and be supportive, at least in the short term. She might not have thought that about the Purls if Elizabeth hadn't suggested this game.

"Yes, Megan, you're the only one left," Dorene said. "Since Ella is a party pooper."

"Well." Megan stalled for time, checking the neat black seam she'd done so far, joining blue to green halfway across the blanket. "My mother used to tell me stories of her grandmother on the Shetland Islands in the 1920s."

"That's not dirt," Dorene complained.

"No." Megan smiled. "But Elizabeth only said something you didn't know, and I've never told any of these."

"But they're not about you."

Megan thought of her high-school tormentor, the original Gillian. "You'd be surprised."

"Tell us," Sally said.

Megan glanced around at the room of eager faces. Even Ella looked curious. "Now?"

"Like we can go anywhere else for a while?" Ella pointed to the half-finished blanket. "Dorene, open another bottle. It's story time and this one's empty."

"Coming right up." Dorene put her hook down and pushed her chair back. "Though you'll probably have to open it for me."

"Geez, Dorene," Ella called after her. "What do you do when you're alone?"

"Drink beer," she called back from the kitchen and cracked herself up.

Megan took another sip, emptying her glass, feeling reluctant and elated at the same time. She'd kept her stories to herself for so long, she wasn't really sure why she'd volunteered to share Fiona and Gillian with these women tonight. And yet . . . if she was going to share lace with them, by telling Mom's stories she could put the craft and the art in context and honor her mother at the same time, help her friends understand what kind of history they were becoming part of.

She accepted a refill from Dorene, took a sip and set it carefully beside her. "All right. I'll tell you my favorite."

Chapter Nine

*E*lizabeth turned on Wiggins Street and dropped to a walk so her heart rate would lower by the time she got back to her garage apartment. She'd been restless all day for the first time since she got to Comfort, the same sort of what-do-I-do-now fidgets she'd suffered through almost daily in New York. That morning she'd tried a drive through Asheville's quaint redbrick downtown, taking her sketch pad in case of inspiration that never came. She'd been in a beauty store for moisturizer, an art store for colored pencils, a kitchen store for cute plates for her room, a drugstore for mountain-view and Lake Lure postcards she wouldn't send, a boutique for some casual dresses, and an antiques store, where she fell in love with a crazy brass planter shaped like a cherub holding up a goblet, which Dominique would probably loathe but which she surprised herself by buying anyway.

Back home she'd unloaded her purchases, found satisfaction in none of them, and finally set out on this punishing run because she couldn't bear the thought that Comfort was failing her, that she might have merely run away, as David had insisted, and brought her problems with her, that her dream about *Babcia* might have been the product of indigestion and random thoughts, not a connection with The Truth.

Yesterday she'd worked again on her pattern, painted it onto thick paper she'd bought at Pearl Paint, her favorite art store, on Canal Street in Soho. The longer she stared at it, the more she became convinced something wasn't right, and further convinced that no one else would appreciate it either the way it looked now or with whatever fix she could muster. She'd completely lost whatever she found that seemed so right at the Lake.

Elizabeth picked up her pace past David's house, not in the mood to engage him. He'd fed a certain place in her soul that one evening in his backyard, but once she'd met Stanley, whose family embodied what she most loved about Comfort, David seemed artificial, self-consciously clever. Maybe the affect was his way of protecting himself, but it wore her out.

At the end of the Morgan driveway she did her cool-down stretches, enjoying the light air and the day's relatively mild temperature. If she ran this hard in New York in mid-July, she'd sweat off half her body weight and inhale enough toxins to kill a small animal.

She rolled her head around, shrugged to loosen her shoulders and ambled down the driveway instead of going through the house, because if Vera saw her hot pink jogging bra and waist-baring tiny black shorts she'd probably drop dead of horror.

Around the corner, she stopped and smiled at the tableau in the backyard. Father and son across the patio table from each other, leaning forward so their heads nearly touched. Jeffrey explaining something on a piece of paper, talking earnestly, gesturing with his pencil.

Stanley caught sight of her first. "Hey, Elizabeth. Been for a run?"

She suppressed a response worthy of David: *Jogging suit, sweaty body, gee, I guess.* "Yes, a great one. It's so pretty here. I felt as if I could have gone on all day."

"All the comforts of Comfort." Stanley made a discreet inspection of her body, which seemed the wrong thing for Stanley to do, but then he *was* a man.

"Elizabeth, come and see."

She grimaced. "I'm all stinky, Jeffrey."

"I don't care. I drew a cool video game. Come and see."

Elizabeth went and saw, listened to his long explanation involving fang-lined tunnels and fights with "bosses" and tremendously unpleasant weaponry. She put herself on autopilot, nodding and exclaiming at intervals, testing out a fantasy of Stanley as her husband, Jeffrey their gifted son, the peaceful sunny yard their own to enjoy on a warm summer afternoon. Domestic. Tranquil.

No panic, but no longing either.

"Jeffrey?" Megan at the back door, folding a bath towel. "Come inside, honey, you owe me a cleanup on your room."

"Aw, Mom."

"You promised you'd get it done before dinner, and dinner's on its way."

"I was showing Elizabeth my—"

"*Jef*-frey . . ." Megan frowned at her son. She seemed taller, stronger somehow. Or maybe seeing and hearing her transformation when she told the wonderful story about her great-grandmother Fiona had changed her in Elizabeth's eyes. She'd been awkward at first, obviously embarrassed at being in the spotlight. Then, as she continued to work on the blanket, her voice had become musical, her eyes lit, the green in them dominant. She'd put her crochet hook down and gestured now and then, a smile hovering over her lips. Elizabeth had been dying to sketch her, but couldn't bear to break the spell.

"Yes, Mom, okay, Mom." He gathered up his drawings. "Hey, Megan, c'n I ask you a question?"

She started laughing before hearing a word. "Yes, Jeffrey?"

"Would you rather throw up on a full stomach or an empty one?"

"Jeffrey." Stanley ruffled his son's hair. "Go help your mom."

"Okay, okay, I was just interested. I'm going." He ran toward the house, clutching his precious papers.

Elizabeth lingered, smiling after him. She should go inside and shower, but her empty apartment didn't appeal and the fantasy of Stanley the father/husband still did. "Your son is adorable."

"Jeffrey is one of a kind."

She tried to picture little Stanley. Tough kid? Class clown? Studious geek? "Were you like that as a child?"

"Nah, I was pretty average." He glanced at her legs again, then leaned back in his chair and kept his eyes on her face. "I didn't make it through college. Jeffrey will, though."

"I'm sure." She dropped into the seat opposite him, wanting to understand why the idea of marriage to Dominique panicked her while this domestic scene hadn't. Why she was becoming restless and dissatisfied in this beautiful place that held such promise for a life solution.

"Something wrong, Elizabeth?" His voice was kind, tender. She nearly got tears in her eyes.

"I'm feeling a little lost, is all."

He covered her hand with his and squeezed gently. "I went through the same thing."

"Recently?"

"When I graduated high school. I was pretty sure college wouldn't suit me, though I did try eventually. The military didn't appeal, neither did getting an entry-level job. I was probably headed down a path toward self-destruction when I started dating Megan."

"She saved you?"

"Just about." He smiled, and Elizabeth felt warmed, even though the smile was for his wife. "After we got engaged I knew I had a purpose in life that didn't just involve me. I had a home to make for her and a future to prepare for children. I grew up in a hurry, settled down and haven't looked back."

It was that easy for him, and nearly that easy for Megan. While Elizabeth flailed, struggled, analyzed and hypothesized, and the closest she got to "I do" was "I do not have a clue." "I better take a shower."

"Did I say something wrong?"

"No. No." She started toward her little door. "I'm fine. Really."

He stood and watched her somberly, big, solid, reassuring man whose wife gave him the only reason for living he needed.

Upstairs, she stepped into the tinny stall and turned on the weak flow, allowing herself to miss the twelve-head Swedish shower Dominique had installed in their master bathroom. She scrubbed off the sweat and tried to scrub off the restless, angry mood with it. Maybe it was best to set Dominique free to find someone who could give him what he needed. She might be on the verge of change or she might never change. It wasn't fair to ask him to live his life without what he wanted so badly just for her sake.

If she did leave him, she'd have to find work, she'd have to support herself, something she'd never done. She had money left to her in trust by her *babcia*, but it could only be used for education and/or the down payment on a house. Emma Burschke had always said Elizabeth should never rely on a man for security. Said it quietly, with a meaningful gesture toward Elizabeth's exhausted mother, for whom Elizabeth had been as much of a trial as her deserter husband and years of dead-end employment.

Elizabeth should call Mom. Maybe repairing that relationship would help, somehow, with this whole process. But what could she say? *Hi Mom, sorry I haven't been in touch, just wanted you to know I'm exactly the failure you worked so hard to make sure I wouldn't be.*

She let tears flow with the hot water, then made herself stop so her face wouldn't be telltale puffy at dinner.

Clean and dried off, with that tremulous hollow feeling inside, like her organs and intestines would drop to her feet at the slightest upset, she sat on the carpet near the open window by her bed, crossed her legs, straightened her back, and began to meditate, the first time she'd needed to since her arrival. If she were a praying type of person she'd pray to God please not to let Comfort wear off yet. Not ever.

She went through the familiar progression of relaxation, focusing on single muscles from her toes to the top of her head, making each let go', imagining herself sinking into the carpet. Then the same process with her thoughts, letting them fade away, replacing them with nothingness which she imagined like the snow on TV channels you didn't get.

Deeper and deeper into peace until she felt the familiar tingling rush of warmth down her arms, and the uncontrollable fluttering of her eyelids signaling her descent into the trance state that would take her over until she broke it.

Silence. Clarity. Peace. Comfort.

Her lips curved; her body swayed slightly. Her calm felt permanent, her joy solidly reinstated. She gave her subconscious free reign to travel wherever it wanted to go.

It headed to Shetland, treeless islands covered in wildflowers, sheep, ponies, a woman striding over hills, arms out, a Scottish Maria from the opening of *The Sound of Music*. Lace flowed from her fingertips like Spider-Man webs, intricate, cobwebby and beautiful, covering the heather, the cliffs, the entire islands, waving in the breeze.

Then 1920s Shetland became Milwaukee, Jones Island on Lake Michigan, houses built on stilts to keep floors dry from storms that swept lake water all the way over the island. Immigrants there, her ancestors, fishermen, hard drinking, hard fighting, law-unto-themselves; children roaming wild, dogs roaming wild, neighbors helping neighbors.

Her Shetland.

She zoomed in for a close-up, saw her great-grandmother and great-grandfather dancing together on the third day of their Polish wedding, the bride playfully trying to avoid having the wedding cap placed on her head, a symbolic acceptance of the end of her girlish freedom. The woman—girl really—turned and Elizabeth was looking at herself, beaming with happiness, finally allowing the cap on her head and turning in surrender to her groom.

Was it Dominique? He was blurry. She couldn't tell . . .

The whole scene went wrong and thrust her out of her trance.

Elizabeth opened her eyes. She couldn't place him there with her at the altar. Not at a peasant wedding on a tiny island in the Midwest. Maybe not in a sunny backyard in Comfort either.

Outside she heard Deena calling for dinner. She got up slowly, calm still, but not joyful-calm anymore, tired and pulled down. Maybe she just needed a good night's sleep. Or one of Megan's wonderful meals. Or a big martini with David. Or a reassuring talk with Stanley. Or to knit out on the porch and learn more about the women who lived here. They seemed to hold the key to something important, but as usual, she was big on hunches, low on the ability to interpret them.

She tried to imagine her friends in New York sitting on her and Dominique's rooftop knitting night after night, sharing stories and themselves, and couldn't. Tried to imagine herself here permanently, without Dominique. She couldn't.

What kind of life did she want?

Terrible questions to ponder on low blood sugar. Downstairs, she crossed the garden, caught sight of David drinking alone in his yard and hurried past to avoid another invitation. Inside, she joined the Morgan family and forced spaghetti and meatballs into her confused stomach, tried to chatter and answer questions from the kids the way she usually did, aware that Stanley glanced at her several times, the only person who appeared to notice her mood.

Vera told stories of Stanley's tremendous gifts and precocious abilities as a child, when he beat every kid in town at a race, when he subdued a rabid dog just with his eyes. Megan for the first time chimed in too, with a story of the year she lived in Minnesota, how a fox family made its den in their back-yard, how in Florida they'd constantly had lizards in the house. Stanley told of a physical therapist client who worked from a home office and had fourteen cats roaming her place. The kids recounted, as far as Elizabeth could tell, every single second of a movie they'd seen the previous night on television, with extra time needed for disagreements and corrections. Still they charmed her; the whole family charmed her.

Afterward, over sweet, too-weakly chocolate bargain-brand ice cream, delicious and totally satisfying, Megan actually let Elizabeth help with the dishes, then received a lingering kiss from her husband before he went upstairs to do some work. The kids dispersed for summertime kid stuff, and Elizabeth and Vera headed to the front porch and their assigned seats in the cooling evening air to wait for Sally, Dorene and Ella to show up for their first lace-knitting lesson.

"Here we are." Megan stepped onto the porch carrying a tray with a pitcher of iced fruit punch, chocolate-chip cookies and a plate of lemon bars Elizabeth had smelled baking earlier this afternoon.

"Megan, you should have told me, I could have helped." Elizabeth guiltily swept the newspaper Stanley had been read-ing off the table so Megan could put out the food.

"Don't be silly. It's no trouble." She sat in her usual chair, took a folder, a flat box and a book out from under her arm. The folder she deposited carefully beside her, the box she stuffed under her chair, the book she opened: *To Kill a Mockingbird*, by Harper Lee, first time Elizabeth had seen her do anything on the porch but knit.

Elizabeth gestured to the book. "That's a classic."

"I read it in high school, and saw the movie with Gregory Peck on TV, but haven't encountered the story since."

"I wish I liked to read."

Megan blinked. "You don't like to read?"

"Nope." Elizabeth yawned to hide her embarrassment. Some people did, some didn't. Dominique didn't. Her mother didn't. *Babcia* did, mostly mysteries and books in her native Polish that Elizabeth hadn't been curious about. Now she was, retroactively, though of course it was too late.

"I don't know what I'd do without my books." Megan laughed self-consciously. "They keep my brain challenged. Raising kids can be mind-numbing."

"I loved every minute of mothering Stanley."

Megan's right leg twitched suddenly, as if it wanted to kick something. Or someone.

"So you've told me, Vera," she said pointedly. "Quite a few times, in fact."

Vera looked startled at the retort. Elizabeth wanted to whoop and offer Megan a high five, though Megan looked nearly as surprised as Vera that she'd said anything, and maybe after finding out about all Vera's miscarriages, she was wishing she hadn't.

Elizabeth couldn't imagine having Dominique's mother around all day long. Natalie DuParc was tiny with a darting head and constantly puckered lips, very French, very disapproving of Dominique's choice of partner no matter how hard she tried to hide it, which Elizabeth suspected at times was not very. Her voice, especially when she was upset, could be a weapon of mass destruction. "Tell me more about your reading, Megan. I should do more. Maybe I'll go to the library tomorrow."

"I read to fall in love, to travel, to learn." She drew her hand down the plastic library cover of the book. "And when I read something really wonderful, not only is it a great form of . . ."

"Escape?"

Megan darted a glance at Vera. "Fantasy, but if the author is particularly brilliant . . . this will sound crazy."

"To a woman who came here because of a tea bag? I doubt it."

Megan laughed, the first time Elizabeth had seen her do so spontaneously, and it lifted her own mood too. "When I feel the world is a cesspool of lies, betrayals and violence, it comforts me that beauty like this is also possible from human hands and hearts and minds. It gives me hope. It raises me above the horrors I can't understand or explain."

Elizabeth nodded solemnly, feeling wistful. She didn't ever have those kinds of deep thoughts, and it had occurred to her a few times that her place in the world might be more assured if she had more of them. She picked up her knitting, thinking that she'd definitely go to the library the next day. Maybe they had another copy of *To Kill a Mockingbird*.

"Here comes Sally." Vera pointed down the street to two women heading in their direction. "And Dorene with her. There's Ella, too, farther down by the Jackson's. I think she's finishing a smoke."

Megan put in her bookmark and put the book down next to her chair, picked up the folder, placed it carefully in her lap and straightened, hands folded, looking ready for a job interview.

"Hey, Vera. Hey, Elizabeth. Hey, Megan." Sally stepped up onto the porch, beautiful and glowing as usual. She reminded

Elizabeth of the old Ivory Girl commercials. "We're here for our first lace lesson."

"Have a seat." Megan poured out glasses of punch and handed them around, offered the plate of lemon bars and chocolate-chip cookies.

While they waited for Ella, Dorene caught them up on Cara and Jocelyn's hedonistic doings in Vegas, then went on to the story of Stacy Pavone and all the shocking things Dorene was sure she was doing with her visiting male "cousin" who sure came to visit an awful lot when Stacy's husband was away. And Janie Lincoln had been seen coming out of Roy Aldernack's garage the previous Thursday, which meant she had the craft-fair contest pretty well sewn up . . .

"Dorene, I can hear you yacking down the block." Ella sauntered up the stairs, grabbed a lemon bar in plum-tipped fingers and sank into the remaining empty chair.

Dorene made a face. "Well, I can smell you smoking down the block."

"Ouch," Ella said mildly. "Megan, these lemon bars would make God Himself happy."

"You girls are lucky you're all so slim. Of course I used to be too, at your age." Vera sighed heavily. "Rocky could pick me up with one arm."

"Yes, Megan, they're wonderful," Sally said. "I'd love the recipe. Foster loves lemon desserts. And speaking of wonderful, I can't stop thinking about that story you told."

"Oh, me neither," Dorene said. "How much of it is true?"

Megan shrugged. "Mom insisted all her stories were true. I think she pulled them out of her imagination to suit the occasion. Gillian couldn't have been real, with all her magic."

"Oh, I *loved* Gillian." Elizabeth felt oddly bereft.

"Wasn't she wonderful? So mysterious and beautiful." Sally bit off the corner of her lemon bar and waved the rest toward Ella. "Like you, Ella."

Ella grinned. "Which makes you Fiona?"

"Oh not me." Sally shook her head. "Megan has that honor. She's her granddaughter."

"That works perfectly," Dorene announced. "Because Megan and Ella were in love with the same guy. Only Stanley chose Fiona instead of Gillian."

Elizabeth looked up from her chocolate-chip cookie. Stanley and Ella. Another piece had fallen into place. Ella's longing looks at Stanley. The strange tension on the porch that evening. The "someone" Stanley was dating when Megan came to town.

"Oh *thanks*, Dorene." Ella rolled her eyes. "We all needed to have that brought up one more time."

"Dorene, I'm telling you, your mouth is like the Energizer Bunny." Vera folded her plump arms across her chest. She looked strange not knitting, as if something were missing from her body.

"Sorry, I wasn't thinking. Sorry." Dorene glanced at Elizabeth. "You have no idea what we're talking about, do you?"

"I have a pretty good idea now."

"I dated Stanley for four years. He married Megan. That's it." Ella put down her lemon bar. "Megan, you'd better teach us this lace thing before I strangle Dorene.

"I can't *wait* to learn." Sally wiped powdered sugar off her fingers. "Especially for my own wedding dress!"

"Here's the idea I had." Megan held up the folder and passed it to Sally. "What do you think? If you don't like it, we can get started anyway. I can always change the design."

Silence on the porch, everyone watching for Sally's reaction, Elizabeth glanced at Megan. She looked nervous and excited.

A gasp first, then a long *ohhh* of ecstasy. Megan's face relaxed. Elizabeth grinned and stood to see with the other women, who crowded around the folder, exclaiming. Megan had made a beautiful sketch and perfect use of lace to trim the plain dress, exactly the way she'd described.

"It's perfect, Megan." Sally's voice was choked. "I can see Fiona getting married in a dress like this."

"How are we going to do all that in a few weeks?" Ella pointed to the paper from over Sally's shoulder. "The panel I can see, but what about the shawl around her shoulders? That would take months."

Vera's head turned abruptly toward Megan. She did not look happy. Elizabeth followed her gaze and found Megan staring back at Vera with guilty defiance. "The shawl is already made. It's right here."

"Really?" Sally clutched the folder to her chest. "Can I see it?"

"Yes. You can." Megan got up and dragged a flat box from under her chair, opened it and pulled out an exquisite lace shawl. "The cream color should match your dress."

"Oh my gosh." Sally's bridal tears flowed; she accepted the lace reverently, then looked up as if she'd seen a ghost. "Oh my gosh. Is this . . . Fiona's wedding shawl? The one she—"

"No." Megan gave a short laugh. "That part of the story was my mother's fabrication. I'm sure we'd still have that one if it were real."

"You didn't wear this at your wedding," Dorene said. "I would have remembered."

"No. I didn't." Megan glanced at Vera and sat back down. "I made it later."

"*You* made this? How can you part with it?"

"Easy." There was an edge to her voice. "It's my wedding gift to you. Enjoy it."

"Oh, gosh." Sally handed the shawl back. "Put it back in the box before I cry all over it. Thank you so much. It's the most beautiful thing I've ever seen. Can I take it home today?"

"Of course."

"Megan." Vera's voice, so distorted Elizabeth had to look to make sure she'd spoken. "That was supposed to be for you and Stanley."

The happiness on the porch froze, dropped, shattered. Even the breeze stopped blowing.

"Vera." Megan stood again, facing down her mother-in-law. "It's mine to do whatever I want with."

"I've never said anything, not a word, but this is beyond anything. Stanley doesn't deserve this." Vera's voice was chilly. "He's been a wonderful husband."

"Yes, he has been." Megan's chin lifted. She came alive the way she had telling the story, eyes flashing hazel, but this time she was angry. "As wonderful as Rocky was to you."

Vera gasped and took a step back. Apparently Megan had scored some kind of victory. Elizabeth discreetly looked around. Everyone else appeared as bewildered as she was.

"Megan. I don't— Are you sure?"

"Yes, Sally." Megan's face softened into its usual peaceful demeanor. A mask, Elizabeth realized in an intuition worthy of *Babcia*. Not her true nature. Was anything in Comfort what it seemed?

"Well," Megan said brightly. "Let's get to business. Vera and I will do the front panel. You ladies can do the trim around the hem. Here's the pattern I picked for that: old shell border with fan edging. It's not too hard, and with all your knitting experience you'll be able to whip through it. The hardest thing is getting used to the tiny stitches and having to count so carefully. But you'll get used to it."

Megan went through the pattern chart, the symbol chart, then passed out lace wool and more of the size two needles Elizabeth had been using while the group sat in an anxious silence.

"You just happened to have this wool sitting around, Megan?" Sally spoke tentatively, testing the atmosphere like an animal sticking its head out of a burrow for an exploratory sniff.

"My grandmother Bridget, Fiona's daughter, kept buying wool even after her arthritis got too bad to knit. She was convinced the quality of what was available would deteriorate and she wanted my mom to have access to the best. When she died, it all came to Mom, and what she didn't use, she gave to me."

"Wow." Even Dorene's big hands handled the wool reverently. "So this is really from Shetland. To think, we're sitting here knitting on a summer night just like all those ladies."

Ella snorted. "If any mermaids pop up let me know."

"Ella, you make me tired, bashing everything." Dorene turned on her. "I dare you to be sappy and sentimental about one thing. One. Right now. In front of everyone."

"Why don't we all do it?" Elizabeth spoke into the abrupt silence. She couldn't bear this evening to go the way the rest of her day had gone. She was already fantasizing about packing her bag and moving somewhere, and she couldn't do that. *Babcia* had to have something in mind for her to learn here, or everything would start to seem pointless and dirtied about the world.

"Good idea, Elizabeth. I'll go first." Megan was expertly

casting on, fingers flying, face lit. "I am really happy to be helping my friend Sally have the wedding dress she wants."

"I'll go next. Mine's easy. I am really touched that my best friends have come together to support me." Sally turned to Dorene. "Your turn."

"I am thrilled to learn to make something so pretty with my clumsy hands," Dorene said. "Ella?"

"Okay." Resigned sign. "I'm very grateful that I am on this porch knitting with a bunch of women instead of riding some well-hung wild male I barely know."

Everyone but Vera laughed, though uneasily.

"Vera." Ella lifted an eyebrow. "You're next."

Heads turned to Vera for reassurance the tension would pass soon. Vera glanced over her red half-glasses at her daughter-in-law. "Lace knitting is like life. Best shared among women."

Appreciative murmurs. Heads turned to Megan for her response. "Thank you, Vera. That was very nice."

"You're welcome." Vera nodded kindly. "Elizabeth, your turn."

And just like that, the storm had blown over. The knitting went on, lips counting, brows drawn in concentration; the silence was peaceful and comforting. Around them night descended, soft and fragrant, embraced the house and stretched beyond, stopped by mountains still reflecting the sun's last glow.

Best shared among women.

"Elizabeth?"

"Sorry." She smiled, made eye contact with Vera, Ella, Dorene, Sally, and finally, Megan. "Mine's easy too. Being part of this group, even as a fringe member, is the best thing that's ever happened to me."

Chapter Ten

Elizabeth opened her eyes, feeling as if she'd been encased in acrylic. She hated afternoon naps, always woke up sick and disoriented and groggy. But today had been warm, she'd slept badly last night, spent the morning trying to sketch, took a long walk, brooded, meditated, brooded some more, then turned down the chance after lunch to go with the family to Hendersonville for shopping and a movie. They'd taken two cars in case Vera got tired and wanted to come home early; Elizabeth had parked hers at David's so they could get back into the garage easily.

Without the Morgans around, her apartment had been too quiet; the yard felt foreign and lonely, making Elizabeth even more miserable and restless than the day before and the day before that, then suddenly exhausted to the point of stupor. Even working on the lace for Sally's dress didn't help much. She'd hoped, having discovered that cherished sense of belonging to the Purls, that the euphoria would carry over, but it hadn't.

She'd dragged herself to bed, even knowing she'd regret it later, and hit a deep sleep almost immediately. Dreams had come, first of Gillian and Fiona in thong bikinis mud-wrestling in a Shetland peat pit surrounded by shouting, leering men. Then of David's wife, Victoria, in black leather chaps and bustier, flogging a group of groveling, naked man-slaves.

Nice.

Slightly more awake, she tried to sit up, failed and let herself flop back down. The brass Cupid next to her bed offered his flowerpot goblet. Honeyed mead? Nectar?

Dust and a dead fly.

Absence of human noise blew through her windows with the breeze undulating the lace curtains. She caught herself wishing even for traffic sounds, a car horn or a shouting cabdriver. Cicadas would have to do, their quintessential summertime buzz a cross between a metal saw and a dentist's drill.

She rolled over, suddenly missing Dominique so badly she could barely stand it, reached into her purse and dug out her cell, dialed his number and lay back, hand covering her eyes.

"Dom, it's me."

"Elizabeth!" He sounded so pleased and surprised, she felt the warm swell in her heart that had been absent too long. "How are things going?"

"Fine. They're fine." She struggled up onto her elbows, brushed the hair out of her face. "I'm actually not in New York."

"Ah, no?" He mumbled something away from the phone. "Where are you, *ma petite*?"

"In North Carolina. Who are you with?"

"Samuel Luxe. You remember him from our Easter party last year?"

"Of course."

"We're having a glass of mediocre wine in a pub after a truly despicable dinner. My God, what these English think passes for food. Bangers and mash? Somebody shoot me."

"Good hunting today?"

"Yeah, okay. Not great, but okay. These are not French quality, you understand, but convincing and less than half the price. I am getting good ideas here, Elizabeth. Big ideas. This will be very exciting for the restaurant. Truffles have such a mystique, you know. Making the dishes more affordable will draw press and crowds. I will combine these cheap English imitations with humble ingredients, risottos, eggs, pasta, simple-simple, but of course exquisite."

Truffles for the Common Man, yes, she knew all about it. "I miss you."

"I miss you of course, *ma chérie*. But only a couple more weeks, yes?"

"Yes." She grinned, desperately relieved to hear him sounding so glad to hear from her after the awful tension before she left New York. "I'm staying with a family here."

"Here where?"

"I told you, in North Carolina. A town called Comfort."

"Yes?" He said something else away from the mouthpiece. "Are you keeping busy?"

"I'm learning to knit lace."

"Lace! *Mon Dieu.* What for?"

"I'm also working on a pattern for a fabric. I'm going to try really hard to make this work."

"Ah, my Elizabeth. I wish you'd give up these big plans. You don't have it in you to work so hard." His I-know-everything voice used to reassure her. Now it set her teeth on edge. "Relax and get an easy job somewhere if you need more to do. I have career enough for both of us, you know this."

She wasn't going to engage him more on that topic. "I thought you wanted to slow down someday."

"Yes, someday, but not now, not while I have this in the works."

Despair hovered on the edge of her already bad mood. Always something in the works, always the next big, bigger, biggest thing, none of it ever having anything to do with her. "I've been doing a lot of soul-searching."

"Yes?" His voice was suddenly tight.

"I want you to come visit here when you're back from—"

"Visit? *Ma petite*, I will have been gone too long from the restaurant as it is."

"It's really important to me, Dominique. To us. After our last fight we need to know exactly where we are and what we want going forward."

His sigh made her want to curl up fetal. "Always the dramatic complications, Elizabeth. I know exactly where I am and what I want. I want the restaurant and I want you. It's you who needs to decide. Going to this little town, what can that possibly accomplish?"

"I think it can accomplish a lot. Getting away from New York, and our life."

"*My* life. That's the problem. You have not built a life there. You stay packed and ready to run."

She rolled to her back, stared up at the ceiling. Always her fault.

"I should get off the phone, *chérie*, Samuel is sitting here, and I can't be rude. I'll think on it and call you later, okay?"

"Yeah. Okay." He wouldn't call later. The promise was his way of getting out of the conversation.

"*Bonne nuit.*"

"Good night." She punched off the phone and heaved her acrylic self up, pushed out of bed and trudged to the front window, hollow and dissatisfied. She hadn't been able to explain to him why she'd come here, what she was feeling. Nor had he asked. He hadn't even seemed surprised she'd left New York. Hadn't asked when she'd be back, hadn't wanted to know about her design. Whereas she knew all about his damn truffles, his restaurant, his menus, his tastes, his goals, his dreams and his every habit.

Below her Stanley's blue minivan pulled into the driveway, chirped into the garage. *He'd* been excited about her fabric pattern and her career and he didn't even know her. Her own boyfriend should be a cheerleader, a supporter, someone who believed in her more than she believed in herself. And he thought she should be panting to marry him? She should want to marry Stanley instead.

He came into view, alone, holding a cell phone to his ear; behind him the garage door started its groaning trip down. The rest of the family must have stayed on in Hendersonville. Elizabeth smiled just at the sight of him, admiring his height and athletic build, the feeling of solidity and steadfastness he projected. The door landed with a final thud, sending the neighborhood back to silence except for the rasping mating call of the cicadas. Would they take any female who showed up, or were they selective? If there were a lot on one branch, did they hold a cicada speed-dating event?

Anything was easier than the way humans paired off.

"I know. I know, darling." Stanley's voice was low, tender. Elizabeth sighed enviously. He was so irresistible to her, this man who adored his wife. "I miss you too, sweetheart. It won't be long, though. I'll be here another week, then we can be together."

Elizabeth blinked. Turned the words over in her head. Here another week and *then* they could be together? But Megan was already—

"Mmmm." He laughed, a deep, sexy sound she'd never heard him use. "I love when you do that. Yup . . . okay, I will. Say hi to them for me. Tell them I'll be home soon . . . Sorry, what?"

Elizabeth retreated from the window until the rocker hit the backs of her knees and she sat with a thump that stung the backs of her bare thighs. He'd be *home* soon? Wasn't he home now?

There had to be some explanation. Maybe he was planning a surprise for Megan and was pretending not to be at the house?

But he'd said he missed her. One more week and he'd see her again.

Elizabeth tried to breathe through the wave of sickening certainty, still hearing Stanley's voice through the window, though the words were now indecipherable.

Was this what David meant when he said he looked forward to her finding out more about Comfort?

Goddamn it.

Elizabeth jumped up, thudded down the stairs, banged open the door and strode over to stand opposite Stanley, reminding herself to be calm, reminding herself not to jump to conclusions, even ones that seemed incredibly obvious, reminding herself that he was innocent until proven guilty, that to assume could make an ass out of—

"Elizabeth." He glanced at her face, said a quick good-bye, punched off the phone. "Your car isn't here."

"I moved it to David's."

"Oh, right. I remember now." He put the phone leisurely in his pocket. "Why don't we sit down and talk?"

"Okay." She was shaking as she sat at the patio table where he'd been so sweet with his son, in the yard where he'd been so loving and romantic with his wife. He sat opposite, smiling easily. His calm was creepy. She'd seen some TV show where a charming, attractive psychopath confronted by his accuser had pulled out a gun and shot him. Smiling.

"I didn't realize you were upstairs."

"Who were you talking to like that? It wasn't Megan."

His smile faded. "I don't think that's your concern."

"No. I guess it isn't." She closed her eyes. A bee buzzed by her ear, and she ducked instinctively. Was this when the gun came out? She almost didn't care.

"Ah, Elizabeth." Stanley blew out a long breath. "I wish you hadn't heard. But since you did, I'll tell you that Megan knows. This is an arrangement that suits both of us."

Her eyes opened as if the bee had stung her. "She *knows*?"

"She doesn't suffer. You've seen me with her, I adore her, and she knows that, believe me."

Elizabeth stared at him, trying to make sense of . . . anything. "Then why someone else?"

"Human nature." He adopted a politely regretful expression. "One person can't complete another, there are always holes left to fill. You know that from your troubles with Dominique. I need her as much as I need Megan. They complement each other. Together they make me happy and fulfilled."

Oh my God. Her dreams were crumbling around her. "What about what *they* might need?"

"I give them both all my love. I give my kids in both families all my love."

"You have other *kids*?" She felt like crying. Lolly, Deena and Jeffrey betrayed, too. "Do *they* know?"

"No." His lips thinned. "They're not old enough yet to understand."

"That their father is cheating?"

"It's only cheating when it's done in secret."

"It's a secret from your kids."

He smiled again, gentle, patient Stanley having to explain something so simple to such a fool. "Most parents will tell you they have plenty of secrets from their kids. We're entitled to some grown-up privacy. No one is neglected; I have to be gone anyway for my job. This way I'm not a lonely married man hanging around hotels being tempted by other women."

"But your wife is a lonely married women. And the other . . . person is probably lonely too." She couldn't believe this. Stanley, her beautiful masculine ideal of a father, husband and man. It was like the head of Homeland Security turning out to be a terrorist.

"The travel demands of my job make my absence inevitable. That has nothing to do with the way we found to make—"

"*You* found."

The gentle smile stretched thinner. "I wanted to keep my family together. I didn't want to keep some mistress hidden away, or get diseases from random encounters, but I needed some way to cope with the isolation. Megan and I rushed into marriage. She'll tell you the same. We're wonderful lovers and friends, but we're not soul mates , we don't complete each other. I couldn't settle for that."

"But she—"

"I'm honest with both women, Elizabeth. I'm faithful to both of them, I married both of them."

"You're a *bigamist*?" She was sick. Absolutely sick. With his wide, I'm-so-honest eyes, he had the smug vapid look of people in fundamental religions or cults, people sure their completely warped reality was absolutely normal and right. She'd missed that look earlier. Because she so desperately wanted to believe in what she thought he was.

"If they accept the situation, which they both do, then who am I hurting, Elizabeth? You?"

She winced. "As a matter of fact, yes. I believed you were better than this."

"Better than what, being able to make two families happy?"

"Megan is not happy."

"Megan has a lot to deal with, three kids, my mother, me away so often." He reached across the table to take her hand, which she put in her lap. "And now you."

"Don't make this my fault."

"You're extra income, but also extra work. That's just fact. But even without the pressure, Megan tends to the melancholy anyway. It's part of what I love about her, her incredible sense of peacefulness. She grounds me, she makes me feel safe and calm, but she is probably a little depressed. I've urged her to see a doctor, try medication, go back to school, find a career, but she wants to be home with the children. It's a hard life to choose, but it's her choice. It's not like I keep her prisoner."

The neckband of Elizabeth's top was squeezing out her air. She wanted to claw at her throat and tear it off.

This was exactly how she felt when Dominique would calmly point out all the ways she was being unreasonable and stupid and above all, *wrong*. When he'd argue the sun went down before it went up, or that the ceiling was actually the floor. It seemed the more sure she was that she stood on solid ground, the calmer he'd get, the more lethal his arguments, the more easily he could shove her over into quicksand.

"What you're doing is wrong." The lame accusation was all she could manage.

"By whose standards? Yours? Do they apply to me and my family?"

"Society's."

"And you, living with your boyfriend without marriage? Ditching your family at age seventeen and going from one man to another?"

She wanted to sock him, then whoever had wasted no time catching him up on her moral failings. Probably Vera.

"You're breaking the law." The quicksand was up to her lips, making it difficult to speak.

"Extramarital sex is against the law too, in many states. And it was once against the law for women to vote. It was once a law that white people could own black people. It's against the law now in most states for gays to marry, but that's changing, slowly. Laws change, people change, realities and human understanding and needs evolve."

Tears of frustration rose in her eyes. She stood. "I can't talk to you about this anymore. You're twisting everything I say."

"I'm stating facts."

She strode past him, no idea where she was going, just sure

she had to get away from this man before he became like Dominique and convinced her Comfort was in Antarctica.

"Elizabeth."

She stopped reluctantly, didn't turn around.

"This is our private matter. I'm asking you not to spread it around."

"I have no plans to." She fisted her hands. "For *Megan's* sake."

"Fair enough."

She managed to walk until she was out of his sight, then broke into a run down the driveway, cold leg muscles protesting the speed after yesterday's repeat marathon. Could she believe in nothing? Would everything she admired or treasured get smashed sooner or later? Was that real life?

She preferred fantasy. She wanted Megan alive with passion telling her Shetland story, she wanted magical and mysterious Gillian to be real, she wanted men to choose honorably, as Calum had, not install the Mrs. Calums, First and Second.

As soon as Elizabeth reached the street she knew where she needed to go. *Call me a sadist, Ms. Detlaff, but I look forward to watching you get to know Comfort.* She sprinted for David's house, banged on the door, waited, panting. He'd said he knew why Megan was unhappy. He must know.

Forever later he opened.

"Well if it isn't Ms.—" He did a double take. "What's wrong?"

"Can I come in?"

"Of course." He moved back, gestured her in. "What happened?"

She started to cry, from her disappointment and frustration and from the kind concern in David's voice. "Something . . . completely unexpected."

"You want to tell me?"

"I just promised Stanley I wouldn't."

"Stanley." The way he spat out the name convinced her he did know. "I saw his car come back and saw him talking to you."

"So . . . you know about—" When he nodded she broke down completely. "How can he cheat on Megan like it's—"

"Shh." David grabbed her arm, turned to look behind him.

The bathroom door in the back opened. Ella came into the front hallway, face pale and blank.

Elizabeth drew in a sharp breath. "Tell me it's not her."

"It's not." David led her toward the dining room table. "I'll pour you a drink."

"Christ, David. Is alcohol your cure for everything?"

"Pretty much." He glanced at Ella, who had followed them like an automaton. "Looks like you'll need one too."

"Stanley's cheating? On Megan?" Ella spoke slowly, staring at Elizabeth, her dark hair and lack of color evoking Snow White.

Elizabeth looked to David in desperation. "I don't . . ."

"I heard you say so." She sounded on the verge of hysteria. "Is it true?"

David nodded grimly.

Ella's mouth opened, worked impotently. A painful gasping sound evolved into a burst of laughter. She bent over the dark chunky table and gave in.

Elizabeth turned murderous. "Shut the hell up, Ella. This is not funny."

"She doesn't think so either." David had pulled out a bottle of bourbon from the built-in cabinet; he poured healthy slugs into two glasses. "Drink this."

Elizabeth slapped her palm on the table. "Stop laughing, for God's sake."

Ella held up one hand, asking them to wait, planted the other on her heaving chest. When she gained control and lifted her face, shiny tear trails glistened on her cheeks. "I'm sorry."

"Not a problem." David held out a second glass to her. "Breathe."

"I don't think I remember how." She laughed again, a short uncomfortable burst. "They were the perfect couple, Barbie and Ken, with their dream house and perfect kids, cuddling like they were still on their Malibu honeymoon. Now it turns out he's been doing Skipper on the side?"

More guffaws, now clutching her stomach.

"David. Make her stop."

"She has to let it out." He pulled Elizabeth to a chair and sat her in it. "Sit and drink. She'll stop on her own."

"I don't want to drink."

"Fine. I do." He downed Elizabeth's bourbon, pushed Ella's glass insistently toward her.

"I don't want mine either. God, oh God." Ella gasped out a last giggle and dropped into the chair opposite Elizabeth, still holding her abdomen. "All those years after I married I spent *pining* for what I could have had, what I thought I *should* have had with Stanley. All that time thinking Megan got what I deserved. And all this time guess what? She got a worse hell than mine. Jesus!"

Elizabeth wanted out of there, out of David's house, out of North Carolina. She wanted to go home. To New York.

No. She didn't want to go to New York. Home to Milwaukee?

Not there either. That bridge had burned to ash. There was no place like home, and she didn't have one to go back to. All she has was Comfort, which had just imploded.

"Well now." David sat between them, at the head of the table. "Isn't this cozy. Me and two beautiful hysterics. You sure you don't want your drink, Ella?"

"How did you find out, David?" Elizabeth asked.

"About Stanley?" He drained the second bourbon. "About a year ago I was visiting Comfort and went next door looking for Megan. I overheard Stanley talking to his other wife."

"Other *wife*?" Ella emerged from her stupor to stare in horror. "Tell me you mean that figuratively."

"The other marriage is illegal, but no one seems to care."

"That is beyond twisted." Ella cringed. "Promise me it's not someone in Comfort."

"I promise you it's not someone in Comfort."

"Thank God for that." Ella fished a tissue out of her shorts pocket and blew her nose, wiped smudged mascara from under her eyes. "I thought Megan was just a cold fish, or that she hated the sight of me because of my past with Stanley. I should have recognized myself—one of the walking dead. I should have known that's who she was."

"Don't beat yourself up. No one knew."

"Except you." Elizabeth's instinct kicked in at the careful look on David's face, and the way he immediately reached for the bottle. There was emotion between David and Megan. Was he the "someone" Megan had been dating when Stanley noticed her? Comfort had turned out to be a regular soap opera. Or maybe David was right, and life was life no matter where you were.

She didn't want David to be right.

"I can't believe it." Ella shuddered. "Stanley. Some Prince Charming."

"Give me a break." David finished pouring, turned to Elizabeth. "Oh God, you're looking misty too."

"He did seem pretty wonderful." Elizabeth sighed wearily. "They seemed so happy together."

"Ken and Barbie." David shook his head. "Ken doesn't even have a penis!"

Ella and Elizabeth burst into giggles.

"You saw in their relationship what you wanted to see. No man is ever going to live up to your fantasies. Love can't fill the holes you've spent years digging yourselves."

"Oh now you're the relationship expert?" Ella jabbed at his arm with her finger. "And how does it work that *we're* deluded but *you're* a noble victim?"

David's eyes narrowed; Elizabeth froze, afraid the situation was going to get ugly. She wished David would stop drinking.

He gave a brisk nod instead. "Okay. Point made. My marriage was flawed, your marriage was flawed, Stanley and Megan's marriage is screwed up beyond all comprehension. Elizabeth's relationship . . . ?"

She shrugged. "As yet undetermined."

"So here we sit on the island of misfit lovers. The broken, the maimed, the malformed, who still, all sensible evidence to the contrary, believe in love, crave love."

Elizabeth fidgeted. Something was bothering her, something was rising in her, and she wished everyone would be quiet so she could figure out what it was.

"We're not at fault. Blame the poets!" He started on his third drink. "Romeo and Juliet were teenagers. They would have moved on. Madama Butterfly wasted her young life over a husband who didn't deserve her. Even pop songs: 'can't live if living is without you.' Anyone who doesn't feel that intensity of longing thinks his or her relationship has gone stale in comparison, because look! Over the neighbor's fence! Great Scott, what a lawn!"

Ella snorted. Elizabeth listened with half her brain, the other still searching for the source of the urgent internal signal.

"But let's look closely at that perfect lawn. The German poet Heinrich Heine wrote some of the most glorious romantic verses known to man over an unrequited passion for his cousin, Amalie, whom he barely knew. After she married, he switched to her equally uninterested sister, Therese. That's not love. That's dysfunction, that's self-isolation. These days he'd be put into therapy and medicated."

"And we'd have lost his art." Ella very casually took the bottle over to her side of the table, out of David's reach.

"So now what?" Elizabeth sounded as cranky as she felt. She hated loud champions of hopelessness. "The party's over, we go miserably on?"

"We become like Albericht in Wagner's Ring cycle and renounce love. In our case the sacrifice earns not power over all humanity but whole, beautiful power over ourselves and our destinies and our happiness, a life free from vulnerability and compromise."

"David." Ella rolled her eyes. "You are drunk."

"And your point is . . ."

Elizabeth put her glass down with a thud. "That is a complete load of crap."

"Yeah?" He turned toward her, eyes showing the pain his sneer couldn't hide. "Then talk me out of it."

"If I thought it would do any good . . ." She stood abruptly, her chair scraping hardwood, moved to the living room and started pacing. The movement freed her from the prison of David's words, made everything clearer. "It's pointless to sit here moaning. We need to help Megan get out of that situation."

"I've got it." Ella snapped her fingers. "I could shoot Stanley!"

"Good idea." David pantomimed cocking a rifle. "I'll shoot at the same time, so they can't tell which of us did it."

"David, you're my hero." Ella reached over and touched his cheek, eyes soft with affection. "Why can't I fall in love with you?"

"Because you're too smart."

"Shh." Elizabeth was on the right track now, the righteous path, and she wasn't in the mood for clowning. "I'm serious about helping Megan. We have to fix this somehow. She's desperately unhappy. I bet that's why she told us the Gillian story."

"Be careful. She might not want to get out."

"I don't believe that." Elizabeth stopped pacing and scowled at David. "And neither do you."

"Ms. Elizabeth, I think you've gotten in enough trouble deciding things are a certain way before you know for sure. Leave this alone."

"No." Elizabeth walked back to the table, confronted him directly. "I need to make something good come out of this visit. I haven't been able to help myself, so there must be some other reason I'm in Comfort."

"Why?"

She frowned at him. "Because otherwise, why was I sent here?"

"You weren't *sent* here. You've assigned meaning to a random set of circumstances and events and called it destiny. If you can not only reject love but toss out the need for meaning as well, you'll have freed yourself forever."

"Oh, right. Gotcha. To be completely happy, you just have to give up being human?" Ella rolled her eyes. "Come on, David, even you aren't that cynical."

"No?" He grinned his handsome Paul Newman grin and Elizabeth no longer felt envious that people like David had found their places and purposes in the world. No wonder he called his life hell. Because he'd retreated. He didn't fight. And neither did Megan. "What do you think, Elizabeth? Am I that cynical?"

"No." Elizabeth shoved at his shoulder. "It's how you protect yourself."

"Women! I told you both the truth and you only see what you want to." His phone rang; he stood and headed toward the kitchen, taking his glass with him. "I give up. Don't finish the bourbon while I'm gone."

"If that's Stanley, invite him over, we'll hide behind the front door and whack him over the head," Ella called after him. "You game, Elizabeth?"

"Absolutely." Elizabeth nodded decisively. "I get the rolling pin."

"Iron skillet for me."

They smiled at each other, then smiling became uncomfortable because the rules of their new co-conspirator relationship had yet to be worked out. David's voice came from the kitchen, too high and strained.

"I'm . . . sorry about Stanley, Ella. I mean that I made you find out."

"It's for the best." Ella closed her eyes. Her color had returned; she was doubly beautiful sad and haunted. "Apparently David is right, and I just loved the idea of him."

"Maybe I just love the idea of Dominique, too. Or of our life together." Elizabeth sat again, traced a thin jagged scratch in the tabletop, throat thick, head aching. "A photography crew from *Bon Appetit* magazine came to shoot a dinner party we hosted last May. They snapped us sipping soup on the rooftop among pots of strawberries and herbs and spring flowers. Snapped us in our dining room tucking into quail with *foie gras* and fresh currants. Snapped us sampling a fabulous array of raspberry and chocolate desserts next to the koi pond in our living room.

"But the truth was, I'd been fighting with Dominique earlier, and he was flirting with one of the guests to get back at me. Her husband was fuming, the other couple was drinking way too much, and it occurred to me that readers everywhere would envy our perfect lifestyle and glamorous friends and fabulous party know-how, when we were all having a miserable time hating each other."

"Oof. I'll have to buy that issue."

"It was painful."

"What's Dominique's story?" Ella glanced toward the kitchen obviously wondering about David, who had gone silent. "Did he come from money?"

"No, neither of us is used to it. Dominique grew up on a small family peach farm in the South of France. Great food, no luxury."

"So you love him for the trappings. And his cooking."

"No, it feels as if I love him in spite of them." Elizabeth plunked her chin in her hands. "But yes, he's a god in the kitchen."

Ella arched her eyebrow meaningfully. "His meat is well done . . . ?"

"Oh yes." Elizabeth waggled hers in response. "Very rare."

They were snickering when David came back into the room

lifting his glass, which he'd refilled to the brim with a clear liquid this time, and only a few ice cubes. Gin from his freezer? The sight was chilling. "Here's to dramatic irony."

"What happened?" Ella sounded worried. "Was it Stanley?"

"No." He drank, laughed and drank again. "It was not Stanley. It was my delightful ex-wife. Victoria."

Elizabeth gasped. "Oh no."

"What did *she* want?"

"She wanted to tell me that she'd hit bottom after the divorce was finalized and had taken the past few months to get her head back on straight. That she recognized what she'd sacrificed to her ambition and her ego." Another gulp of whatever it was, another ghoulish laugh. "She wanted to beg my forgiveness."

Elizabeth covered her mouth with her hands.

Ella gaped. "Oh. My. Sweet. Jesus."

"But wait, there's more." He lifted an unsteady hand, formed the fingers into a gun and pointed it at his temple. "Leaving me was all a horrible mistake, says my Vicky. She is so terribly sorry. She lost her head, then she lost herself. She didn't realize that the life we had was the life she belongs in. She wants us to get together. To talk."

"Are you going to go?" Elizabeth couldn't help train-wreck fascination.

"Of course not." Ella winked at Elizabeth. "She's offering another chance at that horrible disgusting prison called love. After he's made such a strong and healthy choice to avoid it at all costs and hole himself up here all alone, why would he do that?"

"God help me." He lifted the glass and drained the rest, Adam's apple jumping to help the liquid down.

"Um . . ." Elizabeth exchanged alarmed looks with Ella. "Was that gin?"

"Believe it or not, it was water." He lifted the glass and wiped his forehead with the back of his hand. "In light of all that's happened today, I think I've had my last drink for a very long time."

Chapter Eleven

The day of the midsummer dance starts out fine, but clouds move in and the wind makes skirts fly and jackets flutter by the time people begin the walk to the laird's house. Barclay Hunter's magnificent mansion built of stone quarried on the Scottish mainland stands like a monument on top of a seaside brae, or hill; white columns mark its front entrance, buildings spread on either side, for clerks, workers, animals, and for the hard business of farming.

Fiona loves the twice-a-year parties here, midsummer and Christmas, with other locals dressed in their finest enjoying excellent food, warm hospitality, music, dancing and good fellowship. This year, she wants the event over and done. Calum will be there, with Gillian.

Up the steps, she's greeted at the front door by the laird's wife, Effie, in an apricot gown that skims then *forgives her stout figure. Fiona's dress evokes the color of the dawn sky, slender in the waist, narrower in the skirt than her mother wore, lace collar and trim she knitted herself. She even pinned her curls up and got them to stay. Calum will notice her tonight.*

The house is warm and full already, furnished from mainland and continent shops in grand style, drapes at every window, fireplaces blazing in every room, greenery and paper streamers, candles and flowers decorating nearly every surface. The long, fine table in the dining room bears dozens of dishes: hams and legs of heathery Shetland lamb, breads, jellies and salads, puddings and cakes. Whiskey, fruit punch and beer are doled out by servants dressed better than most of those they serve.

Fiona greets friends, neighbors and acquaintances, eyes darting in search of Calum, who is not yet here. She loads a plate with food she has no appetite for, and settles with Aileen Thomson, tries to eat and laugh, gossip and enjoy herself, always on her guard.

The sudden buzz of excitement tells her he's arrived, handsome in his black Sunday best, Gillian in a dress the color of sweet cherries, lips painted to match, breasts pushing the material forward. Her eyes flash green, cheeks pink, shining hair runs down her back, rests on Calum's arm, beckons every man's hand in the room. Taste flees from Fiona's food. She pours back whiskey for courage and smiles, aware of eyes on her, whispers, speculation and worst of all, pity.

In the other room, fiddles tune, including her father's, then fill the house with music. Catriona Tait pulls Gillian aside. Fiona rises and walks straight to Calum, trembling legs hidden under her skirt, and asks him to dance, cheerful, flirtatious, terrified he'll say no.

He accepts, offers his arm and they stroll together into the parlor, Fiona's heart swelling with hope. They dance, matching their feet to the music's joyful rhythm. Fiona could fly across the sea with the pleasure pouring into her when their fingers touch.

The music ends. A new song begins. Calum stays with her; they dance together among fellow islanders, stomping, bobbing, swinging, clapping. Another dance, then calls for a song and Fiona is hoisted onto the platform. She takes in a long breath and sings directly from her heart, For the Sake o' Somebody, *letting Calum know with her eyes who the "somebody" is, blocking out the blot of cherry-red that enters the room and makes its way to his side.*

O-hon! for Somebody! O-hey! for Somebody! I wad do-what wad I not? For the sake o' Somebody. *The song ends to applause, whistles, shouts of appreciation. She steps down and returns to Calum's right, ignoring Gillian on his left. Eric Manson climbs onstage, tells a ribald story of fishing for a mermaid wife. Gordon Smith is next, doing magic tricks; the laird's wife, Effie, plays her fancy carved piano as she does at every party.*

Between each number Fiona joins in the applause, turns to Calum with a smile demanding he acknowledge the evening's joy. He returns her smile gallantly, but not with his whole heart. She refuses to panic. Didn't he leave Gillian alone to dance three dances with her?

Effie finishes to more applause. Calum leads Gillian to the stage, borrows Andrew Tulloch's fiddle and puts it into her hands, bows to her and climbs down, leaving her alone on the platform in the sudden quiet, leaving Fiona alone in the crowd. Her stomach fills with dread.

Gillian lifts the instrument, closes her eyes and begins to play a slow, mournful tune. A trance descends on the listeners. The unfamiliar notes weave in and around them, into their ears, taking hold of their minds, transporting them to places they haven't been in years, to dear ones who have died, to homes they left, to loves they lost.

Gillian's eyes stay closed, her burgundy lips parted, a groove between her eyebrows the only sign of her effort. She sways as if the music's rise and fall pushes her with it, as if her body itself is the instrument.

The song ends on a long, quiet, high note that calls every listener's heart out to its beauty. A breathless hush falls, during which calls of cliff birds take their turn to be heard. Then hands meet, mouths open and the room erupts into applause and shouts, tears streaming down more than one cheek.

Calum climbs to the stage, takes Gillian's hands and kneels at her feet. The room grows still again, this time as if a spirit has passed over and turned the audience to rough stone. Fiona's hands and heart go cold as the sea.

Calum speaks in his deep voice, praises Gillian's playing, praises her grace and loveliness, her dignity and courage, her purity of heart. And there on his knees in front of the laird, all his tenants, and in front of Fiona, Calum asks Gillian to be his wife.

Megan dragged the vacuum cleaner into Jeffrey's room. Clothes were strewn on the floor in a haphazard pattern, shirtsleeves akimbo, pant legs half inside out. In the clothes hamper, only one item: a crumpled, damp bath towel, which Jeffrey carefully deposited there every time he showered instead of hanging it back up in the bathroom, no matter how often Megan reminded him. She grabbed out the towel, sniffed for mildew, and draped it over the rack in the kids' bathroom where it belonged. Back in his room, she bent to plug in the vacuum, sweat prickling under her arms as much from annoyance as the Carolina heat. What wouldn't she give for a few hours on the Shetland coast, comfortable in the welcoming sunshine, salty breeze freshening her skin?

Back, forth, over and over the same worn blue carpet she'd vacuumed the week before, would vacuum again the next week.

"Mom?" Behind her Deena came into the room, shouting to be heard over the motor. "I can't find my drawing pen."

So go look for it! Megan had spoiled these kids out of love and eagerness to make up for their half-absent father. Now she could see she'd also made herself indispensable to give herself some purpose in life. Fifteen years later, the kids were helpless without her, and that purpose was no longer enough.

"You're sure it's in your room?"

"*Yes.*"

"Did you check your desk?"

"*Ye-e-es.*"

"Look under your bed, in chair cushions, and so on. I'll help when I'm done here." She finished the floor in Jeffrey's room, flinging clothes into the hamper, tossing books, empty CD cases, pencil drawings of armed and armored figures onto his desk. Near the bed she always got down on her knees and checked underneath for Lego pieces or coins, stray underpants or dice.

Today she didn't bother, thrust the power nozzle under his

bed. A sudden jolt, the engine roared in protest. Megan should have known better. She wiped her forehead, punched off the machine and pulled the wand back, examined the brush rollers, jammed with a white cotton sock covered in dust and grime. Fine. She was done. Jeffrey's room was clean enough.

"Mom?" Deena again. "I still can't find it."

Had she even *looked*?

"Okay." She went into Deena's room, lifted one piece of paper off her desk, and handed the pen to her daughter with a withering look.

"Oh."

"Yes, oh."

"*Mom?* I'm hungry." Jeffrey this time, from his room next door. "Can I have a snack?"

"I'm ho-o-ome." Lolly, shouting from downstairs; the screen door slammed. "What time is dinner? I want to go to the movies tonight."

Megan leaned against the wall, trying to keep back the angry words forming in her throat. Her kids didn't deserve her bad mood. Her midlife crisis wasn't their fault. "Jeffrey, there are pretzels in the cabinet over the counter, don't have too many. Lolly, dinner will be at six, as usual and yes, you can go to the movies."

"*Sweet!*"

"Okay, Mom, thanks, Mom. I'm pretzel ma-a-an!"

Megan took the vacuum cleaner downstairs, put it away in the closet in the family room, where Lolly gabbed her good news into the phone, then went into the kitchen, passing Jeffrey cupping a handful of pretzels. For dinner, bean-and-cheese burritos with salad from their garden and too-ripe peaches stewed and served over ice cream for dessert.

She leaned on the edge of the sink and sighed. Making the meal seemed overwhelming. Not because of fatigue, she'd been overwhelmed by fatigue before, by indecision, by bad moods—the kids' or hers, by the volume of tasks at hand. This was different. She felt lost, alone in her house in a way she hadn't since she found out about Stanley's other wife.

She'd wanted to leave him then. Or, more to the point, had wanted the symbolism of leaving him, the you-can't-do-this-to-me finality of leaving him. But she'd had nowhere to go, nothing but her husband and coming baby. No degree, no job experience, no skills outside of knitting. Nothing that would make any kind of decent life for her and her child.

So she stayed. Pushed way down inside her every feeling of resentment and anger that she couldn't let out in her favorite spot in the woods. Was it true, what David said, that those denied feelings couldn't be reabsorbed, but bided their time until they could emerge? Was this their time? She had no desire to encounter them again.

Through the window her beloved garden bloomed and flourished, home and restaurant to bees, butterflies and ladybugs. If only she could sit in it, undisturbed, knitting Sally's lace with a cup of tea. For about three weeks.

Fierce concentration was required at the beginning of a new pattern, one stitch at a time. But as the rows mounted she'd relax as always into groups of stitches at a time, rows at a time, whole patterns. Then near-total freedom, thoughts blowing like helium balloons still safely anchored by the tethering yarn. The peaceful, hypnotic rhythm of the clicking needles, the soft-sharp pull of wool over skin, the satisfaction of producing beauty with her own hands . . .

Yet looking now she could see the tomatoes needed water, okra needed harvesting again, green beans needed picking. She should be out there gathering lettuce, choosing tomatoes for dinner; or setting peaches to simmer with sugar, a squeeze of lemon and a hint of nutmeg, perfuming the kitchen with the aroma of fruit and spice. Work had been her solace for fifteen years, it could be so again. This discontent was like a swarm of carpenter ants eating at her from the center outward, starting with David's divorce and intensifying with Elizabeth's arrival. David with his culture and passion, Elizabeth with her freedom and youth, all the things that had passed Megan by.

She took peaches from the refrigerator, peeled the soft fuzzy skin, cut out the brown spots, sliced the remaining fragrant fruit into a pan. Sugar, lemon, nutmeg, and allspice added at the last second. She set the pan on the stove over medium heat, took out the ingredients for her version of burritos, a can of black beans, flour tortillas, garlic, cumin, corn, cheddar cheese, salsa. From her garden she'd need a tomato and ingredients for salad.

On the way out she stopped in the laundry room to pick up her gathering basket: hoop-handled wide curved wicker that fit comfortably over her arm like an old friend. Northern climates might suit her thick blood better, but she did love the long Carolina growing season.

Outside she picked lettuce, a cucumber, pungent fresh basil and soothing mint. Two tomatoes gently twisted off the stem; she never tired of the spicy scent of the plant. The tomatoes were smooth and warm from the sun; she held one up and inhaled, feeling peace returning.

"Megan."

David's tone made her turn abruptly. His haggard look drew her to the fence between their properties. Peace would apparently continue in short supply.

"Reaping nature's bounty?"

She nodded, searching his face. He hadn't been sleeping. But she also didn't think he'd been drinking. "What is it?"

"Victoria." He barely got the word out.

Megan clutched the tomato to her chest. "Is she all right?"

"Vicky could survive a nuclear holocaust. Her, Twinkies and roaches." He laughed harshly; the sound was chilling. "She wants to see me. Apparently being apart didn't work out for her."

Megan put the tomato into her basket, stared down at it, absently appreciating the bright red against the fresh green of the herbs, the dark length of the cucumber and the lighter shade of the lettuce. If she thought about anything else she might develop cracks and shatter, like a cartoon character who's just absorbed a blow. Anvil maybe. Cinder block. Piano.

"What are you going to do?" She couldn't look at him. Basil trembled dark green against the rich auburn wicker. Shaking like a leaf. Haha.

"Megan, I don't know." He was pleading now. With her? With himself? With fate? "She was my wife for nearly twenty years."

"Yes I know." *And you came to me so many of those years when you were here because she couldn't give you what you needed.*

Dear God. She gripped the basket handle. She'd done it again. Completed a man who loved and needed another woman. Maybe Megan hadn't married half a husband. Maybe she was only half a woman.

"I have to talk to her, to put this all behind us, to put it to rest. Work through the bitterness, so I can move forward."

"Ah." Why was he telling her this? She wanted to take her beautifully arranged basket of produce and hurl it at his head. She wanted to run to the top of a mountain, drop to all fours, lift her head and and howl at the moon, throat wide open, soul wide open to whatever God or the stars or the planets could pour into her, something pure and clean and vast. "And if you see her and want more than that?"

"I can't imagine that happening."

"But it might."

He cleared his throat, off balance, uncertain, very un-David. "I guess it might."

"She's determined when she wants something. You've always said so."

A car drove down the street; they watched it bridge the interval between their houses.

"Just tell me. Megan. If there's any hope here for me . . . for us." His voice was low, nearly a whisper, his eyes grazed hers but couldn't land safely.

Then it was easier to speak and to know what she wanted to say. "This has nothing to do with me. This is between you and Victoria. You need to follow your heart."

"After what she did to me I'm not sure I have one left."

"You do." She was tired suddenly of his drama, tired of loving yet another man torn between two women, tired of loving anyone. "And with Victoria you have history, which at one time included a serious vow to be together until death. You shared so much of your life with this woman that even after what she did, after such a betrayal, she's still a deep part of you. All that makes her unexpectedly difficult to throw away, doesn't it?"

He did meet her eyes then, his more intense even than usual in his pale, exhausted face. "Megan . . ."

"Even though you know you should walk away from her without looking back. Even though you need to make that statement, to hurt her the way you've been hurt, to show her and yourself and the world that you're not an object she can use as she pleases, even though you know and feel all of that . . . you can't quite do it."

His expression didn't change. She could have hit him over the head now with her basket, with that anvil or the piano, and he'd still stand there, stunned into total immobility by the mirror she held up to him with her own life reflected in it.

She lifted her head and smiled into his eyes with an unsatisfying sense of triumph. "Well, David."

He didn't move. Waited, hands shoved in his pockets, shoulders hunched.

"Welcome to my world. Enjoy your stay." She turned and went back into her summer-flavored house to make sure the peaches hadn't overcooked. The Purls would be coming; they'd agreed to meet at Megan's now, since she had the materials they needed. A pan of brownies would only take half an hour; she could do those and still get dinner ready on time.

"So then my friend Josh says to me, 'Yes, Joy was over the other evening helping me can my beets.' Ha! I'm telling you, she was doing a lot more than *that*. I wanted to say, 'Oh, *can your beets*? Is that what they're calling it now?'" Dorene burst into gales of laughter. Sally, Vera, Elizabeth and Ella smiled politely. Megan laughed right along with her, because why the heck not? She felt drunk tonight, not having had a single drop of alcohol, aware she was manic, that her power and energy weren't grounded in real happiness or real excitement.

"Anyway, I've gone on long enough. Sally, tell us all about your wedding."

"There's nothing to tell, really." She pulled another length of yarn from the cream-colored ball at her side. "My Uncle Chad is giving me away. We're having a chocolate fountain along with the wedding cake for dessert. And real French champagne. I think Beatrice is ordering it by the truckload."

"Good heavens." Vera pursed her lips disapprovingly. "We only had fruit punch at my wedding. Very sedate."

Megan let out a snort. Open bar from what she'd heard. Everyone had been ripped.

Vera looked at her over her half-glasses. Megan smiled sedately, kept knitting. She was starting at the bottom of the front panel for Sally's dress, Vera at the top. Spiderwebs, spider and diamond pattern center with a ring lace border and lace holes edging. They'd meet halfway.

"When I get married I want everything the way *we* want it, not my parents, and not his," Dorene announced. "No offense, Sally, but the most fun weddings in my book are the casual ones, just picnics. Remember Cara and Frank's at Lake Lure? That was one fun time, volleyball, a cookout, swimming . . ."

"Marriage isn't about the wedding, Dorene." Megan thrust her needle through, veins humming with adrenaline. "That's just the beginning. After that comes the enti-i-ire re-e-est of your life."

She giggled. The women turned to stare at her.

"So take advantage of being single while you can." Megan flung out her arm. "Travel. See the world. Do everything you've always wanted to do. Live in Paris, go on safari in Kenya. Ride an elephant in India. See the pyramids in Cairo."

"Oh." Dorene darted glances at Ella and Sally. "Well, but I've . . . never wanted to do any of those things."

Vera had stopped knitting, sat staring at Megan over her red glasses.

Megan didn't care. "You don't have to do those things exactly. I'm just saying whatever else, don't get stuck sitting on your porch night after night with no damn hope of it ever changing."

"*Megan.*"

"I think what Megan means . . ." The group swung to look at Elizabeth like spectators at a tennis match. "Is that you shouldn't live for marriage. You should only want it if you meet the right person. The travel ideas and the porch were symbolic, yes?"

"Yes." Megan nodded, grateful for the unexpected rescue attempt. "What have you always wanted to do, Dorene?"

"Well that's the thing." She shrugged, needles moving painfully slowly. "I've always wanted to marry and live in Comfort. Though I'd probably want to honeymoon in Orlando."

"Borelando." Ella mimed gagging. "Paradise on earth."

"Maybe it is to her." Megan spoke directly to Ella instead of addressing the floor, which she usually did when she disagreed with someone.

Ella was the one who dropped her eyes, which was very odd. Ella could stare down a mannequin.

"The problem with you girls today is that you want too much. In my day, you married and dealt with it. Nowadays you have to be happy every second or you think you deserve something better. Entitled, that's what they call it. Entitled. At least you have roofs over your heads and food on your tables."

"But your marriage was wonderful, Vera." Elizabeth passed

her next stitch marker and peered at the chart; her old shell pattern was emerging, ragged and amateur, but still beautiful. "You picked the right man."

"Yes. Yes, I did." Vera frowned over her delicate spiderweb. "But I still think young people are spoiled brats when it comes to facing challenges."

"Sally lost her husband, then her mother and father, so she's a spoiled brat for wanting happiness with Foster?"

"That's not what I meant, Megan." Vera whipped off her red glasses. "Is something bothering you today?"

"She's fine." Elizabeth glanced warily at Megan over her knitting, obviously not as sure as she sounded.

"Women today have the option of leaving a bad situation, and that's a blessing, not a weakness, Vera." Ella spoke with passion and sincerity. "It's not the easy way out to divorce, trust me. It's hell. Stand in my shoes for the last seventeen years and see how cowardly you think leaving is."

"Tell us, Ella." Elizabeth was watching Ella closely. Megan didn't wince this time at her insistent intrusion. She had a gift with people, or at least more of one than Megan had. Look what she'd done with the Purls. Megan knew these women better since Elizabeth came than she had for the last twenty years.

"Tell you? Why should I?"

Elizabeth shrugged. "Because we all want to know. And because lace isn't the only thing that's better shared with women. And because we have all spilled and it's your turn."

"Well." Ella's hands were unsteady as she wrapped the delicate thread, but her voice was clear. "Okay. If you want to know. Don was a workaholic, a serious addictive personality. At first I thought he just wanted to get ahead, make money so we could relax. But it didn't work that way. The more he had the more he wanted, the more time he spent away and the lonelier our marriage got. Is that enough?"

"Nope," Elizabeth said cheerfully. "I want to know how that made you fe-e-el."

Ella laughed a shaky laugh. "Okay, Dr. Elizabeth, it made me feel like shit."

"Go with that."

She rolled her eyes. "If he'd had an affair I would have been able to understand. But eternally reaching toward some nebulous idea of success, dedicating your life to the process of achievement, alienating everything and everyone else. I didn't understand that."

"I don't blame you," Megan said. "When your spouse's behavior is beyond your ability to understand, there's no way to put that back together."

Another dagger glance from Vera.

"Exactly." Ella met Megan's eyes with sympathy. "So I walked away from a man I still love, who I couldn't help, to save myself from going nuts. If that makes me an entitled, spoiled brat, so be it."

Vera bunched her lips, and for a few seconds Megan thought she was furious, then she realized her mother-in-law was fighting tears. Immediately she felt a rush of tenderness she didn't know how to offer.

"Rocky—" Vera shook her head and kept knitting. "I'm sure you'll get your life back together, Ella. You're young. You're beautiful. Happiness is out there."

"Thank you." She lifted her eyebrow. "Any chance you can tell it to hurry the hell up?"

"Hey, I'll throw you my bouquet, Ella." Sally's gentle voice eased the tension.

"She's *been* married, what about me?" Dorene huffed her disapproval. "I can't even get a date!"

"At least you still have your youth, Dorene, at least you're healthy." Vera tsk-tsked. "No one is happy with what she has today. No one."

"Not even you?" Megan couldn't help poking. She didn't know why, because on some level she understood Vera's point. Stanley didn't beat or neglect Megan. She had David's friendship, and the Purls, a decent house, enough food. Her children were healthy and happy.

But lately Megan wanted to aim higher. Did that make her an entitled, spoiled brat? When could someone justify breaking out of a bad situation? How bad was too bad? What was that moment that made Ella finally draw the line?

Megan could spend her whole life nobly feeling grateful for what she had. But that also guaranteed that what she had was all she'd ever get.

Sometimes she thought they'd have to bury this porch with her.

From down the street Stanley's van approached, its characteristic chirping getting louder.

"Stanley's home." Vera spoke to Megan, who refused to look appropriately delighted.

"Oh, hey, great, I haven't seen him in a while." Dorene stretched and yawned loudly, wobbly stitches hanging from her needle. "Stanley is one of my favorite people in Comfort. Megan, you sure know how to pick a man."

"I do, don't I." Megan laughed her new manic laugh, noticing that neither Elizabeth or Ella joined in, that Ella's gaze was missing its usual edge.

The garage door closed; the back door opened; Stanley's steps sounded coming through the house.

"I was talking to Grace Atkeson the other day and even she was saying what a hunk he is. You better watch out, Megan, someone will try to take him away from you." Dorene guffawed, showing her large teeth. Megan laughed too—hahaha! Dorene was so funny.

"Hello there, ladies." Stanley grinned at Megan. "What's the joke?"

"Dorene was just saying I'd better be careful or I'll have to share you with some other woman." She gave him an ultra-loving smile she knew would pack a punch.

"No chance of that." He looked away immediately. "Hello there, Dorene, Ella. Sally, you're looking gorgeous. How's the wedding coming?"

She grinned. "Terrific. Thanks to Megan and the Purls."

"Good, good to hear. Elizabeth, how was your day?" He reached to touch the top of her head. She leaned away, keeping her eyes on her lace and he had to draw his hand back.

Very odd. Elizabeth was usually eager-puppy around Stanley.

"Mom? Keeping busy?"

"Of course, son." Vera raised her head from her knitting to beam at him. "How was your game?"

"Good. I played well." He put his hands in his pockets, tall, handsome and dependable Stanley. "It's a beautiful day for golf. And a beautiful day to be sitting out here enjoying the evening."

"Sure is," Dorene said. "I was thinking only this morning that I looked forward to getting here to knit with y'all tonight. Not only because of Megan's incredible brownies either, though boy, that doesn't hurt. I don't know what you make those with, but they're about the best ones I've ever had . . ."

Stanley's phone rang during her predictable prattle. He dragged it from his pocket, checked the display and stiffened, a rare display of discomfort. Over a phone number?

Megan knew who it was.

"Hey, great to see you all." He waved at the group, hearty and masculine, his face strained. "I've got a call to make. You enjoy yourselves."

Megan sat with her hands curled into fists. Her face flushed. Stanley's footsteps went upstairs.

He was going to their bedroom to call his other wife.

"Vera, did I make a mistake on this row? Seems like there's something wrong here." Elizabeth's eyes were on Megan, her expression cautious, concerned.

Megan scanned the other faces in the room. Dorene's blank as usual, Vera's suspicious, Sally's troubled, but understandably. Ella's . . .

Dear God. Did she and Elizabeth know?

"Excuse me." She got up, not sure where she was going, just knowing she couldn't sit there anymore and wonder why Ella was looking at her with something like humanity, or why Elizabeth was avoiding Stanley. Nor could she sit there and think about Stanley, up in the same bedroom they'd conceived their children in, having phone sex with the Gillian-babe that was his alternate life partner. "I'll be back in a minute."

Inside she heard his voice, then their bedroom door closing. The kids were down the street again, Lolly at her movie.

He was all hers.

She pounded up the stairs, barged into the room. "Hang up."

He stared at her, phone pressed to his ear. "Honey—"

"*Hang up!*" She'd never yelled at him like this in her life. "I forbid you to talk to her while you're in this house."

His eyes narrowed in disbelief. "It's an emergency. Tommy fell down and broke his—"

"There are doctors for that." Her voice shook. "I managed *fine* alone when Jeffrey broke his ankle, I managed *fine* alone when Lolly broke her finger, when Deena cracked her head open, when—"

"This will only take—"

"*No.*" She lunged forward, grabbed the phone from his hand and closed it, ending the call. "While you're in this house you have *one* wife, and that's *me.*"

"Stanley?" Vera. Outside the door. Sweet Jesus.

"Everything's fine, Mom." He grabbed the phone back, pushed Megan against the wall by their bed, held her there with his huge hands on her shoulders, face growing red. "Don't you *ever* cut me off from a call like that."

She tried to free herself, couldn't, gave a hoarse cry of rage and frustration. The door burst open. Elizabeth, Vera behind her.

"Get off her." Elizabeth barreled in and shoved Stanley, who staggered away probably more from surprise than her strength. "You bastard. You told me it was fine with her."

"Stanley, what is happening?" Vera, sounding panicked.

Megan stayed against the wall. How had Elizabeth found out? David would never tell. Stanley, never. This was horrible. The worst. She had no right to know.

"Nothing, Mom." Stanley held his hands out. "Everything's fine."

"Everything is *not* fine, you liar." Elizabeth was furious, panting. "Megan, are you okay? Did he hit you?"

"No, for God's sake." She wanted to push her away. Little Elizabeth, living in an all black-and-white world. If Stanley had done wrong, he had to be cruel, too. "Go back downstairs."

"I would never hit a woman."

Elizabeth sneered at him. "Somehow, coming from you, that's not any comfort."

No, no. This was Megan's fight; her shame was none of Elizabeth's business. Damn her coming here and turning everything upside down.

"Megan, if there's anything I can do to help." Elizabeth's super-concerned face, and her I'm-your-friend hand reaching out sent Megan over the edge.

"You can stop interfering in things you don't understand and go back home where you belong."

Elizabeth stepped back, mouth open in surprise.

"Megan!" Vera's outrage came from her daughter-in-law's having violated the sacred laws of Southern hospitality, cracked the polite veneer that hung over all the ugliness. Megan had never felt so foreign as she did then. "You'll speak to our guest with more respect than that."

"Mom, lay off her." Manly Stanley sticking up for his wife except when it mattered. "Megan's upset."

Ya think?

"Nothing is bad enough to make rudeness acceptable."

"Really? Nothing?" Megan thrust herself away from the wall, consumed by fury, not regretting her lost control. "How about your son being married to someone else at the same time as he's—"

"Megan. Don't." Stanley, begging to keep his little secret from Mommy, so she could continue to worship him in the manner to which he was accustomed.

Megan laughed, fists clenched, reveling in the sick surge of power. "It's true, though. Even Elizabeth knows now. Did you tell her when you were in bed with her? Is two women not enough anymore?"

"Megan." Elizabeth looked aghast. "I would *never.*"

"What is she talking about, Stanley?" Vera's voice was high and shaking. "Megan, have you lost your mind?"

"No Vera. She hasn't." Elizabeth put an arm around Vera's soft shoulders. "Your son has another wife and family in . . . somewhere else."

"Roxboro," Megan said. "In the lovely Piedmont region of North Carolina."

"*Stanley!* Are you going to stand there and let them accuse you of such garbage?" Vera drew herself up to her full height, which, given her short stature and dumpling body, wasn't too impressive. "Tell them. You would *never* stoop that low."

"Mama . . ." Stanley sank on the bed, looking like a death-row inmate seconds before his execution.

His phone rang.

"That'll be *her* again," said Elizabeth.

"Why don't you answer it?" Megan taunted. "I'm sure it's for you."

He eyed them miserably. The phone rang again. Again. Twice more and was still.

"God have mercy." Vera put a hand to her heaving chest. "It's true."

"Mama . . ."

"You're no better than your rotten no-good father." Vera pointed accusingly, fingers trembling, blue eyes wide with shock. "If you know what's good for you, Stanley Morgan, you'll get out of this house and won't come back until we decide to let you live."

Chapter Twelve

The days after the announcement of Calum and Gillian's engagement pass in a blur for Fiona. She can't walk the cliffs with the same joy, can't look down at the bright water and the churning white spray without wanting to hurl herself into it. Can't see the birds soaring, diving like missiles for food, calling to one another, without thinking of Gillian and her wheeling flock of skuas laughing at Fiona for thinking she had a chance with Calum. Perversely, with all the thunder and doom in her heart, the weather has been warm, dry and sunny—not a cloud, not a drop of rain, as if the heavens themselves are mocking her misery by celebrating the happy couple.

Yet Calum's troubles continue. Four of his sheep take ill, stop eating and die. He nearly breaks an ankle in a rabbit hole on ground he's walked his whole life. A wild dog leaps his crofthouse wall and makes off with fish the family was drying for winter. Crows peck out the eyes of his favorite old horse, Brodie, killing him.

People murmur about the strange happenings. A premonition of some greater misfortune has seized the islanders. They haven't forgotten the enchantment Gillian wove with her violin, only now, safely away from her spell, the power she wielded seems ominous.

Finally, the winds that so often bedevil the islands catch up with Fiona's mood and roar in, restless and fierce. That same night, Calum's younger brother takes ill again, with high fever and rattling lungs. His mum and Calum take turns with him, sponging his brow, helping him sit up to cough, wondering if it's worth the long journey to fetch a doctor, or if he'll get better on his own. He's too sick to be moved this time.

Also that night, while the unsettling winds lash the village, Fiona has a vivid dream of Calum underwater with fins instead of feet, a merman groom following his mermaid bride, vanishing into unseen depths. She wakens with a bad feeling that persists through the blustery gray day, making her more and more uneasy until she can no longer ignore her instinct.

Taking bread off the fire too soon, she rushes to the waterfront as the men ready their boats to go fishing during the late-night light. Calum is helping her father, his cheeks made rosy by the persistent wind, his eyes dark with worry for his brother and his family. She greets him with clumsy congratulations on his engagement, foolishly still hoping it was all a mistake.

Calum loads bait and another net into the boat, nods

to Fiona's father, who is ready to push off, then puts a strong, calloused seaman's hand on Fiona's shoulder and thanks her, says he hopes he hasn't caused her pain, that he loves her like a sister and always will.

Fiona gives way to despair and anger. She blurts out that there is talk of Gillian's wickedness, that Calum's recent troubles, even his brother's illness are caused by her, that she will bring nothing but pain to the town and to him. Fiona begs him not to get into the Atlantic Lady with her father tonight. Disaster awaits him; all signs have pointed to it.

Calum's face grows grim. He will not listen to silly superstitions attributed to his bride-to-be. Fiona should know better than to believe such gossip. He and Gillian plan to move to the Scottish mainland as soon as possible to escape the small, ignorant minds here in Eshaness. He turns away and strides to the Atlantic Lady, holds the boat steady while Fiona's father steps in.

Fiona forces herself back up to the house, leaving her heart with Calum. That night she picks at her dinner of oats, cabbage and fish, dutifully helps wash up, cares for the animals, and sits again in front of the fire, knitting lace that will never be as lovely as what Gillian can make.

Soon enough wind slams rain down, thunder crashes with rage, and the dread starts. What will happen and when? The power of the gale buffeting the island nearly equals the storm inside Fiona. The Tulloch women knit on, praying for good fortune and safe shelter for their sailors as all women on the island knit and pray through every storm while men are at sea.

Fiona can't help thinking of Gillian, alone with her terror, and feels ashamed of the gossip she repeated to Calum. She prays that he comes back to receive her apology and genuine blessing on his marriage.

The night is long, black and wakeful; the storm abates but worry doesn't. The women are up early, going about their daily chores, making every excuse to go outside, where they scan the horizon for boats.

Breakfast is eaten and cleared, animals fed, garden tended, bread prepared for noon and evening meals. A noise outside stops all movement. The door opens. Ewan Tait stands there, supporting Fiona's father, who has injured his knee, but is alive and well. The women throw themselves on him, crying happy tears. They help Andrew out of his damp clothes and into warm ones, wrap his injured knee, tuck him into a chair by the fire with thick blankets. Fiona sits by his side in an agony of suspense while Mum goes to fetch him broth and some bread.

Dad takes her hand, squeezes it, his face weary and chapped, fingers still cold and wrinkled from the sea. He tells the story of the boat driven off course by the relentless wind, picked up by a wave like the hand of a giant and dumped back down, flinging him and Calum overboard. He was hauled from the waves by Ewan, who saw the Atlantic Lady go down. They stayed as long as they dared, looking for Calum.

Her father closes his eyes, then speaks so quietly she almost can't hear him, and once the words are out of his mouth, she wishes she hadn't. When they reached Eshaness shore this morning after spending the night in the voe of a neighboring island, they found Calum had returned *home first. His body, brought by the waves, had been wedged between two great rocks at the bottom of the lighthouse cliff.*

"Megan, this is Mrs. Temple, I just heard about the . . . situation with your husband, and I want to say that I am absolutely horrified. You poor dear. If there's anything I can do for Jeffrey in school next fall, or anything you need me to—"

"Mrs. Temple. I . . . can't really talk now."

"Of course, I understand. You let me know if there's any way I can help you."

"I will. Thank you." Megan hung up the kitchen phone and leaned over the counter, head pounding, eyes screwed shut. It had been like this for two days. If she ever got her hands around Ella's neck, she'd apply pressure with great enthusiasm.

By the time Megan had gone back downstairs after the horrible scene in her and Stanley's bedroom, Dorene and Sally were still there, but Ella had left. She must have wasted no time crowing her triumph around Comfort. Megan and Stanley's marriage was a joke. Megan had failed as a wife and Stanley had to seek satisfaction elsewhere. Doubtless Ella added that if Stanley had married *her*, he'd be lacking nothing. That obviously he'd made a terrible mistake. Now look what he was forced to do? And on and on, passed from one neighbor to another, distorted like phrases in the operator game until Megan was either a doormat or a dominatrix, depending whose version you heard.

Since then at the Morgan house it had been one call or visit after another—she'd even heard from Cara and Jocelyn in Vegas—sympathy, shock, offers of support. Some were sincere. Others just wanted the delicious thrill of making contact with someone scandal had touched. They wanted to see if there was anything in Megan's voice or face they'd missed all these years, anything that should have tipped them off to the kind of person she turned out to be.

Megan had gotten rid of people as quickly as possible. Little ears all over the house. She knew she'd have to tell the children before—God forbid—someone else did, but she didn't have that courage today. Stanley should tell them, but who knew when he'd dare show his face again?

Vera hadn't left her room for the last two days. Megan had to leave meals outside her door on a tray, explaining to the kids that Grandma wasn't well. She felt like a balloon filling with more and more air, approaching the moment when the pressure inside became greater than outside and she'd explode. Bits of her all over the kitchen, shriveled colorful scraps of skin and innards.

The phone rang again. She considered not answering, then lunged for the receiver. "Yes?"

"Meg, it's your father."

"Daddy." The childish use of his name came automatically. Dear God, things were bad if she was even considering turning to him.

"How's things?"

"Fine. They're fine." She couldn't tell him. He'd show up and try to take over, threaten Stanley, cause an even bigger fuss around town than there was already. "Kids are getting restless."

"You should teach those girls to knit. That's what you and your mother did all summer long. All year long. I remember it that way anyway."

"Yes." She moved to the window. Back to the room. She'd

buried dreams of teaching her daughters when she'd given up lace. But yes, she could do that now, she should. "That's how it was."

"I was calling because I found a box in our attic with your name on it in your mother's writing. Rectangular, like a shirt box, you know what it is?"

Megan frowned. She and her father had gone through everything. "No."

"I'm sending it to you, just wanted to let you know it's on its way."

"Okay, thanks, Dad. I'll look for it."

He cleared his throat, henh-henh-*henh*. "You sure everything is okay?"

The question hung in her ears. She wanted to break down, run to his knee, show him her hurt spots and have him fix them. But all her life he'd diverted her pain to Mom, so she'd learned not to run. And yet, now he was asking.

"Stanley and I are having a . . . rough time."

"How rough?"

"I'm not sure yet."

"Okay." He blew out a long breath. "If you need to, you can come up here to stay for a bit. Bring the kids. I know Tricia will want to meet them. And I'd like to see you."

Her throat cramped. He called to check on her often, but this was a first. "Okay, Daddy."

"I hope everything works out so you're happy."

"Thanks, Dad."

"Welcome." He sniffed, was probably scratching his balding head, which he did when he felt uncomfortable. She tried to picture him, still lean in his older years, still handsome, with the green-brown eyes he gave Megan. "Well, I'll let you go."

Megan grinned, shaking her head wearily. "Yes. Okay. Bye, Dad."

She moved back to the mixer, scraped batter for a Mexican chocolate cake into prepared pans. Maybe she would go visit. Take the kids up to New Jersey, take them to the shore there. Jersey beaches were much prettier than they sounded.

"When are you going to tell us, Mom?"

Megan whirled to face her eldest daughter. "Lolly, don't sneak up like that. You scared me."

Lolly stood hugging herself, face pale, hair disheveled, wearing a Jonas Brothers T-shirt and faded cotton shorts, every inch the child she was instead of the woman she was becoming. "Well?"

Megan wasn't prepared, had no idea how to handle this. The only person she could go to for help was the problem in the first place, and he conveniently wasn't here to face the fallout. "When am I going to tell you what?"

"Whatever it is you're not telling us."

Behind her Deena and Jeffrey peeked anxious faces around the doorway.

"Something is going on, you might as well tell us what. All these calls and visits, and you telling everyone you can't talk about it. At this point whatever it is, we can imagine something worse, so you better just tell us."

Jeffrey came into the room hugging his favorite stuffed dog. "Are you sick? Is Daddy?"

"Does he have cancer?" Deena followed him. "Is that why he left? Is he in the hospital?"

"No." Megan gathered the kids to her. Deena and Jeffrey clung; Lolly moved away. "Nobody's sick. I promise you. Your

Dad and I had an argument. We're upset right now. Like when you guys fight, you don't want to be around each other, so he thought he'd leave for a while."

"Mom?" Jeffrey's voice was high and small, like he was five years younger than nine. "Are you getting a divorce?"

The word hung ugly in the air. Divorce. Dear God.

"Your dad will come home when we've both cooled off and we'll talk our disagreement over. Just like I teach you guys to do."

"Really?" His need to believe nearly broke her barely held composure.

"Really."

"Why does the whole town know?" Lolly, not satisfied yet.

"Someone must have heard us."

"Your fight was that loud?" Jeffrey was horrified.

"No, of course not. But people were here, and someone must have said something by mistake. Now. Who wants to scrape the bowl?"

Jeffrey and Deena volunteered for the honor with one tenth their usual excitement. Megan grabbed two teaspoons from the flatware drawer and handed one to each. They jostled for position more solemnly than usual, but at least with enthusiasm. Megan held the thickly chocolate-coated spatula out to Lolly.

"No thanks." Lolly held her gaze, not angry or defiant but disappointed, hurt and still worried, which was much worse.

"It's your favorite."

"I know. I'm just not in the mood." She turned and walked out of the room. Chocolate didn't work at her age. Soft-pedaling a crisis didn't either. Megan had blown it. She needed to treat Lolly as the near-adult she was.

Tears rose. Megan fought them back, clenching her throat,

swallowing convulsively. The tide barely faltered. She wasn't going to be able to beat this one.

"Deen', Jeff, going for a walk, back soon." She managed to sound mostly normal.

"Okay."

"Okay, Mom, bye Mom." Jeffrey spoke through a spoonful of cake batter.

Outside she hurried toward the woods, past David's empty house, letting the tears go, but not giving in to sobs yet.

"Megan."

"Hey, Megan."

She didn't stop. What were Ella and Elizabeth doing at David's house? Was he back? She wouldn't let herself hope. He'd be a wreck, no matter what happened with his ex. She couldn't help him in this state and he couldn't help her.

"*Megan.*"

Their footsteps pounded the asphalt behind her, flashing her back: new-in-school nerd pursued by a gang of popular girls. As then, she could run, but what was the point?

Not bothering to hide her misery, she turned. Maybe they'd been at David's printing the latest issue of *Bigamist News*.

"What do you want?"

"We want to see how you are." Elizabeth reached to touch Megan's arm and then changed her mind when Megan flinched.

"David asked me to e-mail him some files off his computer." Ella met her eyes, still looking human, throwing Megan off balance.

"How is he?"

"So-so. Vicky is pitching hard. He's not convinced, but he's staying to hear her out."

"I see." Megan tried to swallow over the weighted medicine ball in her throat. David had called Ella for the files. He'd told Ella about Vicky.

"He said to say hello and—"

"Who is spreading my story around town, Ella?" She tried to make it clear in her voice who she thought, but uncertainty made her miss the mark. Ella wasn't behaving like someone who'd just succeeded in destroying Megan's life and wanted to gloat.

"Dorene told Cara. She only told *her*, and only because Cara called when Dorene was still really upset on your behalf, but of course . . ." Ella's face tightened into anger. "Cara told everyone. You know how it goes here. I'm sorry, Megan."

"Okay." She didn't know whether to believe her or not.

"Did you think it was me?" Ella arched an eyebrow, but didn't seem surprised.

Megan shrugged. "It would have made sense."

"Except, believe it or not, I'm on your side."

"Really, this whole thing is my fault. I should have minded my own business when I heard Stanley talking to . . . her." This time Elizabeth did touch Megan, laid her hand on her shoulder. "But I want to make it right."

Megan nearly laughed through new tears. For all Elizabeth's loyalty, sometimes Megan just wanted her to go away. "What can you possibly do?"

"Ella and I were about to go out for ice cream." Elizabeth squeezed her shoulder and let go. "Come with us. That'll do for a start."

"I don't think I can."

"Come on, Megan." Ella rolled her eyes. "Do something impetuous and stupid for once."

"I did that when I married Stanley. It didn't work for me."

A startled silence, then Ella and Elizabeth saw Megan's smirk and burst out laughing.

"Come on." Ella giggled again. "Let's go put a dent in one of the Chit Chat Café's Bucket Sundaes."

"But my kids . . . I have a cake in the oven . . ."

"Not a problem." Ella whipped out her cell phone, dialed with nails whose burgundy polish was chipped on two fingers. If that wasn't a sign of the apocalypse . . .

"Lolly, honey, it's Ella. Elizabeth and I are kidnapping your mother and taking her to the Chit Chat for ice cream, can you take the cake out when it's done? And be in charge of the little guys?" She listened to the response, met Megan's eyes and smiled so warmly, Megan dropped hers. "Yeah. Okay. I'll tell her. I will. Okay, honey. You be good."

Ella flipped her phone closed. "She said she had that chocolate spatula after you left, it was really good and thank you. She said she was glad we were taking you out because you seem sad."

Megan nodded, wiped away two more tears. "Do I have *any* makeup left on?"

"No, you're hideous."

"You're gorgeous." Elizabeth socked Ella playfully. "Let's go, I'm hungry. I think I skipped lunch."

Megan followed Ella and Elizabeth, feeling apprehensive and third-wheel. Last time she'd been to the Chit Chat for ice cream was to celebrate Jeffrey's ninth birthday in May. Stanley had been away and she'd had eight crazed children to cope with by herself; she hadn't ordered anything but coffee. She was due for a splurge, but she wished it was under other circumstances.

They drove the short distance to downtown Comfort, parked by Tucker's Hardware and filed into the Chit Chat Café, its scarred red vinyl booths and chrome-edged counter stools nearly deserted on a Monday mid-afternoon. Tyler Pinkton and Andrew Gellar were at the counter drinking coffee and reading newspapers. Gladys and Stellie Jacob sat at another table finishing a late lunch.

They sat, Ella and Elizabeth on one side, Megan on the other. Kerry Banks came to wait on them, grinning while her eyes stayed bored. She'd been head cheerleader at Comfort High ten years earlier. Apparently life had been downhill ever since.

"Hey there, girls, how y'all doing today?" She glanced at Megan curiously.

"We have never been better." Ella's tone challenged her to think otherwise. "We'd like one bucket sundae and three of the biggest spoons you've got."

"Yes ma'am, coffee too?"

"Coffee too."

Kerry nodded and strolled away. Megan examined a burn mark on the Formica table, body buzzing with unpleasant adrenaline. In her peripheral vision she saw Tyler staring, Gladys glancing over, then bending her head toward Stellie. Why had Megan come here with these women? She should have stayed home with her kids and summoned the guts to tell them the truth, a truth she owed them years ago, but Stanley had been so adamant they shouldn't find out. He said it was best for them. Now it seemed painfully obvious it was only best for him.

"Well . . ." Ella leaned languorously back against vinyl that clashed with her nails. "Another lovely day in Comfort."

Elizabeth sighed. "I liked it better when I thought the town was perfect."

"Get real. People suck everywhere."

"Oh stop, you sound like David. And speaking of, do you think he'll go back to his wife?"

"If you ask me . . ." Ella answered, looking at Megan, "he'd be a fool to."

Megan had no idea how to react to this version of Ella. Did she know about David, too? Had he told her of his feelings during one of those drunken evenings they spent together? Megan didn't want to think about it.

"So Megan, what are you going to do now?" Elizabeth asked. "Stay? Leave?"

She flinched. "I don't—"

"Here you go." The waitress set down the plastic bucket heaped with eight scoops of ice cream: strawberry, vanilla, chocolate, cookie dough, chocolate chip, Oreo, butter pecan and Rocky Road. Pooling and dripping over them, chocolate, caramel, marshmallow, butterscotch, pineapple and strawberry sauces. Above this ice-creamscape, clouds of whipped cream, walnuts, pecans, almonds, chocolate jimmies and colored sprinkles. The crowning touch: three maraschino cherries. Three long-handled spoons stuck straight out of its considerable depth.

Megan flashed back to the table of nine-year-olds, plunging in spoons, shoving full loads gleefully into messy mouths. She remembered sharing a sundae here the summer she and Stanley got together. He'd bragged about their engagement to anyone who would listen. She'd had no appetite for ice cream, only hunger for the handsome man who would introduce stability and peace to her life, impatient for the wholesome and bright future they'd share.

"On your mark . . ." Ella picked up the spoon closest to her and waited until the others followed. "Get set . . . *go*."

Megan dug her spoon into the cold gooey sundae and came up with a mix of butter pecan and pineapple that tasted like heaven.

"Oh, that's orgasmic." Elizabeth's eyes rolled back in her head. "All the more for being a caloric nightmare."

"Eaten at a completely inappropriate time of day."

Megan took another spoonful, vanilla with butterscotch, walnuts and whipped cream. She'd probably be sick the rest of the day.

"I wanted to let you know I'm leaving Comfort, Megan." Ella spoke calmly, filled up her spoon again. "Pieces of my old life have been collapsing for so long, it's time. You know how I felt about Stanley . . ."

Megan nodded at the bucket. Yes. She knew.

"Or how I *thought* I felt about Stanley. Finding out that he— Well, it was the last piece of the old skin. Shedded now. I'm ready to move on."

"Where will you go?"

"I have a second interview for a job in Atlanta as assistant to the president of Savannah College of Art and Design. My gut says they'll hire me."

Megan ate another spoonful without tasting it. She felt close to tears again, and didn't trust herself to speak. Even two days ago, if someone told her she'd be mourning Ella's departure, she'd have laughed for a week.

"I'll be here for Sally's wedding next month either way. And I'll finish my part of the lace."

Megan took a sip of coffee to clear her throat. "I hope they do hire you, Ella. And I'm glad you'll be at Sally's wedding."

"Of course I will be." Ella watched Elizabeth clean a thread of caramel sauce off her chin and miss half of it. "Would you get married again, Megan?"

"I'm married now."

"But I mean if you leave him."

Megan shrugged. She'd stayed with Stanley knowing about his other wife for fifteen years. The only thing that had really changed now was that the lies about it would stop. She didn't want to hear that other people were planning the end of her marriage. "I don't know."

"I don't think I'll ever marry again."

"Oh, come on, Ella." Elizabeth fought her for a spoonful of Oreo with hot fudge. "Of course you will."

"Why? Because everyone does?"

"No, because you're so . . ." Elizabeth waved her spoon around, fishing for the words. "Into men."

"Ha! You try going through a divorce, see what it does to you. When I found myself alone after I left Don, all I could think about was finding a replacement as soon as possible." Ella shuddered. "Let's just say I'm better now."

"Thanks to Stanley?" Megan didn't try to keep the irony from her voice.

"At least in part. Killed off my perfect man fantasy pretty quick."

"Then all this has been good for something." She forced a smile, wanting to go home, wanting to get as far away from this conversation as possible, to dive into bed and pull the covers over her head like Vera had, not come out until she felt ready to face the world.

Except she'd spent the last fifteen years unable to face the world. What made her think a few days in bed would change that?

"I bet this mess will turn out to be good for lots of things." Elizabeth wiped at the caramel drip and missed again. "I bet you look back someday and realize it's one of those this-is-the-first-day-of-the-rest-of-my-life moments."

Ella looked sick. "Elizabeth, you could put ipecac syrup out of business."

"I was just—"

"Good afternoon, ladies. Ella, Elizabeth." Mr. Coughlin, who supposedly worked at the mayor's office, only "work" didn't appear to be in his job description. "And Megan . . . my dear. How are you *doing*?"

Megan sighed. She was really starting to hate that tone.

"Hey, she's got a Chit-Chat ice-cream bucket in front of her, how can she be anything but euphoric?"

Frank chuckled and pointed a finger-gun at Ella. "You kill me, girl."

"I'd sure like to," she mumbled.

"If you need anything, Megan honey, advice, a shoulder, a place to bunk down, you let me know, okay? Marge and I will be glad to help."

"Thank you." Megan managed a polite smile, wanting to throw down her spoon and run. She couldn't live here and be treated like a terminal-cancer patient. She'd take the kids and go . . . somewhere. To New Jersey with Dad? Would Stanley move with them? He might leave Comfort now. But they couldn't abandon Vera, and she'd never leave.

"Take care, y'all. Stop by the office anytime if you need to talk." He waved cheerfully and strode out of the café, whistling.

"Oh, right, his office is the first place you'd go." Ella shook her head, making her dark hair swing. "I won't miss this small-town shit at all."

"Oh, but it's so wonderful that everyone comes together in a time of crisis and supports . . ." Elizabeth trailed off at Ella's withering look. "Okay, never mind. Anyway, I still believe this will turn out for the best. I believe in aiming high, expecting good things to happen. If you don't, life is chaos. And so sad."

"Oh my God," Ella groaned. "Why do I like you again?"

"Because I'm yang to your yin; you're incomplete without me." Elizabeth turned to Megan, that tiny thread of golden sugar still glistening on her chin. "We got interrupted last time I asked. Megan, what are you going to do now?"

"Oh . . ." She wanted to dip her napkin in water and wiped away that caramel. She wanted order and neatness, she wanted peace, and happy, busy kids with stable, comfortable lives. And she wanted to knit lace by the ocean for weeks at a time. "Probably what I do best. Just go on."

Ella made a pained sound. "God, does that sound pathetic."

"I think you should leave him."

"Easy for you to say." Megan spooned up Rocky Road with marshmallow sauce. "I have no income of my own. And I have three children."

"And he has two wives," Ella said.

"Uh . . . I knew that." Megan licked marshmallow from her lips. How would life be different if Stanley had stayed only with her? His salary would go twice as far. She could afford help around the house. Trips with the children, to expose them to more than rural North Carolina. And she'd have him to herself. Would that have made her life so different? Maybe. Maybe not.

"Have you ever met her?" Elizabeth inadvertently added a stripe of chocolate to her chin. "The other wife? I wonder what she's like."

"Gillian to my Fiona."

"How do you know that?"

"I found her picture in his wallet. Years ago. But I knew anyway. He dated you, Ella, for years, look at you." She gestured to Ella's perfect makeup, chic black sleeveless top and well-muscled arms. "Where else would he turn when Fiona didn't measure up?"

"Oh, give me a break. What makes you think you're the problem?" Ella threw down her spoon in disgust. "Why isn't it just some sick deviance in your darling husband? From what Vera let slip to me, the apple didn't fall far from the tree. I guess Rocky kept his Bullwinkle busy, too."

Elizabeth put a hand over her mouth to keep from spitting ice cream. Even Megan started giggling.

"Oh God," Ella whispered. "Duck. It's Betty Ethers. She'll want to join us and eat the whole sundae."

"Too late," murmured Megan.

"Hey, girls." Betty waddled the last few steps to their table, forehead creased with concern. "Megan, you just can't imagine how sorry I am to hear about that rat husband of yours. Is Vera okay? She hasn't shown up to play cards all week. Tell her us girls are worried sick about her."

"I will. Thanks, Betty."

"Oh my." Her eyes lit up at the half-empty ice-cream bucket. "Doesn't that look good."

"Yup." Ella defiantly ignored etiquette and didn't ask her to join them, shook her head when Megan started to. "It's delicious."

"Oh . . . Well . . ." She waited a few more hopeful seconds. "You enjoy yourselves. I'll be getting home now. Got to put up some peach jam."

"Okay, then." Ella all but shooed her away.

"Nice to meet you, Betty," Elizabeth called after her, then settled back in to the table. "Okay, I get it. Small town. Not much privacy."

"Like a nudist colony," Ella said.

"But all these people care about you. If my life fell apart in New York, I could cry for three hours in a café and no one would even take notice."

Megan watched Betty waddle away. At least one decision had been reached today. She had to move away from Comfort. She couldn't stay here.

"How y'all doing?" Kerry walked by and patted their table. "Is that bucket okay?"

"Needs more fat and sugar." Ella's smile turned weary when Kerry didn't seem to get the joke. "We're fine. Thank you."

"You know what I think?" Elizabeth waggled her spoon thoughtfully.

"No, but we're about to find out," said Ella.

"I think you should meet her." Elizabeth lifted her caramel and chocolate-speckled chin. "The other wife, I mean."

Megan stiffened. "What on *earth* for?"

"I'm not exactly sure. I just have this idea that she holds the key for you."

Megan put down her spoon, picked up her coffee, not sure she should be trading a sugar buzz for caffeine when her hands were already shaking. "The key to what?"

"Figuring it all out."

"Figuring all *what* out?"

Elizabeth looked up from the bucket in amazement, as if the answer was the most obvious thing in the world. "Who you are. And what you need to do now to change your life."

"What makes you think I want to?"

Elizabeth looked at her with sympathy. Megan wanted to lunge across the table and dump the bucket on her head. "You can't go on the way you have been, Megan."

"You may be onto something, Ms. Elizabeth. Gillian came to Fiona after Calum was gone. You mix it up and go to Gillian. Talk to her and decide either to fight for Stanley or go the opposite route and tell her she can have the jerk."

Megan put the cup down. The ice cream and caffeine were mixing with stress to make her stomach gurgly and unstable. She was afraid she might cry again. "But I don't know which one I want. If either."

"Go see her. I'll come with you if you want." Elizabeth nodded firmly, a trace of whipped cream lodged in the corner of her mouth. "I guarantee she'll have your answer."

Chapter Thirteen

$\mathcal{D}$inner was the quietest since Elizabeth had arrived in Comfort three weeks earlier. The kids were somber. Neither Elizabeth nor Megan had appetites due to stress and ice cream. Vera had finally emerged from her room, but barely spoke beyond assuring the children she was feeling better, and saying yes, no, please and thank you to offers of potato salad, hot dogs and carrot sticks. Even Jeffrey only asked what Elizabeth would rather have, a seal that shot rockets or a rocket that shot seals.

Afterward, plates in the dishwasher, leftovers back in the refrigerator, pots scrubbed, dried and put away, the kids went to play with similar-aged friends down the street. Vera, Elizabeth and Megan intersected in the hallway outside the kitchen.

Megan sent the front door a look of loathing. "Why don't we have the group sit out back in the garden tonight? Vera, we can move your rocker if you want."

"The garden? What for?"

"We're living on the edge." Elizabeth didn't wait for Vera's response, went out onto the porch with Megan. They lifted the rocker together and carried it down the driveway, settled it on the patio where it looked oddly out of place. Elizabeth went upstairs to get her knitting and something warmer than her sleeveless top. She was pleased with how her part of Sally's hem decoration looked, but as much as she loved the idea of creating something so beautiful, she was discovering pretty fast that lace knitting wasn't her thing. Maybe Vera could manage to connect spiritually to all the women of Shetland throughout time, but Elizabeth was just connecting to crankiness and impatience. Following the chart was grueling and the ultra-thin thread meant progress was measured in millimeters. Elizabeth liked bulky knits you could add six inches to in an evening.

In her dresser, stuffed under a cotton sweater, she came across the Ingles Market bag containing her very first attempt at lace and the thick rolled paper on which she'd painted her fabric design. She'd meant to ask Megan's opinion, but the time had never seemed right, and Elizabeth hadn't been inspired to work on it further. Maybe tonight, since she and Megan finally managed decent bonding earlier over ice cream.

She brought the painting downstairs and outside into the still, cool evening, where Vera and Megan were knitting away already, the pattern falling from their needles delicate and intricate, a graceful interweaving of diamonds, fans and spiderwebs.

Elizabeth put her painting on the patio table, feeling awkward and vulnerable. "I brought something to show you, Megan. It's a fabric design, inspired by the mountains and hawks around Lake Lure. But it's missing something, it's not quite . . . I just can't tell."

Megan unrolled the watercolor, which looked even more rough and amateur under the gaze of the woman who'd produced the gorgeous garden around them, and all that lace.

"Oh, it's lovely." Her voice was overly polite. Even though Elizabeth expected the reaction, agreed with the implied assessment, her heart sank.

"But . . . ?" she asked hopefully.

"I'm no expert. But I'd say it needs more movement here." She pointed to a spot between two brown squiggles. "And less here. You're trying to create a flying motion with these birds, and you almost have, but they're not quite going anywhere. It's static. The colors need to shift here to here, and deepen there, so that you can direct the eye—"

She looked guiltily up at Elizabeth. "Sorry, I'm getting carried away."

"No, no, it's fine." Elizabeth forced her frozen smile to thaw. "It's exactly what I asked you to do."

"I wouldn't get so excited about fixing it if I didn't really like it to begin with."

"Yes, I know. I appreciate it." She took the pattern back, pretended to study it and consider Megan's suggestions. She couldn't see what Megan meant or how she envisioned fixing the problem, couldn't even connect with the flash of inspiration she'd had at the lake, or remember what had been so exciting about the moment.

She wasn't a designer. Dominique was right. She was a pretender. And if she wasn't a designer—she was back to square one, lost again. Maybe she should marry Dominique just to keep from being swallowed up by her own insignificance. "Those were great suggestions. I'll work on it tomorrow. Thank you."

"You're welcome." Megan picked up her lace eagerly, diving

again into the pattern with barely a glance at her chart. "I hope you go far with it."

"Me too." Like all the way to the garbage.

Vera held up her part of the panel. "I've gotten off somewhere on this part and I can't catch it. Help me fix this, Megan. I've just gone back to the diamonds after the spiders."

Megan dragged her chair next to Vera and bent over the complicated pattern, counting stitches, examining the flow of the threads.

Elizabeth wanted to scream at the unfairness of it all. Here she was, floundering around, only half good at anything, grabbing on to whatever she could in order to put herself out in the business world and succeed, and this woman sat here, boiling over with genuine talent and wasting it in her backyard.

"Have you ever considered selling your work, Megan? You'd make hundreds on each piece. A *lot* of hundreds."

"I thought about it at one time." She answered distractedly, not even titillated by the thought of cash, not even tempted by the lure of success. "Vera, here's where you got off, see? After this web."

"Oh, yes. I should have known to weave in a lifeline." She took the lace back, scowling.

"What's a lifeline?" Elizabeth slumped into her chair, figuring it was another thing she could be bad at.

"It's a thread you insert through the loops of a row, usually before you're about to start a pattern change or before an increase or decrease," Vera said. "I use a contrasting color so I can see it easily. If you make a mistake after that row, you just rip out. The thread will protect and hold what came before, and you can start over with the hard part."

"Wow." Elizabeth stared at Vera's thick, lined fingers flying with the wool. The idea caught her instantly, as if *Babcia* were whispering for her to pay attention. "Do they make those for your life?"

"Wouldn't that be something!"

"Hi, guys." Ella, lugging a chair from the porch, new energy to her step, smile lacking caution or irony. She'd gotten the job in Atlanta, was leaving within the week. "Sally and Dorene are on their way. I know it's not an official meeting, but we were lonely knitting at home and figured we'd stop by. Is that okay?"

"I'm glad you did." Megan's enthusiasm was open and genuine. "Can I offer you some—"

"Not a thing. Sit and relax. We're taking care of it."

"Here we are." Sally, Dorene with her, also carrying chairs from Megan's front porch. Sally put hers down next to Ella and looked around, inhaling deeply. "Oh it's so pretty. Why haven't we been meeting back here all along?"

"It's the week for getting out of ruts," Megan said drily.

Elizabeth dragged her lace out of its protective bag, thinking it was her week to get more stuck in hers. Worse, she wasn't immediately calculating how to bounce out.

"What ruts?" Dorene set her chair opposite Vera and collapsed into it. "Break out the food, Sally, I'm exhausted. Today was the craft-fair entry deadline and I was all day logging entries. So many people wait until the last minute."

Vera peered over her glasses at Ella. *"Imagine* that."

"I brought Mike's Hard Lemonade and a package of Oreos." Sally unloaded a cloth shopping bag. "Megan, we didn't want you to have to do anything."

"Oh, you are sweet." Megan's hazel eyes were warm with

gratitude. She'd blossomed, strengthened. Even the clothes she wore were brighter today.

"Cara and Jocelyn are back." Dorene accepted a lemonade from Sally.

"They were *not* encouraged to attend tonight," Ella said. "Or any other night. As long as they both shall live here."

Megan's hand froze reaching for her bottle of Mike's. "Never? Because of me?"

"The Purls have come unstrung." Ella pulled her lace out of its bag; she'd done a good few inches and it looked perfect.

"But . . . what about your Thursday nights at the Anchor Bar?" Megan scanned her peacefully knitting friends, obviously having a hard time processing this. "And Wednesday-morning manicures? All the time you've spent together . . ."

"Didn't you say it's the week for getting out of ruts? But wait, there's more." Ella turned to her left, tapped Sally's chair, the careful languor she'd cultivated having given way to new purpose. "Hey, you. Anything you want to tell us?"

"Foster and I are moving in September." Sally's gentle voice was eager; her hands moved gracefully over her lace. "His brother is taking over the hardware store. Foster wants to go back to school and get a business degree from UNC Greensboro."

"And the most important reason . . ." Ella lifted her drink in a triumphant toast. "He wants to get Sally away from his mother. Finally."

Toasts all around. Elizabeth drank too much from her bottle. Ella, freed from her bitterness, Megan evolving, Sally escaping into new love—Elizabeth felt orphaned and, childishly, betrayed.

"Wow." Megan tried to smile bravely. "I'll miss you and Ella both. But I'm very happy for you, Sally, you'll be able to start your marriage with just the two of you. That will be wonderful."

"Ahem." Vera sent her a sidelong glance.

"Oh. Vera." Megan blushed. "I didn't mean—"

"Well, I'm staying here." Dorene's needles twirled bizarrely; her lace straggly and misshapen. "You'll never guess what happened. Never."

"You met a guy."

Dorene gaped at Ella. "How did you know that?"

She shrugged. "It's the only thing I'd never guess."

"Ha ha ha."

"Who is he, Dorene?" Sally asked.

"Well." Dorene settled herself for the forthcoming epic. "Yesterday afternoon I was sitting at the Chit Chat waiting for Cara and Jocelyn."

"*Et tu*, Dorene?" Ella said.

"I know, I know." She glanced apologetically at Megan. "But they wanted me to hear their stories about Vegas. Anyway, I was knitting, and I was thinking about Gillian, how she went after everything she wanted like she owned the world, and how if I could be like her I'd have men all over the place. Anyway, right when I was thinking that, I look up and there's this guy who's just come in. He sits in the booth next to mine, gets a cup of coffee, then he starts looking at my lace. And then he looks at me. And then the lace. And then me. And—"

"Got that bit, Dorene."

Dorene ignored Ella. "I thought, What would Gillian do? So I smiled at him like I'm some way-hot mermaid, and we start talking. He turns out to be Josh Holscombe's cousin! Then right before Cara and Jocelyn came in, I gave him my phone number. Two days go by and I'm thinking my Gawd, if he doesn't call I'll throw myself off a cliff. But he did! He called and we had a nice talk and we're having coffee next week."

More congratulations, more toasts. Elizabeth drank deeply again. Colorful, vivid women all around; she felt gray, misty and indistinct.

"Thanks, guys." Dorene was flushed pink, eyes bright. "I swear all the time we were talking, I felt Gillian there through the lace, helping me find my strength."

Megan laughed uneasily. "Dorene, my mom made Gillian up."

"I know. But she's fabulous, such a beautiful, powerful, magical woman. I picture her as Angelina Jolie."

"No-o-o." Ella shook her head. "More wholesome-sexy, like Jaclyn Smith."

"Demi Moore," Sally said. "Elizabeth, you're quiet tonight. What do you think?"

"Oh. Wow. I guess I hadn't really thought about it." She riffled quickly through some movie memories. "Selma Blair?"

"Cyd Charisse," Vera said emphatically.

"Good one." Sally lifted her chin toward Megan. "You own her more than we do. How do you picture her?"

Megan's shrug lifted her knitting. "Genevieve."

"Oh, Megan." Sally's needles stilled; she bit her lip. "I'm sorry. I should have thought."

"It's fine. Don't be silly."

"Oh, darnation." Dorene peered at the chart, back at her knitting and back at the chart. "I did something wrong again. I don't have enough stitches in this section."

"Give it here, I'll look." Vera beckoned the lace over. "You need a lifeline about every row, Dorene."

"I know," she groaned, getting up to surrender her latest disaster. "This lace stuff is killer. Give me a good stockinette scarf anytime."

Vera's expert hands checked Dorene's knitting. A squirrel chattered nearby, broadcasting triumph over unfettered access to David's yard. Breezes offered scents of Megan's garden. The more beautiful the surroundings, the more vibrant and cohesive the Purls, the more pale and tortured Elizabeth felt. Where now? What now? She was out of energy to reinvent herself. Too late now, but there must have been a way to avoid hitting this painful and lonely bottom. Somewhere along the way . . .

"I need to know something from each of you." She pulled up her needle and turned the work around. "If you could have—"

Ella groaned. "Can we have *one* get-together without your mind games?"

"No." Elizabeth put up a hand to shush her. She was onto something; her instincts were buzzing like the bees around Megan's mint. "If you could have a lifeline, for your life, where would you weave it in?"

"Elizabeth." Sally chuckled softly. "You don't mess around with small talk, do you?"

"I don't see the point of having regrets," Vera said. "If you went back and did one thing differently, you'd just blunder into other mistakes. That's what life is. Here, Dorene, I added another stitch to your section. It won't show."

"Thanks, Vera." Dorene retrieved her work. "Megan, you better put my bit in the way back of Sally's dress."

"Nonsense. It's beautiful." Megan gestured graciously, a woman ruling with real power now. "Why don't you go first, Elizabeth? It's such an interesting idea."

"It's a trap." Vera shrugged. "Yammering about what might

have been only sets you up for disappointment in what you have now."

"Maybe." Elizabeth hung on to her patience. "But let's try anyway."

"I'd weave it in the night I had with Jess." Dorene took her repaired lace back to her chair. "Right before I seduced him."

"You'd change your mind." Vera nodded approvingly.

"No, no. Then I could keep going back and doing it over again."

She gave her goofy grin and everyone lost it, even Vera. A gust of wind blew at the same moment, as if the garden surrounding them was laughing, too. Elizabeth's smile cut out early. She wanted to absorb as much of this evening as she could: the friendship, support, camaraderie, the effortless feeling of belonging. The Purls wouldn't be here to come back to when she left.

"I don't think I'd change anything in my life." Sally shifted in her chair. Her neckline gaped and Elizabeth caught a glimpse of the scarring on her shoulder. "So much of it was hard, but I learned and grew, and now I'm so happy I can't imagine doing anything differently or I might not end up where I am."

"Smart woman." Vera nodded in smug satisfaction.

"I'd put one in before I married Don, to avoid that mistake. But yes, like Sally, I trust I'm heading toward happiness now." Ella threw Megan a significant glance. "At least I'm no longer cemented in misery of my own making."

Megan flinched. "Oh, *thanks*, Ella."

"Don't mention it. And it's your turn now, so go. We need to get back to gossip and insignificant chatter, where we belong."

"I'd put my lifeline in right now. Tonight." Megan looked up from her knitting toward the mountains, the sun's dying light glowing on her skin and in her eyes. "Because I'm so unsure what to do going forward, that if I choose wrong I'd want to be able to come back to this night with you all here, and have you help me do it right the next time."

Elizabeth looked down to hide a surprise attack of tears.

"So that's mine. Elizabeth? Finish this off for us."

She cleared her throat. "I still don't have one."

"You made *us* all play."

"I know, Ella." Elizabeth hunched her shoulders. "But I've made so many bad choices I've ended up nowhere with no idea what to do next. Right now I'd say I need a lifeline back to when I was born."

"The problem with you girls is that you overthink everything." Vera peered over her red glasses. "And you have too many options. In my day, you got married to the guy who asked you and you stayed married and you—"

"Pretended everything was fine," Megan said with some heat.

"The worst kind of life a woman can have." Ella echoed Megan's passion. "That was mine in Florida. And Megan's here. We need to be able to make ourselves happy, both because it's good for us and because men shouldn't have to bear that burden."

"The hardest part, I think," Sally said, "is finding the balance between making yourself happy and making other people happy."

"Bingo." Ella jabbed her needle toward Sally for emphasis. "And deciding how much needs changing in a bad situation and when. No one can tell you that. You have to get there on your own."

Elizabeth's stomach turned sick. She didn't even know what would make her happy. She couldn't even figure that out.

"You all make me tired." Dorene shook her head. "Do men worry about this stuff?"

"No." Sally, Ella and Megan all spoke at once, making Dorene chortle.

"Hey, we should write our own version of *When Women Rule*, where we have each woman ruling over herself, not over men."

"You get right on that, Ella." Megan smiled up from her knitting. "And by the way, we're not letting you off the hook, Elizabeth. Just ramble on about your life and see what comes to you."

"Yes," Sally agreed. "God knows we've been through enough trouble collectively, that we should be able to help."

"I'll try." Elizabeth pushed her stitches down the needles and let them rest. She had nothing to lose. "After I left Mom's house and moved to Boston, Alan and I had this starving-artist life we both loved. He was a painter with a hobby as a waiter. I was a waitress with a hobby as a painter. But then the whole thing gradually started feeling . . . I don't know, wrong."

"I know what went wrong." Vera scratched beside her nose with a knitting needle, looking disgusted. "You grew up."

"You're probably right." Elizabeth picked up her lemonade, took another swig; it tasted too sweet now. "Then I met Dominique and we did the starving-artist thing for a while, too, only his art was cooking. I had a job as secretary at a law firm, but I was trying to get other businesses off the ground. Meanwhile, Dominique's took off, and I let it take us. For a long time it was thrilling. And then . . ."

She froze in her chair. She couldn't go back to that life in New

York. She realized it like a thunderbolt had split the darkening sky and zapped her in her chair. Not after being here with all this life and warmth surrounding her. Not back to those long, lonely days in her own company, watching TV, scouring the Internet for entertainment, sending e-mail, shopping, calling friends to schedule a social life, always an effort.

How could any of these women leave Comfort?

"Something started feeling wrong," Megan prompted.

"And then I came here." She looked around the group of concerned faces and the lightning struck again. Megan's house. Megan's friends. Megan's town. Dominique had been right about this too. First Mom's life. Then Alan's. Then Dominique's. Now Megan's.

Elizabeth's rut was longer and deeper than she'd ever let herself see. But now that she finally understood its nature, she had a 100 percent better chance of hauling herself out.

"I know where to put it." She turned to the woman *Babcia* had sent her to, both to help and to learn from. "Like Megan, I'd weave my lifeline in right now, tonight, sitting here, knitting lace with all of you."

Chapter Fourteen

The family stays inside that day, nursing Andrew and grief. Late at night Ewan Tait again comes to their house, breathless and nearly frantic. Along with the miraculous news of Andrew Tulloch's return, news of Calum's death has spread. Crofters have gathered, but their sorrow and their talk have turned ugly. They believe Gillian responsible for the tragedy, or others of her kind—witches, fin-men or evil spirits. She has brought bad luck on Calum and will continue to poison their village with more of the same. A group has marched to her house. They want her gone from Eshaness.

Fiona gasps and flees into the summer twilight. She arrives at Gillian's house, too late. A mob drives the beautiful grief-stricken woman before them. Gillian is pale, stumbling, her face tearstained. She glances at

Fiona, gives a sad smile and mouths something Fiona doesn't catch. Fiona pushes among her fellow islanders, grabs at shoulders, shoves bodies, trying to get someone, anyone, to listen to reason, to stop this wicked blaming of an innocent woman for a death that is so much part of their life. She finds Calum's mother, pleads with her to stop, but she and the others have lost one of their favorite sons, and someone has to pay for their pain.

At the road out of Eshaness, Gillian suddenly veers toward the cliff by the lighthouse site, where she ran from Fiona and Calum on their walk so long ago. The mob falters. Alban Tait follows and tries to pull her back, but she yanks herself free, hissing like a raging cat. He steps away, hands up in surrender, foolishly afraid of her power.

Gillian faces them, pale and lovely, dark hair blowing. She unties her black cloak and throws it to the ground, uncovering a white dress decorated with the magical, beautiful lace she's knitted herself. She grins, laughs her big wild laugh, turns and runs toward the cliff, spreads her arms and dives off its rocky edge.

A few shouts, screams, most of the Shetlanders stand stunned. Several men rush to peer over the cliff, but in the dim twilight they can see nothing. Quiet settles, bringing uncertainty. Prayers are muttered. Another death, another tragedy, will this end the curse? Fiona pushes out of the group and walks home, knowing this night has changed her life. She cannot feel the same way about her neighbors or her community or Shetland again.

***

Megan lay in her bedroom, eyes open, watching the ceiling, watching the window, watching the clock numbers roll on from midnight. She could hear Jeffrey's regular snores out in the hallway, impressively loud for a skinny nine-year-old. His wife would be doomed to a marriage of nighttime earplugs.

She turned restlessly, adjusted her pillow, fussed with the cotton blanket, then sat up with a groan and pushed the hair out of her face. This was hopeless. Her brain whirred like the Wheel of Fortune, clicking through all the worries and obsessions keeping her from sleep. Click, click, click. Where would it stop this time?

Out of bed, to the window, she pressed her face against the cool glass, gazed out at the stars pricking the sky.

Click, click, click. Stanley. She could settle down and accept again what she'd accepted fifteen years earlier, or insist he choose. If he chose Genevieve, she'd have to find the strength to build a new life alone. If he chose Megan she'd be left with a husband for whom she wasn't enough.

Click, click, click. David. He and Victoria might have gotten back together, or they might not have. She couldn't count on him in her future, but she couldn't make herself rule him out either. They'd shared so much.

Click click click. Fiona, Gillian, Calum. After the Purls left two nights ago, Megan had stayed out in the garden, working on Sally's dress panel. In the near-darkness, crickets accompanying her stitches, she'd thought of her mother, of her stories, fell deeper and deeper into the past, and gradually slid into a trance, the first one in so many years.

In the phantom warmth of a smoky peat fire, she'd sensed the ghost presence of Shetland knitters all around her—Fiona;

her mother, Mary; her Aunt Charlotte; Granny Nessa and hundreds of others spread out over the islands.

She missed the sea, had been away from it too long, its smells, its creatures, its plants, its moods and constant surprises. Could you ever evict your childhood home from your soul? Or maybe this longing ran deeper, back to her ancestry.

The bedroom seemed suddenly stuffy. She slid open the screen, stuck out her head, breathing in the placid night air, identifying scents of flowers and forest. No salt here, no peat, no angry storms and boiling blue oceans. Just peaceful gardens, quiet woods and sedate mountains.

Megan turned abruptly to dig her phone out of her purse. She was going to call Stanley, and if he didn't answer, she'd keep calling. If he was with Genevieve he could bloody well answer her call the way he'd answered Genevieve's here. It was ridiculous, this silence between them. They weren't children, and they weren't enemies.

She powered on her cell, was in the midst of dialing when the notifier chimed, announcing voice mail from an unknown number. Probably a wrong one. She dialed into the service and listened to the mechanical operator instruct her about things she already knew. The message started. She inhaled sharply at the sound of David's familiar deep voice, clear and alert.

"Megan. Hope you don't mind me calling. I figured I'd be sure to get you if I called your cell; you must have given me the number at some point. Ella told me what happened—no, not like it was gossip, so stop getting all pissed off. She knew I'd want to know. Dorene is a bigmouth, but Cara and Jocelyn are toxic cows. I hope you're all right. I'll come home if you need me. Call me, I'm worried about you."

The mechanical operator told her the message had come

in three days previous. Megan quickly deleted it to avoid the temptation of listening again and again, then immediately felt the loss. *Call me, I'm worried about you.*

She peered at the clock. 12:30 A.M. Maybe he'd still be up? Or asleep with his phone turned off, so she could leave a quick message, tell him not to come, to worry about himself, that she was fine.

Bad idea, to risk him answering. Not now, when the night was summery and soft and Megan was the only body awake in the house, lost and vulnerable in her isolation. She'd probably make a fool out of herself, put out some hint of how she still felt about him, and then he'd tell her he and Victoria had just finished having make-up sex all over her house.

She'd call Stanley.

The phone rang only once before he answered, shocking her, so that she was at a loss what to say.

"Megan?" He sounded worried, wide awake. "Are you there? What is it? One of the kids?"

"Everyone's fine." She drifted back to the window, leaned against the sill, looking out into the dim shapes of her garden. "Where are you?"

"At a motel in Reidsville, up by the Virginia border. I have a meeting with clients in the morning, thought I'd allow myself extra sleep by getting here tonight instead of having to drive from headquarters at the crack of dawn."

"Oh." He sounded as if everything were normal between them. It gave her an eerie, disoriented feeling, as if she'd imagined all the uproar. "How are you doing?"

"Miserable without you, Megan." His voice dropped, became husky. "I miss you."

She ignored the tug on her heartstrings and forced herself

to pay attention. *He* missed her. *He* was miserable. David was worried about *Megan*, hoped *she* was all right. Ditto the Purls. Ditto everyone in Comfort.

"Things are pretty bad here, Stanley. Your news spread all over town." She waited hopefully for his reaction. *I'm worried about you, Megan. I'll come home if you need me.*

"Oh Lord. I'm toast there. I can never go back. I'll be crucified."

Megan closed her eyes. He wouldn't change. Vera had never taught him and Megan had never demanded. She'd toiled making life comfortable for everyone else, never saying, *Enough. My turn.* Her mother had done the same. So had Vera. How many other women? Was that the driving force behind Victoria's leaving David and writing the book? Too many years of isolated martyrdom and then the explosion, *you bastard, what about me?* Victoria regretted that explosion now.

"Megan, let's move away from Comfort. You and me and the kids. Start over somewhere."

She took two quick steps toward the middle of the room, said the first thing that came into her head. "What about your mother?"

"I don't think she'd leave. Comfort has been her home her whole life."

"Yours too."

"Yeah, but I'm not tied to it the way she is. I've been thinking." She heard him moving. Turning over in bed? He slept in boxers and she pictured his familiar strong body, white hotel sheets emphasizing the deep gold of his skin more than their beige ones at home. "I have a bunch of clients close by here. The town is really nice, larger than Comfort and a lot going on. Real estate isn't too bad either, we could get a good down payment by selling our house. What do you say?"

"What about . . . her?"

"Mom?"

She grimaced. "No, *her.*"

"Megan." He used his gentle teacher voice. "I made a vow to Genevieve, too."

Right. How selfish of her.

"The kids will like it here. I found a house that needs some work, but it has a pool. They'd love that. The schools are good . . ." He was pleading in that sexy, charming way he used to persuade her to do what he wanted. The way he'd pleaded with her not to leave with her family after high school, to stay in Comfort. He'd marry her, they'd have a boatload of kids and live well. He'd get a good job and spoil her like crazy. "Just you and me and the kids. We could start over, Megan."

She moved away from the window, sank down on the bed. What were her other options?

"Megan? You still there, sweetheart?"

"Yes."

"I love you. You know I love you." He sounded close to tears. "That has never ever changed."

"I know." She let herself fall back, stared at the ceiling. Moving with Stanley to another town, where nobody knew the Big Secret. She and Stanley would still be together for the kids, who'd be protected from rumors and slander, the inevitable fallout here. Megan wouldn't have to worry about earning enough money to make it on her own. The children wouldn't suffer from her breaking up the family. A new life.

Except it would be the old one in a new place.

"Let me think about it." She knew what her answer would probably be; she just couldn't say it yet. She wanted to pretend for a little while that she was like her father, believing the world held boundless possibilities. Like Fiona, forced into a new life, making hard choices with the world at her feet.

A childhood memory resurfaced, of a storm forecast to hit their town—which one, where? Mississippi? Florida? She didn't remember. Just that the sun was still shining but her mother had been hard at work preparing the house and yard for the strong winds expected with the rain. Megan had been huddling inside, small and scared, while Mom was out closing the shutters. Bang. Bang. Bang. One by one they swung shut, cutting back the light in the house until it was safe and protected from the gale to come, but dark and airless and still.

God protect her from having closed all her shutters.

"Tell you what, Megan, have Mom watch the kids and you come here for a couple of days. It'll be just the two of us at this motel. We'll have a second honeymoon, you and me, and I can show you around Reidsville, you can see the town for yourself. Would you like that?"

A tear rolled from the corner of her eye, across her temple and landed in her ear, cold and annoying, like the wet willies Lolly loved to torture her siblings with. A second honeymoon, for the rebirth of a dying marriage. "I'll see if I can manage it."

"I miss you, sweetheart." He spoke with passion. "I want us to be together again. Without you . . . I'm only half here."

She said good night, shut off the phone, tried to sit up but couldn't find the energy. Without her he was only half there. Which half? Did Genevieve get the part with the manly bits or could Megan have that one?

The giggles started. She put a hand over her mouth to stop the noise, snorted and teared until she realized there was nothing funny about the situation. Two wives, one husband who claimed to need them both. Even Calum had chosen, Gillian over Fiona. If Megan pushed Stanley to choose, would he do the same? Genevieve's Gillian over Megan's Fiona? She couldn't risk the ultimatum until she was sure she could live with the outcome.

Propped on her elbows she tossed the phone onto the pillow in disgust. So, what now? She should go spend the days with Stanley. Her first responsibility was to patch up the marriage, for the kids' sakes if nothing else. She could arrange to have Vera babysit or cash in on sympathetic friends' offers to take the children for sleepovers when things got too much. She could see Reidsville. Maybe a new beginning would work.

She sighed, thinking of Fiona and Gillian's story, how their mutual pain helped draw them together emotionally after Calum's death. Two women who loved the same man.

Megan sat the rest of the way up, feeling that strange combination of excitement and dread from considering a difficult decision.

Elizabeth had offered to come with her if she went. Megan could ask to be dropped at Stanley's hotel afterward. It would only be an hour or so out of the way back to Comfort from Roxboro. Maybe Elizabeth wouldn't mind the detour. Genevieve might not want to see Megan, nothing might come of their meeting, the idea could be completely crazy, but it was something Megan could *do*.

She was finally fed up with sitting back and letting life happen.

* * *

"Okay, I think we're ready." Megan put her overnight bag in the trunk of Elizabeth's rental car and slammed the lid. She hadn't packed much. A couple of clean shirts, shorts, and for the two days she'd spend with Stanley in the motel, the red lace lingerie he'd given her years earlier. She wasn't really excited at the prospect of wearing it—if for no other reason than she thought it made her look like a pudgy over-the-hill stripper—but when you got to spend alone time with your husband for the first time in a decade plus, she supposed sexy underwear was the thing to bring.

She turned to her kids, hugged Lolly first. "Bye, sweetie. You're in charge, okay?"

"Why can't we come?" Jeffrey pouted at his mother. It seemed unbelievable, but the nights, weeks and years had come and gone since Lolly arrived squalling, into Megan's shocked stupor over Stanley's dual life, and Megan hadn't ever managed to go anywhere without kids in tow, even for a girls' overnight locally.

"You'll have a great time with Grandma."

"I'm going to let you gorge yourself with candy and play computer all night long." Vera hugged Jeffrey to her.

"Really?" Jeffrey's eyes grew wide with bliss.

"Not exactly." Megan pulled her second daughter toward her, held her tight and kissed the top of her head, which she wouldn't be able to do much longer without a stool. "Bye Deena, you be good. I know you will be."

"Why 'not exactly,' Mom?" Jeffrey had extracted himself from Grandma's arms and was back at Megan's side.

"You'll have a sleepover at Michael's house tonight, Jackson's tomorrow and Curtis's the next day. You'll hardly notice I'm gone."

"I don't know. I think I will notice."

She gathered him in for a fierce hug she made sure wasn't longer than the ones she gave his sisters, tousled his hair and got into the car, as anxious to get going as she was anxious over leaving her children.

Two nights ago in the wee hours, she made up her mind to follow Elizabeth's suggestion and go on this crazy trip. In the morning, she'd cleared the details with Elizabeth, who was enthusiastic as always, then summoned all her courage to call information for Stanley's other home number in Roxboro. And if that took courage, then it made sense that she sat for long minutes on the bed with the phone in one hand, the number in the other, unable to make herself dial, thinking back to high school in Portland, Maine, when she had a killer crush on Jeff Huskins and could barely bring herself to call him on the harmless pretext of getting a math assignment.

Finally the prospect of the kids' return from a trip to the drugstore for gum—*straight* over and *straight* back she'd told them—spurred her to make the call, then launch herself off the bed and start pacing. Genevieve had picked up after the third ring, her voice deep and slow, changing Megan's image from a strong, dynamic Ella type to a languorous nymph whose full-time job was lounging around in negligees drinking cocktails and oozing sexuality.

The conversation had been brief, to the point, and ten times more awkward than asking Jeff Huskins for math. Genevieve had agreed to her visit, but Megan had a feeling it was more because she was so taken aback at the request than from any desire to meet the other Mrs. Morgan.

Amazingly, Megan hadn't given in to her instinct, which was to tell Genevieve sorry, she'd lost her mind briefly, but it was back now and please forget she ever called.

She buckled her seat belt, waved out the window to her kids. "Call my cell if you need anything, but not if it's to remind you where you put your socks. Bye! Back in a few days!"

"Have a good time." Vera gathered Jeffrey to her. "You'll miss the craft fair judging, but we'll let you know the results when you're back."

"Okay. Bye, everyone! Love you!"

Elizabeth pulled the rental out of the driveway, kids calling good-byes, Jeffrey running after them, waving, until the car picked up speed and left him behind. Downtown they turned off Main Street and joined Highway 140. As they traveled down from the mountains, Comfort lifted away behind them and Megan's spirits lifted with it. She was free. On her own, with highway spinning out in front of her.

"How are you doing? Freaked out or okay?"

"Both." Megan turned to smile at Elizabeth. "It feels wonderful to be going somewhere. Like getting out of jail, much as I love my kids. I get to be a woman again, instead of a mother or wife."

"Yeah, that is really great."

Megan pulled her lace for Sally's dress out of its bag. Elizabeth didn't understand. She got to be a woman anytime she wanted to be. "This was an incredible idea. Thank you."

"Don't thank me yet. Did you sleep last night?"

"Not much. You?"

"I had a dream. *Babcia*, my grandmother again."

Megan wasn't sure she wanted to hear this. Especially if Granny predicted a fiery road crash or duel to the death between Stanley's wives. "What did she tell you this time?"

"Always to pimp my friends." She glanced at Megan ruefully, then back at the road. "I'm serious. She was all somber, shaking her finger at me with this warning voice, 'Elizabeth, Elizabeth' . . . and then that's what she said. 'Pimp your friends!'"

Megan burst out laughing. "Should we stop and pick up some fishnets and black leather for me?"

Elizabeth lifted her hand, let it smack back on the steering wheel. "It really unsettled me. I mean what if my whole journey to comfort turns out to be a completely stupid misinterpretation of nothing, like David said? Then what is this all for?"

"To help me?"

"Help you learn to prostitute yourself?" She looked so miserable, Megan felt a surge of protective sympathy.

"How about to help me see my life more clearly? That's pretty worthwhile. To me anyway."

"You would have done that on your own. So far I've just gotten you into a huge mess, which the trip today could make worse."

"Maybe. You shouldn't give your grandmother all the credit, though. Even if you assigned more meaning to the dream than it deserved, you knew you needed distance from your situation or you wouldn't have jumped on her suggestion."

"I like that interpretation." She looked in the rearview mirror and changed lanes. "Dominique would say I'm running away."

"Have you spoken to him?" Megan turned her work, started on the next row.

"I'm avoiding him. And he's avoiding me." Elizabeth wrinkled her nose. "Maybe I'll figure out what I want before I die. Ya think?"

Megan didn't have an answer for that. She'd died in their house in Comfort with Stanley and hadn't noticed until David started coming by on his visits home and brought her back to some semblance of life. Then Elizabeth, in all her bumbling earnestness, furthered the process. Soon—maybe today?—Megan hoped to complete it.

She tried to enjoy the trip, knitted, watching the mountains flatten to gentle hills, the forests thin and give way to patches of farmland, felt the heat climb and bear down on the car, the humidity creep into the interior in spite of the air-conditioning, making her perspire uncomfortably. Reidsville, where Stanley wanted them to live, wasn't far from here. About an hour northeast, half an hour north of Greensboro where Sally and Foster would move to. Hotter even than Comfort. Megan would melt.

Highway I40 joined with I85; they left both for Route 49 northeast through Prospect Hill and Bushy Fork toward Roxboro. Megan put her knitting away. The lovely suspension of time in the car was nearly over and Megan's tension rose. She'd worn one of her favorite skirts, black flowered rayon that would be too warm in this climate, had fussed with her appearance as if she were going on a date, French-braiding her hair instead of pulling it into a ponytail, wearing muted lipstick and a little mascara. She might as well look her best meeting this Gillian who completed her husband.

By the time they reached Roxboro and turned right on Allgood Street, Megan was ready to hyperventilate. "It's Number One-ten."

The street looked vaguely like theirs in Comfort, the houses similar in style and economic level. Good so far. If he had Genevieve/Gillian in a mansion, Megan would show up to meet Stanley in the motel later tonight wishing she'd brought a weapon.

"There." Megan pointed. Elizabeth slowed and they watched the house growing closer. "That's it."

"Okay, then." Elizabeth put the car in park. They sat staring at the modest colonial, white with forest green shutters. The neighborhood was still enough to look fake, until a calico cat chased a butterfly across the neighbor's lawn. "Well."

"So." Megan giggled, she couldn't help it. What had seemed a good idea at some point was absolutely stupid now and utterly beyond her. "Here we are."

"Yup. We're here all right."

"Okay. We're doing this. One, two, three . . . *go*." Megan picked up her wrapped lace gift and pushed open the door into the horrid sweltering heat. Elizabeth emerged on the other side.

Their doors closed. *Thunk. Thunk.*

And then, unfortunately, there was nothing to stop Megan from walking up the front path meandering through a lawn remarkable for being picture-perfect green next to the neighbors' patchy yellowing grass, and being bordered by expertly varied masses of African daisies, baby's breath, marigolds and snapdragons. Hedges grew in perfect rounds under the front windows; impatiens and larkspur flourished around the bottom of an oak.

His other wife was a gardener too.

On the front step Megan felt herself going faint. "I can't do this. I feel terrible."

"Just press the doorbell and get it over with." Elizabeth touched her arm gently. "It's the heat. Don't forget to breathe."

Megan filled her lungs, lifted her hand and pressed the glowing orange rectangle.

A woman opened the door. Megan took a step back. Not the woman from the photo. Who was this?

"Hello." She had light brown hair pulled back in a ponytail, pretty, bland features, a few extra pounds camouflaged by a blue-and-white floral dress with short sleeves and a full skirt. She looked from Elizabeth to Megan, expression neutral. "One of you must be Megan."

The voice. The voice was the same as on the phone, slow, Southern and rich.

"I'm Megan's friend, Elizabeth. You're Genevieve?"

"Yes." She flicked a nervous glance at Megan, forced a smile. "Come on in."

Megan didn't move. Elizabeth had to give her a gentle shove to get her across the threshold. This couldn't be Genevieve. Genevieve was dark, model-beautiful, voluptuous . . . the Gillian other-half Stanley needed. This woman was no more any of those things than Megan was.

Inside, the house smelled like fresh homemade cookies. Which meant the other Mrs. Morgan must be a baker too.

Genevieve ushered them into her living room with reluctance that made Megan even more uncomfortable. If she didn't want them there, why hadn't she said so?

She answered her own question: because Genevieve was the type to put others' needs ahead of her own, and Megan had needed to come.

That sounded familiar too. But not as familiar as the room's furniture—the type, the quality, even the arrangement. Stanley's same recliner, the very same model, the very same reddish-brown color, with probably the same-shaped butt-depression from him being parked in it. And look! The chair sat in front of an older model Sony TV, almost exactly like theirs. Not too big. Cable connection. No doubt Genevieve was enjoying Megan's old coffeemaker and whatever else Stanley had brought over from his other house.

Interchangeable. Houses, appliances, wives.

This was unbearable.

Cross-stitch on the wall, faded floral rugs. No lace. Thank God no lace. Stanley had to have something to orient him in the morning as to which house he'd woken up in.

Megan took another look at their grudging hostess. If this was Genevieve, who was the woman in Stanley's wallet?

If he had three wives, she was going to kill him. Maybe if Genevieve didn't know about the third woman either, she'd like to help with the murder. Maybe Gillian and Fiona found out Calum had someone else too, so they got together and tossed him off a cliff, then blamed the storm for his death. Megan was starting to see how these things could happen.

"Have a seat." Genevieve gestured to a sofa, which, amazingly, was blue. Megan's was beige. "Would you like some lemonade and cookies? I made them this afternoon."

"Thank you, that would be nice." When Genevieve left the room, Elizabeth shot Megan a wide-eyed look of disbelief and pointed to the recliner, the cross-stitch picture, the old TV.

"I know," Megan murmured.

"Here we go." Genevieve brought in a tray on which she'd put three iced glasses, a pitcher of lemonade and a plate of cookies.

She served her guests and sat on the edge of a gold wingback, clutching her glass as if it were the saddle pommel on a bucking bronco. "Sure is hot today."

"Yes," Megan finally found her voice. "It's cooler in the mountains, where we live."

"Is it?"

Horrible silence while cookies were nibbled, lemonade sipped. Even Elizabeth must be at a loss. This was Megan's show. She had to start it. "I brought you something."

"Oh?" Genvieve looked apprehensive, as if she were afraid Megan had hauled over Stanley's laundry.

Megan stood and crossed to where Genevieve sat, held out the rumpled package, a lace doily she'd done shortly after she'd settled in Comfort, before she married. "A peace offering, I guess."

Still cautious, Genevieve unwrapped the lace. "Oh, thank you. This is lovely."

"Shetland lace," Elizabeth told her. "Megan made it."

"She did? You did?"

"Yes." Megan went back to her seat. "Do you knit, Genevieve?"

"Quite a lot. This is so beautiful." She held it up to the light. "I'd love to know how to do this."

"I'd be happy to teach you." Megan spoke automatically and then wanted to kick herself. The three of them sat frozen, each undoubtedly pondering the absurdity of what she'd just said.

"You know . . ." Genevieve frowned down at the doily. "I'm not sure where to put this. I don't know how Stanley would react."

Elizabeth gave a blast of laughter worthy of Dorene; Megan giggled along with her.

Genevieve looked startled, then gave a small smile, laid the lace on the arm of her chair and stroked it. "So. I made sure the kids would be out when you came . . ."

The expectation was clear. Megan sat up straight, bracing her feet on the floor. "I wanted to meet you."

"Why? I mean why now?"

"Because this situation is . . . no longer tolerable." She heard herself saying the words and nearly scared herself to death.

Genevieve put a hand to the gold cross around her neck, an instinctive gesture which meant she probably wore the necklace all the time. So Stanley could tell his wives apart in the dark? "No longer tolerable?"

"I mean . . ." Megan felt the dizziness coming back and made herself breathe, steady and low. "I don't want to do this anymore. To share him."

Genevieve swallowed, turning paler by the second. "You want me to give him up?"

"No! I'm not—"

"I haven't worked in fifteen years." She darted glances between Elizabeth and Megan, still clutching her throat. "He said I'd never have to again."

"I'm not asking you to give him up."

"Oh." Her hand dropped to her lap; she grabbed it with her other one. "Then . . . why come here?"

"Because this isn't right."

She took in a long, slow breath; looked from Megan to Elizabeth and back with the sad, empty eyes Megan had seen so often in her mirror. "I'm happy with Stanley. He's good and kind, and he cares more than most husbands I see around. My friends are always telling me how wonderful he is, how lucky I am to have him."

Megan could have been listening to a tape recording of her

own rationalizations for the last decade and a half. It sickened her hearing them now. All those wasted years buying Stanley's crap about needing another type of wife to complete him.

"Do your friends know he's got another wife?" Elizabeth asked.

"No. It's not up to them how I choose to live."

"Of course not." Megan wanted to shake Genevieve, tell her to come back to life, that being the walking dead was the worst possible sentence, that there was a world out there beyond the Stanley threshold, and they should both be taking those first steps to reach it.

But looking at Genevieve's blank eyes and worried forehead and fingers anxiously clutching the cross of Jesus again, Megan knew there was no point saying any of it. She wouldn't have listened to anyone either, until she was ready to hear. Least of all her husband's other wife. The most she could do was plant the seed, let Genevieve decide if she'd water it back to life or not.

"I came to get an answer, Genevieve." Megan sent a grateful look to Elizabeth. She'd been so right that Megan would find that answer here. "About why he needed two of us. And meeting you . . . I've gotten that."

Genevieve's eyes grew rounder. "What is it?"

"He *doesn't* need two of us. He's lazy and greedy." She put her lemonade down before her shaking hand made her spill. "Now I'm just asking why I put up with this for so long. Why I was too scared to question his selfishness, why I made myself too blind to see it for what it was."

"Please." Genevieve jumped from her chair as if it had caught fire. "I can't listen to this. I'm sorry."

"You should listen," Elizabeth said. "He's taking advantage of both of you."

"No." Genevieve shook her head. "It's not like that."

It was exactly like that. "You can marry Stanley for real. With my blessing. I'm . . . leaving him."

"Megan!" Elizabeth jumped up from the couch and pumped her fist. "Yes! You are *woman*!"

Megan started laughing, unable to believe what she'd just said. Her mouth had opened, the words had come out. She wasn't even sure it was true. Yet.

Genevieve stared at Elizabeth and Megan as if they were aliens. "What is going on?"

"She's set herself free." Elizabeth laughed jubilantly. "If you were smart, you'd do the same. Dump the cheating bast—"

"Elizabeth." Megan held her hand up, a stop signal. Genevieve wasn't ready. Who knew if she ever would be? Sometimes people stayed dead their whole lives.

"This is so . . . I'm not ready for this change." A tear rolled down Genevieve's pink cheek. "What will he do? Move back in here? What if he needs someone else again?"

"I wish I knew what to tell you." Megan looked into her exhausted, dull eyes and knew she had to help this woman. Somehow. "Forgive me. It was selfish of me to come."

"Does Stanley know you're here?"

"No, but I'll see him tonight and tell him I met you, if that's okay."

"Yes." Her voice came out a husky whisper. "I don't want to lie to him."

Elizabeth snorted. "Why not? He lies to you."

"No." Genevieve shook her head; another tear rolled down her face. "He was honest with me from the beginning."

"He told you he was married?"

"Yes." She wiped her tears. "He told me. And that he had an

arrangement with his wife—with you, which meant I could be part of his family honestly."

Megan inhaled sharply. A buzzing started in her ears. She no longer felt faint, but flushed with extra blood in her head, in her cheeks, behind her eyes. This much she could do for Genevieve now, though she wouldn't be grateful. Not yet. "Five years into our marriage, when I was pregnant with our first child, I was going through some papers and found one referencing your house, which he'd filed there by mistake. He never told me. There was no arrangement."

Genevieve turned pale, put her hand to her chest. "Why did you tell me that? Why did you come here?"

Megan pulled a scrap of paper from her purse and a stubby pencil, and wrote down her cell number on it. "Take this. When you get over the shock, if you need to talk, please call me."

"Why are you doing this?"

Megan wasn't sure what "this" she was referring to, liberating her with the truth or destroying her pleasant illusions? Probably both.

"Because you deserve to know who you married." She gave the paper an insistent shake toward Genevieve, who'd made no move to take it. "Because I know what it's like to feel so completely isolated in this bizarre situation. Because I can be an honest friend to you."

Genevieve took the paper as if she were moving underwater.

Megan thanked her for the lemonade and cookies, said good-bye and followed Elizabeth down the flower-bordered path, looking back once to find the door already closed.

In the car, Elizabeth started the engine, then turned, beaming. "You rock."

"Thank you for coming with me. I couldn't have done that without you." She rummaged in her purse with shaking hands. The fallout was just hitting, but if she waited until the shock was over, this call would be so much harder. For once, she was cleanly angry, with no guilt or regret, not at Genevieve, not at Elizabeth, not even at herself, for a change, for being so weak as to put up with Stanley's betrayal.

"Elizabeth." She pulled her cell phone out of her purse. "I'm going to call my husband. It's going to be ugly."

"Oh goody. Do you want me to wait before we start driving?"

"No, you're fine. I just have to do this right away before I lose my nerve." She didn't think she would. Her declaration of independence might have been impulsive, but it felt now as if the truth of wanting to leave Stanley had been hiding behind a locked barricade and once she'd said the simple phrase, *I'm leaving him*, the lock clicked magically open and the feelings poured out.

His number connected. She was shaking so much she was starting to get dizzy again and had to remind herself—again—to breathe.

"Hey, Megan. You on your way?"

"Not anymore."

"What happened?" His voice was gentle with concern. "Are you all right?"

"I stopped by to see Genevieve this morning in Roxboro."

A choked sound made with vocal cords cut silent by shock.

Megan braced herself for the lies, the justifications, even for his anger. Then decided she wasn't going to wait around for any of it. "Just one question, Stanley. What part of you can this very sweet and pleasant clone of me fill that I can't?"

More silence. She started laughing, sick, painful laughter

that hurt her throat. "Oh, I lied, I have another question. And boy, it feels good to be the one lying this time."

"Megan . . ."

"Who's the woman in your wallet? Brunette, sexy lips, big eyes, lots of makeup . . ."

In the corner of her eye, she saw Elizabeth's wide-open mouth of horror.

"Hey, now wait." His disappointed schoolteacher voice. "Why were you going through my wallet?"

She laughed harder. How was it that she could see him so clearly all of a sudden? "Are you married to her, too?"

"*No.*"

"What, she turned you down?" She waited for his answer, watching Route 49 go by on its way to I85, which would change to I40, then mountains, Comfort, and in the not-distant future, a new life somewhere else that would belong to her.

"She's a woman I—"

"You know, what? I changed my mind. I don't want to know. I really don't, because it doesn't matter. I thought it was a picture of Genevieve. All these years, I thought at least some part of me understood and accepted that I wasn't enough for you, that you needed this other glamourous Ella-type as well, and I put up with it. But the woman in your wallet isn't Genevieve." Her laughter turned brittle. She prayed to God she wouldn't cry. "Genevieve is just another Fiona."

"Megan . . . sweetheart. Look, just come up here and we'll talk this all out. Everything's ready, I have a reservation for the two of us for dinner at this really nice steakhouse. I haven't taken you out in way too long. We'll talk about it, I'll explain the whole situation, which I swear is totally innocent." He chuckled unconvincingly. "In fact, you'll probably laugh when you find out—"

"I'm not coming, Stanley." Time seemed to stop while she thought of more words she didn't have the courage to say, then took a deep breath to say them anyway. "And . . . I want a divorce."

Beside her Elizabeth let out a silent shriek and pumped her fist in the air. That, and the sound of her own voice still in her ears, were the only proof that she'd actually spoken.

"Megan . . . honey." His voice dropped. "You're just angry now, you don't know what you're saying."

"Yes. I do."

"No, no. Drive up here. We'll talk about it."

"Elizabeth's taking me home now."

"Elizabeth." His voice rose bitterly. "She put you up to this? God I knew it had to be something like that. You'd never turn your back on me by yourself."

"Why not?"

"Because you're not like Elizabeth, Megan. You don't put yourself before everyone else, your needs before everyone else's."

"Nope. That's your job." She was so angry she could barely speak, as if all the anger from all the years putting up with his self-indulgence was hitting her now. This was her explosion, her very own *When Women Rule*. Only she wrote hers honestly, and she wouldn't regret leaving Stanley.

"What will you do? How will you live? You need me." He drew the words out, at his most earnestly seductive. "You need me to love you, Megan, and to take care of you, my sweetheart, and to be there for you."

"Half the time." Some part of her said it wasn't fair to him, that she should have been stronger at the beginning, let him know then the situation wasn't acceptable, insisted he leave Genevieve or she'd leave him. But it was too late for hindsight; she was only going to look forward now. "As for me needing you, I finally figured out it's the other way around, Stanley. It took me fifteen years to realize it. You can't make it without me, or you wouldn't have another Megan set up here in Roxboro."

"That's not true and you know it." His standard defense when he was running out of arguing room. "How can you manage on your own?"

"I won't be on my own, Stanley. I have my father and his new wife, and a lot of really good friends." She hung up quietly, turned the phone off, knowing he'd call again. Ahead of her there would be more. Plenty more. At times unbearably more. But this was enough for today.

"Wow. Wow!" Elizabeth banged on the steering wheel and let out a war whoop that was much too loud for the car. "You are awesome, you are *incredible*."

Tears came. Megan laughed uncertainly through them, not seeing well, still trembling, still breathing too fast. "I hope so. Because all I feel right now is really manic, really relieved . . . and really, really scared."

Chapter Fifteen

*E*lizabeth drove down Route 49 humming, feeling alive and excited and happy to be where she was, better than she had in years. No, that wasn't right. She'd been happy plenty of times, but this happiness felt more powerful, more stable and real.

Megan was going to leave Stanley, get herself out of that hell-of-a rut and live. Finally, Elizabeth had done something here other than make things worse for people.

Maybe that was the difference in this happiness. She'd brought it to someone else and it reflected back on her. She looked over at Megan, who was knitting at approximately the speed of light, beautiful in her skirt and blouse, hair French braided, color high.

"How are you doing, Megan?"

"I feel like I've launched myself out of a plane with no parachute." She gave a shaky laugh. "Leaving Stanley with no job, no degree, no experience—"

"Are you kidding me? You're gifted many times over, you have tons of options. You could landscape people's garden and yards, you could cater parties, open a bakery, you could make *lace,* for God's sake. I would *kill* to have your talent."

"Come on."

"I'm serious. I'll get friends to bid for your next lace work. David can hire you to do something with his ugly yard. You can cater Sally's wedding."

Megan laughed, but did slow her crazed fingers somewhat. "You're going to take charge of my career now?"

"Sure, I'll be your manager. No, your *pimp*! Just like grannie told me to. I charge a very reasonable commission."

"You don't let reality get in your way much, do you, Elizabeth?"

"Absolutely not!" Elizabeth pounded the steering wheel, feeling as if she were on the verge of figuring out everything in the universe. "Reality is vastly overrated. Look at my *babcia*'s dream. It might or might not have meant anything, but because I believed it did I came here and changed my life and yours. And your mother's story had huge power over your interpretation of the situation with Stanley's other wife."

"Her story doesn't apply anymore." Megan sounded almost wistful. "Genevieve turned out to be another Fiona."

Elizabeth drove on, mind buzzing. Everything felt right, which meant they must be looking at something the wrong way. She glanced again at Megan, knitting beautiful lace, her green eyes troubled.

There it was.

"*You're* the Gillian character." She cackled triumphantly. "You brought lace to miserable Fiona back there."

"She's not—"

"The real Gillian is guiding you, like *Babcia* is guiding me. She led you to your Fiona in her time of need. Even Dorene said she felt Gillian through the lace, remember? And you're ten times more intuitive than she is."

"Elizabeth—"

"Best of all, now that you're at a crossroads, the spirit of Gillian can be the one to—"

"Elizabeth!" Megan smacked her on the shoulder.

"Ow." She cracked up. "Okay, okay, sorry, I'm just so excited."

"Really? I couldn't tell." Megan rolled her eyes. "That's a nice idea, but for one minor point. Your grandmother was a real person, and Gillian wasn't."

"Oh." Elizabeth wrinkled her nose. "Okay, but . . ."

"Give it up." Megan put her busy hands down, leaned back and blew out a breath. "It's a beautiful concept, but life doesn't fall into place quite that neatly."

"I wish it—" A billboard caught her eye and she gasped and swerved onto the shoulder. "Oh my God. Look!"

"What?" Megan clutched the dashboard. "What is it?"

"*Truffles!*" Elizabeth came to a stop that threw her and Megan forward, then back again. "*Perigord* truffles. Those are the French ones, the best quality. Can that be right?"

"Geez, Elizabeth, you nearly gave me a heart attack over fungus?" Megan glanced at the sign, calming hand to her chest. "Yes, I've read about them. I guess our climate is right."

"Grown right here, on that farm? I can't believe it. Wait until Dominique finds out."

"Wouldn't a chef know already?" Megan spoke gently. "I mean if *I* do . . ."

"You're right. He must." She wrinkled her nose at the colorful sign. This was important. This fit in somewhere. She knew it. She felt it. "Do you mind if we stop?"

"Go for it."

Elizabeth read the billboard again: *take the next right, go five miles, then follow signs.* She got back on the road, blood pumping crazily. Truffles. Dominique's heart's desire here in his own backyard all the time. This was too incredible to be a coincidence. *Babcia* led Elizabeth to Comfort for Megan and led her here for herself.

They drove the five miles, and yes, there was the sign showing a picture of fields and trees with a big red arrow, *Hellmer's Farm. Finest truffles in the New World.*

Left turn, then bumping down a shorter road through fields of traditional crops, tobacco among them according to Megan—Elizabeth wouldn't know a tobacco plant if it rolled into a cigarette and smoked itself—another turn, then ahead, a white two-story farm on the side of a hill.

Close by the house Elizabeth parked and pulled off her seat belt, adrenaline racing. "Want to come with me?"

"Sure." Megan pushed open her door to the blast of heat, still carrying the lace. "But I need another ball of wool, would you open the trunk?"

"Okay." Elizabeth pulled the release lever and walked around to the back of the car, gazing at the house, hand up to shield her eyes from the hot sun. Beautiful house, shaded by large, leafy oaks. A wonderful steep roof interrupted by dormers, a latticework balcony on the second floor, a matching porch on the first. An old house, probably early nineteenth century.

She wanted one just like it. She wanted to live in a house like this, on a farm like this. The certainty of it nearly buckled her knees.

The front door opened; a friendly-looking middle-aged woman in jeans and a pink cotton sweater emerged and came toward them. "Hi there."

"I saw your sign." Elizabeth gestured toward the road, bursting with all the questions she wanted to ask. "I hope it's all right we came by. I'm Elizabeth Detlaff. This is Megan Morgan."

"Hi, Elizabeth. Hi, Megan."

"Nice to meet you." Megan smiled, lace cascading from her needles halfway down her thighs.

"I'm Clair Hellmers." She watched Megan fold the lace. "What can I do for you?"

"My boyfriend is a chef in New York, Dominique DuParc."

"DuParc?" The woman tore her eyes from Megan. "Sorry, don't know that name."

"He has a restaurant and show, *French Food Fast,* on the Food Channel." She dug in her purse for one of his cards. "He's developing a restaurant menu around truffles, so I stopped to see what you have. I know yours aren't in season now, but maybe you have some flash frozen I could let him try?"

"We like getting to know chefs." She spoke distractedly, took a step toward Megan, who was about to zip up her case. "Excuse me. Megan, was it?"

Megan turned from the trunk clutching her new ball of wool. "Yes?"

"Is that knitted lace?"

"Oh." Megan looked startled. "Yes."

"Shetland lace." Elizabeth stepped back to give Clair better access. "Megan has it all over her house. Curtains, doilies, tablecloths, all incredible quality, all handmade. Show her, Megan."

Megan gave her a look, then unfolded the panel again. Elizabeth smiled back sweetly. Megan had the talent, Elizabeth had the chutzpah. Together they could be a small business waiting to happen.

"Our daughter is getting married at Christmas. She saw a lace veil in a shop once, with hearts and roses on it, and is having trouble finding one like it." Clair waited eagerly for Megan to unfold the panel, pushing back a lock of gray hair the hot breeze had dislodged. "Oh, that is exquisite."

"It's for a friend's wedding dress."

"Karen would be thrilled." She reached for it. "Do you mind? I just washed my hands."

"Go right ahead." Megan was deliberately ignoring Elizabeth's big-eyed exaggerated excitement. When they got back into the car, Elizabeth was going to enjoy a nice fat told-ya-so. Pimp her friends? No one could argue her out of the workings of destiny now. Not even David.

"This is incredible." Clair examined the work reverently. "I'd love to commission one from you. Do you sell your work?"

Elizabeth lifted her eyebrows and nodded at Megan behind Clair's back. This was the first bit of her leaving-Stanley parachute.

"Yes." Megan's voice was small but firm. "I do."

"How much?"

"I—"

"Eight hundred dollars." Elizabeth grinned, enjoying Megan's look of horror. About time she figured out her value.

"Hmm." Clair held the piece up. The white lace stood strong and clean against the green background of the rolling hills, wind ruffling it gently, sun throwing dappled patterns through the oak. "Did you design this or is it traditional?"

"I designed it. But it was traditional for Shetland women to knit their own designs. So I guess it's both."

Clair lowered the lace, folded it carefully. "May I take a picture of this and call my daughter? I'm pretty sure this is the style she's been searching for."

Megan nodded, looking as if she couldn't decide whether to celebrate or cry. Elizabeth wanted to throw her arms around her, tell her everything was going to be fine, wonderful and happy-ever-after now. Megan had taken the leap, the arms of the universe were rising up to catch her. How many times had *Babcia* told Elizabeth that was how the world worked, and how often had Elizabeth sneered at her? When she got settled, she was going to call her mother and invite her to visit. Or maybe she'd go back to Milwaukee. It was time for a reconciliation with her past.

"Come on up." Clair led the way into the house, which was cool and smelled of coffee and pine, then into the kitchen whose white counters and cabinets emphasized the fresh airy space, and whose retro appliances fit the old and the new perfectly. Elizabeth turned, absorbing the light and comfort of the room, the glimpse of green hills out the window.

This was what she wanted. A farmhouse in the country. She could see herself living here, quietly, simply, surrounded by beauty, growing her own food, raising an animal or two, living close to the land like her Milwaukee ancestors on Jones Island, part of a real community.

The certainty was quiet, simple, nothing like the adrenaline rush of her business ideas, nothing like the impulsive thrill of taking on a new challenge. It was as if she'd been peeling back layers over the last few weeks and was finally able to gain access to her true core.

If Dominique wanted part of this new life, she'd take him, make whatever compromises necessary so they'd both be happy. If not, she'd find a way to do it herself. Use her inheritance for a down payment. She was meant to be here. *Babcia* had known all along.

"Have a seat." Clair gestured to the natural wood table, opened her cell phone and took a picture. "I'll just be a second."

"No problem." Elizabeth smiled politely until she left the room, then opened her mouth in a silent scream of excitement.

"I can't believe this is happening today, already, just now," Megan whispered. Her eyes were shining, cheeks pink; she looked ready to take on the world.

"It's a sign that you did the right thing." Elizabeth squeezed her hand on the table. "This is enough to make me believe in fate all over again."

Megan nodded gravely. "Maybe Clair will have my fishnets and black leather."

They were still giddy when Clair returned, holding the cell triumphantly aloft. "She loves it. If it's okay I'll give her your number and the two of you can talk details."

"Absolutely." Megan scrawled her number on the pad Clair proffered, while Elizabeth started mentally designing business cards. She wouldn't just be handing out Dominique's anymore.

Clair poured them coffee, offered raisin oatmeal scones she'd baked that morning and homemade strawberry jam. Elizabeth ate in ecstasy. Someday the jam would be hers, the scones made with her own hands.

While they sat, she questioned Clair about hazelnut trees and oaks, inoculated roots and fungus, dogs vs. pigs, summer vs. winter, whole and pieces, oils and canned, fresh and jarred, getting more and more excited.

If Dominique decided he could do business here, they could buy a place, plant truffles of their own, retire here when he was tired of the race. They could split living in North Carolina and New York. Maybe Dominique could open a second restaurant in North Carolina, specializing in local truffles, open only during the short season, December to March, leaving his New York restaurant in charge of others while he was gone.

She could be instrumental in helping Dominique settle his career the way he wanted, at the same time living her life the way she wanted. And this close by, she could still help Megan and keep in touch with the Purls until she planted her own roots, maybe by starting her own knitting group. Or book group. Or art group. Something.

Finally, Clair hinted she had other things to do and Megan hinted they'd better be back on the road, and Elizabeth reluctantly agreed. She bought a bottle of truffle oil and vacuum-packed whole truffles, then promised she'd be in touch in December when the local harvest began. Dominique could use this to his advantage, *Buy American; We Support Our Truffles*. A marketer's dream.

"Thank you for letting us drop by." Elizabeth gave Clair a hug, probably surprising the life out of her. "I'll have Dominique call you when he's back in the country."

"We're hoping for a good harvest this next season so we can get him a good deal. More and more people are growing truffles locally. I imagine the price will eventually come down."

"Wonderful. Thank you!" Elizabeth bounced back to the car, waited impatiently for Megan to follow, then pulled away from the house, bumped to the five-mile stretch of road before they reached the highway again, and pulled to a stop on the shoulder. "I can't wait to call Dominique, do you mind?"

"Not at all. I'll take a walk."

"In this heat? I don't mind if you stay."

"Whew. Thanks." Megan fanned herself. "I'm not made for this climate. And thank you for pimping my lace."

"I told you it would sell. Clair's daughter will get married in your veil, *everyone* will want to know where she got it, and you're on your way. You can get choosy and start charging thousands, especially for big-city customers." Elizabeth opened her cell. "I'll hurry to make this call, and we can get you back to your kids."

Megan's face fell, and Elizabeth wished she hadn't said anything. Lolly, Deena and Jeffrey would have to find out about their father's other family, about Megan leaving him. Rough times ahead.

Elizabeth dialed, feeling somewhat less fizzy. Dominique picked up on the second ring. *"Bonjour, ma chérie."*

"You won't believe this. Guess where I am."

"Where have you gotten to now, Elizabeth?" He sounded annoyed. "What about our koi?"

She rolled her eyes. "The doorman is feeding them. Since when are you so concerned about fish?"

"Since when are you all over the country?"

"I'm not all over the country, I'm still in North Carolina." She shook her head woefully at Megan. When Dominique was like this she wanted to slug him. "And you still haven't guessed where I—"

"Elizabeth, it's late here, I am very tired."

"Okay." The bubbles in her fizzy mood were popping in bunches. "I'm right near a truffle farm."

"Oh, yes?" Distracted, he wasn't listening.

"Black Perigord truffles, the real deal."

"Elizabeth. The real Perigord is in France. It is not in North Carolina. I know there are people trying to grow them there, but they can't—"

"*Listen* to me. Just listen. Because I have something important to say."

"Okay."

She was so surprised at his backing down she nearly forgot how to continue. "They *are* growing them here. I met one of the farmers and bought one to try. Maybe these truffles are better than the summer ones in England, or better for your menu at least. The whole patriotic angle would work really well. I bet most people don't know truffles are grown in this country. They'd eat them up. Literally and figuratively."

He forced a chuckle. "So what, you are going to run my business now?"

"That's not what I'm saying."

"Sorry, *ma petite*. I am grumpy today. I'm sure your truffles are very nice. Buy me one and we can eat it together. When are you coming back to New York?"

She stared at the green hills surrounding her. The air in the car was becoming stifling. "When are you back?"

"Next week, Monday. The first of August."

"Okay." She twisted her lip. There was so much still to learn and do here. Megan would need her. "We have to talk."

"About what? You'll be back by then, yes?"

She turned the ignition key, pushed the A/C fan up to high. Cool air started flowing again, but didn't stop her perspiring. "I'll come back for a while. I have a friend here who needs me."

Megan looked up from the knitting she'd been doing to pretend she wasn't listening, and smiled warmly.

"*Elizabeth*." Dominique sighed heavily. "We have a life together in New York. You have a business you're supposed to start. The fabrics, remember?"

"I'm . . . not so sure about that now." She winced, expecting the exasperated noise French people did better than anyone else on the planet. "You were right. I'm not much of a designer. And you're right, I've been trying to force myself into businesses I had no aptitude for. And I haven't built a life of my own, I just lived yours, you were right about that too. But I've figured it out now, for real. I love it here. This is where I belong. This is where I want to—"

"How long are you going to do this running away?" His voice was so loud Elizabeth took the phone from her ear. Megan could probably hear him. "All your life you haven't been able to settle!"

"I know. I know. But I'm ready now, Dominique." She wanted to scream at the irony. Girl who cried wolf asking him to believe her one more time. "I know what I want. This time I really do."

"North Carolina." His voice dropped, broke.

"And you, Dominique. I want you. I just don't want to live your life. I want our life. And part of 'ours' has to belong to me before I can buy into it. I can't live in New York anymore, not all year long. I need what I've found here."

Silence while she prayed he wouldn't give up, hang up. Then the sound of a long patient exhale. "Okay. So now what?"

"I'll come back to New York and we can talk it out, find a compromise."

"And marriage? Is that still on the table?"

"I think . . . that can work, yes." She made it through the sentence with only one nervous squeak.

"Elizabeth." He pronounced it the French way, *eh-leez-a-bette*, and the surprised warmth in his voice steadied a large portion of her nerves. "I am actually speechless."

She smiled, not scared, not wanting to back out, still ready to move forward. This was going to work. "Your part of the compromise is not spending all day trying to take over the food universe. You need time to help me raise our kids."

"My God, whatever you're smoking down there, keep at it." He laughed his big infectious Dominique laugh, which could cause an entire crowd to go silent looking for the source. "Okay, *ma chérie*. We'll talk. I want you to be happy. Come home soon. *Je t'aime beaucoup*."

"I will. And, um." Elizabeth glanced at Megan, who'd started humming politely. ". . . same here."

She hung up, face hot, fizzy again with joy and, oddly, relief.

"You okay, Elizabeth?"

"Yes." She exhaled hard. "I think I'm really fine."

"You'll marry him?"

She turned, grinning, and pointed to Megan's lace. "Will you make me a wedding shawl? Cater the ceremony? Landscape my yard?"

Megan laughed, tears starting, and Elizabeth realized how strange it was for Megan to be ending a marriage and Elizabeth planning to begin one, all on the same day. Yin and yang.

She put the car in gear, moved out onto the road. "Let's go home."

The second the words were out of her mouth, happy tears started. Not her home. No matter how long she stayed, how much she grew to love Megan and the kids—and tolerate

Vera—the house in Comfort would never be her home. The condo in New York was Dominique's. The apartment in Boston had been Alan's. The duplex in Milwaukee her mother's.

But the life she would build here with Dominique, the degree she earned, the career she started, the friends she made, all those would belong to her. And all those put together would be the comfort *Babcia* wanted her to find.

Chapter Sixteen

The next day the clouds have blown past, but the village of Eshaness is somber and still. Crofters wake to shame, to grim acknowledgment of what they've forced on Gillian, driven by sadness and anger and whiskey. Fiona goes through the long hours of sunshine numb with grief. At night she cannot sleep, finally gives up, wraps a thick woolen shawl around her and stokes the fire, takes up her knitting, trying to focus on anything but the nightmare images crowding her mind. After an hour, three hours, three minutes, she doesn't know, doesn't care, the door to the house opens so quietly Fiona can only tell someone is there by the sudden freshening of the air.

Alarmed, she turns, half expecting Calum, even knowing from having said her final wrenching goodbyes earlier, that his body is laid to rest at home.

It is Gillian, still dressed in white trimmed with lace, a dress fit for a bride. She carries a small sheepskin bag, smiles at Fiona's shocked face, and comes closer to the fire, eyes haunted and dark. It's then Fiona notices she's shivering and damp. Can ghosts be cold?

Fiona starts to speak, but Gillian shakes her head, puts a finger to her lips and points to the enclosed beds where Fiona's family sleeps. She sits near the fire, opens the bag and passes over wool such as Fiona has never handled, soft like rabbit fur, exquisitely even in color, nearly white, a remarkable, impossibly delicate thread, thousands upon thousands of yards from a single ounce. In spite of her pain and misgivings, in spite of questions about how Gillian can have survived her leap off the cliff, or whether she did indeed survive, Fiona feels a thrill of pleasure.

Gillian nods, pleased by Fiona's reaction. She reaches into the bag again and pulls out two pairs of tiny silver needles, smooth and strong as steel. For the rest of that night and for many, many more nights after, Gillian appears and teaches Fiona to knit in a way Fiona never dreamed she could. Hours they spend, and though words are rarely spoken, a bond grows. Together they are knitting the most beautiful wedding shawl Fiona could ever imagine.

For a time after the night of tragedy, villagers claim to catch sight of Gillian back among them. The same rumors of her first weeks return. Some insist she still swims naked every morning by Eshaness's highest point where the lighthouse will stand, where Calum's body was found. Boys patrol its cruel drop—for the safety of the town, they say. Wives pull equally defense-minded husbands back home to their duties. Eric Manson reports seeing her late at night at the spot where she fled the mob. He called to her, but she shook her head and dived again from the cliff. All he saw below, though he waited several minutes, was a seal floating peacefully through black waters, eyes and sleek fur glinting in the moonlight.

Weeks go by and Fiona and Gillian's lace emerges, swirling with patterns of seas and sky, birds and flowers—Shetland itself captured in the threads. Every night, all night long they knit, Fiona falling into bed just before dawn and waking refreshed mere hours later, as if she has spent the whole night sound asleep. Gillian has powerful magic indeed.

One stitch at a time, the work nears completion. When the shawl is finally finished, Gillian places it gently around Fiona's shoulders and embraces her, lays a soft hand against her cheek before she leaves as quietly as she came the first time and every time after. She never returns. Night after night Fiona waits, but the hours out of bed tell on her, she is no longer able to stay awake without suffering during the day. The full grief of the town's tragedies comes upon her, and she spends miserable months mourning Calum's death, mourning the loss of Gillian, her mysterious rival and friend.

Eventually, though winter is still upon them, though cold and winds whip the islands unmercifully, Fiona's heart knows the birds will soon return, signaling the renewal of springtime, and that spring will bring her a new life. She will leave Eshaness for another city, another island, another country, another world. Wherever she settles, she will meet a fine young man who will love her best of all women. And on her wedding day she will wear the shawl she and Gillian have knitted here in Eshaness during long summer nights. Down the aisle, she will walk to her groom, thinking of a green-eyed, wild-haired, lovely witch named Gillian, who must still be swimming the blue water among the green, treeless islands of Shetland.

Elizabeth drove into Megan and Stanley's driveway, put the car in park, turned off the engine and leaned back against the headrest. Megan sat, unable to move, listening to crickets chirping in the near-darkness. The trip was over. They were home. But getting out of the car meant facing what she'd done and all the pain she'd cause her children and Vera and herself.

She wished God would send down a flashing sign, *Megan, you did the right thing*. Throwing away a decent, peaceful life for what? Instability. Uncertainty. A whole assortment of devils she didn't know.

Door pushed open, she stepped thankfully into the cool air of Comfort, then back to the trunk to haul out her overnight bag. The kids were at friends' houses but Vera would wonder why Megan had come back with Elizabeth instead of staying in Reidsville with Stanley. There was no postponing the show.

"Megan? Who's there?" On cue, Vera's voice from the garden, sounding thick-throated and groggy. Had she been asleep so early?

"Yes, it's me." She handed over Elizabeth's bag and hauled hers into the garden. "Hi, Vera."

"I talked to Stanley." Even in the dim glow reaching her from the back door light it was obvious her eyes were swollen with tears. "He says you left him."

"Yes." She had no idea what else to say, so she stood with her bag, feeling like a schoolgirl facing her headmistress, aware of Elizabeth hovering behind her.

"He wants me to go to him."

"Will you?"

Vera nodded. "Yes. I'll go."

"That's good." Megan was suddenly and desperately tired; the adrenaline she'd summoned for this encounter had given up early. Or maybe she'd run out altogether. "He'll need you."

"He was devastated. I've never heard him like that." Her voice broke. "Is this for real, Megan?"

"Yes." She made herself sound as gentle as she could. "I'm sorry."

Vera took in a long, shuddering breath, let it out with practiced suffering. "John Foley is driving me over in the morning. Stanley asked him to. He's heading to Greensboro anyway."

"Okay."

"David's back, he came looking for you." Vera lifted her soft chin with unmistakable disapproval. "I told him you were on a second honeymoon with Stanley."

"Ah." She couldn't summon excitement about David's being back or annoyance at Vera using irony as a weapon. The part of her brain controlling emotion must have blown a fuse.

"Is he getting back together with his wife?" Elizabeth finally spoke.

"I didn't ask."

"Okay." She sounded disappointed.

Megan wanted bed. Like she'd never wanted anything before.

"I'm leaving early in the morning," Vera said.

"I'll get up and see you off."

"I'd rather just *go*." Her expression softened. "But thank you."

"Anything you want me to put out for you, or—"

"I'll be fine." She turned to go into the house, then stopped. "I'm sorry for the pain Stanley caused you. You know that. Maybe there was something lacking for him here . . ."

Megan gave a short laugh. If Vera wanted to preserve what remained of Stanley's perfect-boy image, she was welcome. Megan had spent years married to the idea that she was somehow at fault. Now she was divorcing that, too.

"Though . . . it doesn't excuse what he did."

"Thanks, Vera."

"Well." She stood uncertainly. "Good night."

Megan walked forward and gave her mother-in-law a hug that lasted longer than she intended, felt more sincere than she expected. "I'm sorry for all this."

"I can't bear what you're doing to your children. I stayed with Rocky for the sake of my son. You girls now . . . you want it all for yourselves." Tears caught up with her, she shook her head and walked into the house.

"Kaboom." Elizabeth stepped near and slung her arm over Megan's shoulders. "Don't listen to her. She just wanted the perfect exit line."

"She found it." Megan closed her eyes. "What if she's right?"

"*He* broke your vows, *he* violated your marriage. You stood it for fifteen years. That's more than most women would do."

"Uh . . ." Megan opened her eyes. "That doesn't sound like a compliment."

"Oh." Elizabeth frowned. "Well, I meant it that way."

"Hey." David's voice out of the darkness over the fence. "I heard the car."

Elizabeth tightened her arm around Megan's shoulders and leaned close. "I'll go upstairs. Come up if you need to talk later."

"Good night, Elizabeth." She hugged her back. Never in a million years could she have imagined that first day standing in the garden with this flaky, exuberant woman, that she'd come to lean on her so hard. "And thank you."

"Don't thank me, thank *Babcia*. And Gillian."

Megan kissed her cheek, watched her make her way over to the garage, then headed toward the fence, head aching, limbs shaky and tight. She didn't want to face David. Not tonight. "Welcome home."

"Same to you." His features were barely visible, but his grin caught the last of the evening light. "I came back to make sure you hadn't been torn apart by the Comfort vultures. Vera said you were with Stanley in Reidsville?"

"I left him."

The grin disappeared. "Left him in Reidsville . . . or left him?"

"I went to visit his other wife this morning." She laughed wearily. "Feels like a week ago already."

"My God, Megan."

"It was Elizabeth's idea. All these years I assumed Genevieve gave him something I couldn't. But she turned out to be me." She shrugged, knowing he'd understand.

"Jesus. The guy is an egomaniac."

"Some of us are drawn to them." She raised her eyebrows. "How are you getting along with yours?"

"Ha." He shook his head. "The answer is we're talking, but I'm not packing up to move out west and she's not packing to move here."

"So now what?"

"I'm here in Comfort for my sabbatical year. Then I go back to Boston. As it was." He sidled closer and nudged her with his shoulder. "Congratulations, you're the one with the big decisions."

"Yeah, thanks."

"None of which you have to make tonight." His voice turned tender. "Get some sleep, Megan. We'll talk later. Whatever crap you have to go through, I'm here. Maybe I'll learn to knit and become a Purl."

She giggled at the thought. "When you're not chasing squirrels."

"You know." He nudged her again, intimate in the darkness, bringing back a lot of memories of a lot of years ago. "I've decided to embrace my squirrels, Megan. They were driving me crazy, and I wasn't fazing them at all."

Megan laughed in the darkness, astounded that she could feel at all happy. "That sounds very Zen and very smart."

"Get some sleep." He put his arm around her, pulled her in to him across the fence. She rested her head briefly on his shoulder, allowing herself a minute of his strength and familiar scent before she had to face the night alone. "Maybe in time we can both allow ourselves to believe in something better, Megan. Something really big and magical and lasting so we won't be alone. And maybe we'll have the courage to go after it. I think we're taking the right first steps."

"I hope so." She lifted her head, stepped reluctantly away from his arm, wishing it could be as easy as the two of them picking up where they left off, but knowing it wasn't what she wanted. Not now. She'd leave Comfort, maybe move east near Elizabeth and Sally, nearer to Genevieve and Stanley so he could see the children often. If she was meant to be with David, that would happen in its own time. "Good night."

"Sweet dreams, Megan."

Back into the dark house she climbed the stairs feeling as if she had weights on her ankles. In her room, she flicked on the lights, stared at her and Stanley's bed for several minutes, then took her bag into Lolly and Deena's room to sleep there. Or try to sleep.

Most of the night she dozed fitfully, waking again and again, blinking through confusion for a second or two each time, before she remembered. She was leaving Stanley. Right or wrong, how would she support herself, what damage would the children suffer, could she really manage alone, and on and on and on.

The slam of a car door woke her a final time, an engine started and pulled away from their driveway. Megan dragged herself out of Lolly's bed, went to the window, pushed aside the curtain and peered out. Vera, gone already, on her way to Stanley's side, first in Reidsville, then who knew. Maybe she'd come back to live in Comfort. Maybe she'd move in with Stanley and Genevieve.

Megan needed to take this one hour at a time.

She crossed into her room, showered quickly, dressed in loose jeans and a yellow cotton sweater, and thudded downstairs.

Welcome to what was destined to be one of the hardest days of her life.

Yawning, she stepped into the kitchen and stopped dead. Balloons, streamers, glittering confetti stars, and a posterboard with huge letters drawn with markers. *CONGRATULATIONS! Love, the Purls.* Signed by each.

Megan stared, feeling sick. This was their idea of a celebration? The dissolution of her marriage? Maybe someday she'd celebrate, but not this soon, and not in this way.

She strode forward, intending to sweep it all into the trash, then she noticed the blue ribbon, the shiny gold plaque, first prize, Comfort Craft fair, and an envelope with her name on it.

The rainbow blanket *won*?

Which of the Purls slept with Roy?

Envelope opened, she read the contents of the letter and sank into a chair, blinking in disbelief. A check for five thousand dollars, made out to Megan.

The Purls had entered the shawl she made for her vow-renewal ceremony, the one Sally would wear at her wedding.

She'd won.

What's more, Addy Baker needed permission to give out her contact information because so many people who'd traveled from Hendersonville and Asheville for the fair had asked where they could get lace.

Megan blinked some more, allowed herself a smile, then a grin and a warm swell of love for her Purls. How she'd miss them.

This was all really hard to take in.

Coffee. She needed coffee. Megan stared again at the check. First thing after breakfast she'd buy herself a new maker, the kind she liked, a machine that would keep her faithful company until the end.

One step at a time, so the uncertainty ahead, bad and good, yin and yang, wouldn't become overwhelming. She needed Elizabeth's *Babcia* to guide her through this, to give her confidence that she could fly off into the murky future and find sunshine.

She needed Gillian.

Coffee brewed, she took her cup outside, wanting to get away from the riotous mess of the kitchen. On the stoop she paused to inhale the garden-scented morning air, benefiting from the suspended animation of having made an enormous decision she didn't have to put into action just yet. The last peaceful sunrise of her old life. She could still pretend the kids were innocently asleep upstairs as usual, Vera in her room, Stanley away on a sales trip.

Down the steps, she saw on the patio table a package, folded note stuck to the top with *For Megan* written in Vera's careless scrawl. Megan's shoulders slumped. End of being able to pretend nothing had changed.

She drew out her chair but didn't sit, set her coffee down carefully, opened the note. *Megan, this came from your father the day you left.* Megan ripped off the paper, rolling her eyes at the way Dad always wrapped packages with enough tape to keep Harry Houdini out. Inside a stained cardboard box. A note from Dad that simply said, *From your mother.* Fighting tears, she lifted the lid, pushed the rustling tissue aside.

Lace.

Megan lifted, unfolded, caught her breath. A wedding shawl, delicate beyond anything she'd ever be able to manage, complicated beyond anything she'd ever be able to imagine, nearly magical in its perfection. Holding it, gazing rapturously, trying to take in the extraordinary details—fans, birds, trees, diamonds, flowers, curling ocean waves—she was swept by emotion, not pain, not joy, but with elements of both added to humbling awe. This was the work of true genius, a lace-knitting Mozart.

Breeze blew; the shawl rippled sensually as if delighted to be freed from the confines of cardboard. A slip of paper fell from its folds, cut with uneven edges from a larger sheet. Megan picked it up and read, read again to make sure she really understood, trying to take in the hope spreading through her for the first time in fifteen years.

On the paper in her mother's unmistakable loopy handwriting: *Wedding shawl, knitted in memory of Calum Jamieson during the long summer nights of 1925 in Eshaness, Shetland, by my grandmother, Fiona Tulloch, and her too-briefly known and long-missed friend, Gillian Halcrow.*

A⁺
AUTHOR
INSIGHTS,
EXTRAS &
MORE...

FROM
**ISABEL
SHARPE**
AND
AVON A

Interview with Author Isabel Sharpe

Q: Your book has a flashback story that takes place on the Island of Shetland in the mid-1920s. Can you tell us how you did your research?

I'm usually not big on research, to be honest. I'd much rather focus on the characters and their stories and emotions. However, this time I was hooked. I probably couldn't have written this book without the Internet, or at least I couldn't have finished it by my deadline! I not only found terrific sites, like the Shetland Museum website, which has archives with amazing pictures from that period, but I also came across references to very helpful books, including *The Last Lighthouse*, by Sharma Krauskopf, about her successful quest to purchase the Eshaness lighthouse being built on Shetland during my story, and *Heirloom Knitting*, by Sharon Miller, an invaluable resource for anyone wanting to knit lace. I even found a movie, *The Edge of the World*, which was filmed on the Shetland island of Foula in 1937, but which took place during the 1920s, and which used native Shetlanders as extras. There was even one quick shot of women knitting lace! I nearly jumped out of my seat with excitement.

Q: Is your story historically accurate?

I did mess with facts a little. There is an area called Eshaness on Shetland, with a lighthouse, but I couldn't find evidence of a town with that name—that is my invention. And I might have pushed it a little having superstitions about witches and selkies and finmen linger as long as the mid-1920s. But they were too good to pass up, and who knows? People do cling to that kind of story. I tried to have mainly the older generation talking about the legends.

Q: Have you ever been to the Shetland Islands?

No, but I'd love to go! At one point I did some research on travel options, thinking it would be the chance of a lifetime, and what better way to write about a place than from firsthand experience? But at the time I checked, it would have cost three thousand U.S. dollars for one person just to get there and back, which is over my travel budget.

Q: How did you get the ideas for the flashback characters?

Oh you're really testing me here, it was a long time ago. Their story came partly from the characters I was working with in the main story, and partly from who they were. Gillian arose as a contrast to Fiona and from the legends of the finmen and the selkie. There's a movie set in Ireland, *The Secret of Roan Inish*, which I stumbled over while writing the book. I'd picked it out because I thought it might appeal to my sons (it didn't, but I loved it!), and then there was all this great stuff about selkies relevant to my book! Serendipity.

Q: Can you tell us more about the finmen?

Fishing, then, as now, is a very dangerous way to make a living. The sea around the Shetland Islands seems to have been particularly difficult due to sudden and severe storms. In earlier, more superstitious days a lot of the losses—boats, people, nets, lines—were blamed on amphibious creatures called fins. The finmen, who resented mortals for competing on their fishing grounds, did whatever they could to cause trouble for them. I guess it was more comforting for Islanders to imagine their loved ones had been snatched by sea people than drowned. And easier to blame bad luck (or maybe carelessness) on some faceless other species.

Finmen were obsessed with silver ("white metal") and loathed the sign of the cross. Fishermen would cut crosses in their floats and sinkers, and toss silver coins into the water if they suspected they were being chased. The finmen would become distracted by the silver and pursue it, allowing the men to escape.

There were also legends of finwives, who began life as mermaids, many times more beautiful than mortal women. If these mermaids were able to marry mortal men (consummation was the key), they could retain their beauty and live happily. Hence, tales of mermaids trying to entice men with their beauty and glorious singing. If they failed, they were forced to marry finmen. Gradually they'd lose their beauty until they became hideous finwives.

The idea of finwives resembles other cultures' ideas of witches. Unlike finmen, who avoided humans, the finwives would move onshore to live among them, though staying relatively solitary. They would knit or spin and practice healing arts—the classic suspicious single woman suspected of witchcraft. In return for healing and for selling needlework, the finwives would earn silver, which they would dutifully forward to their greedy finhusbands.

Q: Who are the parallel women to Fiona and Gillian?

I didn't want to make direct parallels. At various points in the story, various people have aspects in common with the characters in the Shetland story. Ella can be a Gillian to Megan's Fiona as well as Genevieve, Stanley's other wife. Elizabeth is a newcomer who shakes up Megan's complacency, and who develops a relationship of sorts with David. Elizabeth and Megan start out as antagonists and then bond, so their relationship can be compared to Gillian and Fiona as well. I didn't want it all to jibe too neatly.

Q: Have you ever tried lace knitting?

Yes! When I started this book. Of course I had to try. I learned to knit as a girl, and have always enjoyed it. I also loved crewel and cross-stitch embroidery, needlepoint, and made my own clothes for many years. I make a point in my regular knitting to find the most complicated patterns possible to keep me challenged and interested. So I felt entirely up to the job of taking on lace. Uh, no. No matter how carefully I counted every stitch, by the next row I was always missing one somewhere. I did stick with it long enough to develop a recognizable and very beautiful pattern, but it went too slowly for impatient me, and I never got far enough for the pattern to become instinctive. My hat is off to anyone who can make it through a project. I found pictures online of lacework that was absolutely stunning.

Q: Where did the Shetland women get the wool for their work?

They'd raise the sheep themselves, then in the summer, when the animals were molting naturally, they'd pluck *by hand* the softest hairs from the sheep's necks and behind their ears. This was to keep the hairs as long as possible (shearing would shorten the individual strands). They'd mix the wool with seal oil, which they'd wash out for regular knitting, but leave in for strength when making the finest threads. Then they'd card the wool and spin it. The best spinners could get nine thousand yards from a single ounce of wool!

To avoid spoiling the most delicate yarns, they did everyday knitting with thicker wool outside while they did other chores (they'd rig one needle so they could knit one-handed!), and they worked on the fine lace inside by fire and lamplight in the evenings. One source said it took up to nine months to spin the yarn for a shawl and six weeks to knit it. This they did in addition to making thicker mittens and caps and stockings for their families and to sell.

What the women on Shetland accomplished is mind-boggling. Their lives were so hard, they had so much to take care of—house, garden, children, animals—yet, somehow they managed to create all this gorgeous and amazingly complex lace. I have no idea when they slept!

Q: What is the history of Shetland lace?

Shetland sheep produce especially warm and soft wool, better suited to knitting than weaving. Knitted wear was already important to the local economy by the sixteenth century, when natives traded stockings, caps and gloves to northern European merchants and fishermen. Lace knitting grew out of this tradition. In the nineteenth century, the height of the lace industry's prosperity, gifts to England's royal family paid off when Queen Victoria (herself a knitter) wore collars and stockings of Shetland lace, and lace patterns were printed in English magazines. In 1851 Shetland lace was displayed at the Great Exhibition at London's Crystal Palace. By the early twentieth century, Fair Isle sweaters had taken over as the main commercial knitted product from the islands, and the demand for lace died off.

Q: Knitting has been very important to Megan's life. What part has knitting played in your life? Have you ever belonged to a knitting group?

I've never belonged to a group. For me, knitting is a blissfully peaceful and solitary activity, but then I'm an introvert, so that fits me. My paternal grandmother was a knitter. She was incredible. Her stitches were so even (mine aren't) they looked like they came out of a machine. She also never used a pattern. My mother also knitted, and she taught me. Three kids to raise, a full-time teaching job, and Mom managed to knit me beautiful sweaters! Once she even made a cable sweater for my Barbie (Mom, where did you find the time?). I need my hands busy when I'm listening to music or an audio book, or just letting my mind wander, and needlework is perfect for that.

Q: On to the characters in your book. Did Gillian exist or not?

You can decide! The shawl that shows up at the end could have been knitted by Megan's mother, or it could have been the real one passed down. Maybe there was real magic and the box and shawl appeared in Megan's father's attic when Megan needed to see it. Maybe Fiona was altered by the shock and grief of losing Calum and imagined Gillian while she knit the shawl herself. There are many possibilities. Me, I'd love to believe the Shetland story as written.

Q: Why is Megan so sure Gillian isn't real?

First, in a literal sense, because Gillian suddenly appeared in her mother's stories when Megan had a difficult girl at school to deal with, and because her mother often told the Shetland stories as morality tales to fit Megan's life. And of course the "magic" side of Gillian would not have held water for Megan.

Second, symbolically, the book is about Megan's world expanding. She lived all over the country as a girl, but stayed very closed and small in her life, directed very inward. Her memories are more of knitting with her mother than the cities and towns around her. In fact, she often confuses where she lived at any given point. Her eventual opening up to believe in Gillian is part of her opening up to external experiences and aspects of herself that she denied for too long.

Q: Do David and Megan end up together?

I'll leave that to you! But yes, I believe they do. I think David keeps Megan's world from closing in on her and I think she keeps him humble. They're a good match in temperament, too.

Q: What do you see as Elizabeth's future?

In my mind Elizabeth is still going to need a few years to settle down and make peace with her mother and herself. In my original draft, Dominique was an overbearing jerk and she left him at the end of the book, but that was too many women leaving relationships, so I changed it. I think her process of maturation works better this way. I'm still not sure Dominique is perfect for her, but she loves him, and he definitely adores her. I do think she'll go to college, and become a more mature and grounded person. Having career goals of her own will help their relationship too.

Q: Can you relate to Elizabeth's aimlessness career-wise?

Yup. Until I started writing, when my first son was a baby, I had pretty much resigned myself to wandering from one job I didn't much care about to the next. I had no career aspirations simply because nothing made me catch fire. Writing changed my life. Maybe Elizabeth will find something to catch her on fire. Truffles? That farmhouse in North Carolina? Being a bigger part of Dominique's life and world? Something will. She's too stubbornly enthusiastic and creative to remain down for long.

Q: Why truffles?

I must have come across an article about them—I didn't realize they were being grown in the United States! I'm a foodie, so all things about food interest me, and I was fascinated. Truffles are why I set the story in North Carolina. The western mountains became the perfect place because of their beauty, but also because they seem in many people's minds to be the opposite of ocean, which is where Megan and her ancestors come from. And truffles represent Elizabeth's fancy life in New York, which she leaves, but which are still part of her in the form of Dominique, so she embraces them again at the story's end.

Q: What about Ella's future?

Ella will always land on her feet. I'm not worried about Ella. Watch out world, here she comes.

Q: Anything else you'd like to tell us?

Check out the information online about the Shetland islands! A truly fascinating place with a dramatic history. And if you're already a lace knitter or brave enough to try, I'd love to hear from you. E-mail me through my website, www.IsabelSharpe.com.

ISABEL SHARPE was not born pen-in-hand like so many of her fellow authors. After she quit work in 1994 to stay home with her first-born son and nearly went out of her mind, she started writing. Yes, she was the clichéd bored housewife writing romance, but it was either that cliché or seduce the mailman, and her mailman was unattractive. After more than twenty novels for Harlequin and the exciting new direction of women-focused stories for Avon Books, Isabel admits her new mailman is gorgeous, but she's still happy with her choice.

www.isabelsharpe.com

Isabel Sharpe

ALSO BY ISABEL SHARPE

AS GOOD AS IT GOT
A Novel
ISBN 978-0-06-114056-3 (paperback)

At a retreat for the suddenly single, three women discover they have a lot to learn about love, life—and themselves.

All Cindy wants is for her cheating husband to return to her. Ann thought she had it all. She'll get something out of this mindless camp, even if it kills her. Martha has spent her whole life being the shy, fat girl—but not anymore! One thing is certain—no one is going home unchanged.

"Sharpe delivers a cheeky overcoming-adversity narrative that's laced with wisdom and humor." —*Publishers Weekly*